KU-335-030

SPECTRUM ONE

£4.70

SPECTRUM ONE

Narrative Short Stories

Edited by
BRUCE BENNETT
PETER COWAN
JOHN HAY

LONGMAN

LONGMAN GROUP LIMITED
Longman House,
Burnt Mill, Harlow, Essex CM20 2JE, England
and Associated Companies throughout the World.

Copyright © Longman Group Ltd 1970
All rights reserved. No part of
this publication may be reproduced,
stored in a retrieval system or
transmitted in any form or by
any means, electronic, mechanical,
photocopying, recording, or
otherwise, without the prior
permission of the copyright owner.

First published 1970
Eleventh impression 1984

ISBN 0 582 34313 5

Printed in Hong Kong by
Wing King Tong Co Ltd

PREFACE

Writing short stories is a comparatively modern art. It was first given serious consideration in the early part of the nineteenth century and is still, today, undergoing radical experiment and change. Yet paradoxically, the short story derives from the ancient and unsophisticated tradition of the prose tale, the earliest of which, *The Shipwrecked Sailor*, was recorded in Egyptian papyri about 4000 B.C.

The transition from the predominantly oral tradition of the prose tale, to the written tradition of the short story, is recent and complex, and, like the short story itself, resists simple definition. Perhaps the most useful descriptive criterion for the short story is the criterion of limitation. To the inexperienced this can be deceptive. The relative brevity of the short story, its traditional focus upon a single episode, and its radical limitation of detail in both characterization and setting, might suggest simplicity. In fact it requires the exercise of the fullest capacity of the conscious artist. Short stories, however simple they may appear to be, reveal an awareness of technique on the part of the author. The American writer, Edgar Allan Poe, discussing his fellow writer, Nathaniel Hawthorne, insisted that in Hawthorne's stories 'every word *tells*, and there is not a word which does not *tell*'.

In this two volume anthology we have included stories which are intrinsically interesting, and which illustrate the diversity of themes and techniques used by short story writers. We have arranged the stories in an order which begins with simple reportage of an anecdote by a detached narrator, and ends with the complexity of symbolic short stories in which plot seems to have vanished. As much as other works of art, short stories resist classification, and forcing them into categories according to theme, or to specific technical characteristics limits the ways in which different readers might respond to them. By calling the anthology *Spectrum* we hope to emphasize the relationships which exist between apparently different stories.

In providing prefatory notes to each story, our intention has been to offer enough brief biographical and critical comments, and suggestions for further reading, to provide a perspective which will increase the reader's understanding and enjoyment of the stories.

CONTENTS

INTRODUCTION

This volume contains a range of 'narrative' short stories. 'Narrative' refers to their common characteristic of a firmly defined sequence of actions and events. At one end of the range, first in this anthology, is a story that has its roots in oral tradition, Hardy's A TRADITION OF EIGHTEEN HUNDRED AND FOUR, in which, like the Anglo-Saxon *scop* and the minstrel of medieval times, the narrator recounts a tale he has been told. At the other end of the range is Bradbury's THERE WILL COME SOFT RAINS, where the narrator is completely absent and we are given a camera's view of post-nuclear civilization. Between these extremes of narrative approach and subject are stories with a multiplicity of themes and techniques, arranged in a rough order of increasing complexity, both of technique and of implication.

Of central importance in an appreciation of the stories within this range is the notion of plot. One test of the effectiveness of a story's plot—perhaps most briefly and usefully defined as its causal sequence of events—is to ask whether the final situation differs in any significant way from the initial situation. Most of the stories in this volume will provide fruitful analysis of this question. As stories with a strong narrative component, they will be found to move forward, often in exciting and unexpected ways, to a resolution. In so doing, they testify to the reality and significance of the events they depict, a generalization that applies as much to the 'remote, intimate airways' of Walter Mitty's mind as it does to the circumstantial realism of London's TO BUILD A FIRE.

Narrative stories differ in this respect from many modern short stories modelled on the work of Chekhov, Mansfield, and Joyce, in which an apparently unshaped 'slice of life' leads to no formal resolution, but is intended, often, to illuminate certain moods, attitudes or feelings. Narrative short stories often suggest more than they state too: it would be difficult to read TO BUILD A FIRE without feeling something about human courage and endurance; or THE KNIFE without sympathizing with the problems of migrants. But the immediate situation and events are always central. We are never tempted to interpret setting, characters or events symbolically, as we are often led to do in Camus, Kafka, and the writers mentioned above, nor do moods or feelings take primacy over the more solid world of objects and events.

It is hoped that this book will provide enjoyment and a growing appreciation of the many possibilities of the narrative short story. Its humorous possibilities are suggested in stories as different as CHAMPION OF THE WORLD, THE BRIDE COMES TO YELLOW SKY, and THE SECRET LIFE OF WALTER MITTY. THE KNIFE and THE ONLY ONE WHO FORGOT indicate its possibilities in dramatising social problems, while its potential as a medium for science fiction is suggested by THERE WILL COME SOFT RAINS. Themes will be seen to recur: the pains and difficulties of 'growing up'; prejudice against those who appear 'different'; the jarring opposition of real and dream worlds. On a more technical level, it will be observed how orthodox chronological development is varied and intensified to good effect in FLIGHT and THERE WILL COME SOFT RAINS, and how the flashback is employed in THE OCCURRENCE AT OWL CREEK BRIDGE. The degree of involvement of the narrator in his story will also be noticed, ranging from the total involvement of the first person narrator in I'M A FOOL to the highly implicated narrator in ON SATURDAY AFTERNOON and the completely detached teller of Solomon Selby's tale in A TRADITION OF EIGHTEEN HUNDRED AND FOUR.

Along with such critical considerations, it is hoped that this volume will provide a basis for fruitful discussion of the many human values and attitudes contained in its stories.

ACKNOWLEDGEMENTS

We are grateful to the following for permission to include copyright material:

The Trustees of the Hardy Estate and Macmillan & Co. Ltd for 'A Tradition of Eighteen Hundred and Four' from *Life's Little Ironies* by Thomas Hardy; Penguin Books Ltd for 'The Piece of String' from *The Penguin Boule de Suif* translated by N. P. Sloman; Harold Ober Associates Incorporated © 1922 by Dial Publishing Company, Inc. Renewed 1949 by Eleanor Copenhaver Anderson for 'I'm a Fool' by Sherwood Anderson; Curtis Brown Ltd for 'Through the Tunnel' from *The Habit of Loving* by Doris Lessing; Laurence Pollinger Limited and Jonathan Cape Ltd for 'The Black Boxer' from *Country Tales* by H. E. Bates; Murray Pollinger and Michael Joseph Ltd for 'The Champion of the World' from *Kiss Kiss* by Roald Dahl; Hamish Hamilton Ltd for 'The Secret Life of Walter Mitty' from *Vintage Thurber* by James Thurber, © 1963 Hamish Hamilton London; T. A. G. Hungerford for his story 'The Only One Who Forgot'; The Cheshire Group Publishers for 'The Knife' by Judah Waten from *Two Ways Meet*, ed. Rorabacher; Rosica Colin Limited for 'On Saturday Afternoon' from *The Loneliness of the Long-Distance Runner* by Alan Sillitoe (W. H. Allen and Co.); Harold Matson Company, Inc. for 'There Will Come Soft Rains' by Ray Bradbury, Copyright 1950 by Ray Bradbury; McIntosh and Otis, Inc. for 'Flight' from *The Long Valley* by John Steinbeck, published in Britain by William Heinemann.

Thomas Hardy born 1840 in a Dorsetshire cottage at Upper Bockhampton, England. Trained as an architect, he was intensely interested in old buildings, both for their design and for their association with the old village way of life, which was being threatened in his lifetime by industrial expansion. His life-span spread from a time when Wordsworth and the Duke of Wellington were still living until ten years after the First World War.

Aware of the changes that occurred in his lifetime, he carried this historic sense into his novels, poems, and stories. The novels, for which Hardy is best known, are mainly set in Wessex, a partly real partly dream country, topographically recognizable as the south of England but incorporating a way of life that was rapidly disappearing. THE DYNASTS, Hardy's long epic-drama contains nineteen acts and thirty one scenes in blank verse and a variety of other metres, along with some prose. Besides the major scenes centring around the figure of Napoleon, THE DYNASTS contains many short episodes similar in idea to 'A TRADITION OF 1804', showing how historical events affected the private soldier, the camp follower, and the English country people. Hardy's ability to accurately reproduce the accents and rhythms of speech of his rustic characters is exemplified in 'A TRADITION OF 1804'. Its narrative organization—in the form of a tale re-told—is one of the earliest and simplest methods of short story construction, but its more complex possibilities are later exploited in the stories of Joseph Conrad.

Suggested for further reading: Short stories: 'THE THREE STRANGERS', 'THE MELANCHOLY HUSSAR OF THE GERMAN LEGION', in WESSEX TALES, 1888. Novels: FAR FROM THE MADDING CROWD, 1874, THE MAYOR OF CASTERBRIDGE, 1886, TESS OF THE D'URBERVILLES, 1891.

A TRADITION OF EIGHTEEN HUNDRED AND FOUR

Thomas Hardy

THE WIDELY DISCUSSED POSSIBILITY OF AN INVASION OF ENGLAND THROUGH a Channel tunnel has more than once recalled old Solomon Selby's story to my mind.

The occasion on which I numbered myself among his audience was one evening when he was sitting in the yawning chimney-corner of the inn-kitchen, with some others who had gathered there, and I entered for shelter from the rain. Withdrawing the stem of his pipe from the dental notch in which it habitually rested, he leaned back in the recess behind him and smiled into the fire. The smile was neither mirthful nor sad, not precisely humorous nor altogether thoughtful. We who knew him recognized it in a moment: it was his narrative smile. Breaking off our few desultory remarks we drew up closer, and he thus began:—

'My father, as you mid know, was a shepherd all his life, and lived out by the Cove four miles yonder, where I was born and lived likewise, till I moved here shortly afore I was married. The cottage that first knew me stood on the top of the down, near the sea; there was no house within a mile and a half of it; it was built o' purpose for the farm-shepherd, and had no other use. They tell me that it is now pulled down, but that you can see where it stood by the mounds of earth and a few broken bricks that are still lying about. It was a bleak and dreary place in winter-time, but in summer it was well enough, though the garden never came to much because we could not get up a good shelter for the vegetables and currant bushes; and where there is much wind they don't thrive.

'Of all the years of my growing up the ones that bide clearest in my mind were eighteen hundred and three, four, and five. This was for two reasons: I had just then grown to an age when a child's eyes and ears take in and note down everything about him, and there was more at that date to bear in mind than there ever has been since with me. It was, as I need hardly tell ye, the time after the first peace, when Bonaparte was scheming his descent upon England. He had crossed the great Alp mountains, fought in Egypt, drubbed the Turks, the Austrians, and the Proosians, and now thought he'd have a slap at us. On the other side of the Channel, scarce out of sight and hail of a man standing on our English shore, the French army of a hundred and sixty thousand men and fifteen thousand horses had been brought together from all parts, and were drilling every day. Bonaparte had been three years a-making his preparations; and to ferry these soldiers and cannon and horses across he had contrived a couple of thousand flat-bottomed boats. These boats were small things, but

1

wonderfully built. A good few of 'em were so made as to have a little stable on board each for the two horses that were to haul the cannon carried at the stern. To get in order all these, and other things required, he had assembled there five or six thousand fellows that worked at trades—carpenters, blacksmiths, wheelwrights, saddlers, and what not. O 'twas a curious time!

'Every morning Neighbour Boney would muster his multitude of soldiers on the beach, draw 'em up in line, practise 'em in the manoeuvre of embarking, horses and all, till they could do it without a single hitch. My father drove a flock of ewes up into Sussex that year, and as he went along the drover's track over the high downs thereabout he could see this drilling actually going on—the accoutrements of the rank and file glittering in the sun like silver. It was thought and always said by my uncle Job, sergeant of foot (who used to know all about these matters), that Bonaparte meant to cross with oars on a calm night. The grand query with us was, where would my gentleman land? Many of the common people thought it would be at Dover; others, who knew how unlikely it was that any skilful general would make a business of landing just where he was expected, said he'd go either east into the River Thames, or west'ard to some convenient place, most likely one of the little bays inside the Isle of Portland, between the Beal and St Alban's Head—and for choice the three-quarter-round Cove, screened from every mortal eye, that seemed made o' purpose, out by where we lived, and which I've climmed up with two tubs of brandy across my shoulders on scores o' dark nights in my younger days. Some had heard that a part o' the French fleet would sail right round Scotland, and come up the Channel to a suitable haven. However, there was much doubt upon the matter; and no wonder, for after-years proved that Bonaparte himself could hardly make up his mind upon that great and very particular point, where to land. His uncertainty came about in this wise, that he could get no news as to where and how our troops lay in waiting, and that his knowledge of possible places where flat-bottomed boats might be quietly run ashore, and the men they brought marshalled in order, was dim to the last degree. Being flat-bottomed, they didn't require a harbour for unshipping their cargo of men, but a good shelving beach away from sight, and with a fair open road toward London. How the question posed that great Corsican tyrant (as we used to call him), what pains he took to settle it, and, above all, what a risk he ran on one particular night in trying to do so, were known only to one man here and there; and certainly to no maker of newspapers or printer of books, or my account o't would not have had so many heads shaken over it as it has by gentry who only believe what they see in printed lines.

'The flocks my father had charge of fed all about the downs near our house, overlooking the sea and shore each way for miles. In winter and early spring father was up a deal at nights, watching and tending the lambing. Often he'd go to bed early, and turn out at twelve or one; and on the other hand, he'd sometimes stay up till twelve or one, and then turn in to bed. As soon as I was old enough I used to help him, mostly in the way of keeping an eye upon the ewes while he was gone home to rest. This is what I was doing in a particular month in either the year four or five—I can't certainly fix which, but it was long before I was took away from the sheepkeeping to be bound prentice to a trade. Every night at that time I was at the fold, about half a mile, or it may be a little more, from our cottage, and no living thing at all with me but the ewes and young lambs. Afeard? No; I was never afeard of being alone at these times; for I had been reared in such an out-step place that the lack o' human beings at night made me less fearful than the sight of 'em. Directly I saw a man's shape after dark in a lonely place I was frightened out of my senses.

'One day in that month we were surprised by a visit from my uncle Job, the sergeant in the Sixty-first foot, then in camp on the downs above King George's watering-place, several miles to the west yonder. Uncle Job dropped in about dusk, and went up with my father to the fold for an hour or two. Then he came home, had a drop to drink from the tub of sperrits that the smugglers kept us in for housing their liquor when they'd made a run, and for burning 'em off when there was danger. After that he stretched himself out on the settle to sleep. I went to bed: at one o'clock father came home, and waking me to go and take his place, according to custom, went to bed himself. On my way out of the house I passed Uncle Job on the settle. He opened his eyes, and upon my telling him where I was going he said it was a shame that such a youngster as I should go up there all alone; and when he had fastened up his stock and waist-belt he set off along with me, taking a drop from the sperrit-tub in a little flat bottle that stood in the corner-cupboard.

'By and by we drew up to the fold, saw that all was right, and then, to keep ourselves warm, curled up in a heap of straw that lay inside the thatched hurdles we had set up to break the stroke of the wind when there was any. To-night, however, there was none. It was one of those very still nights when, if you stand on the high hills anywhere within two or three miles of the sea, you can hear the rise and fall of the tide along the shore, coming and going every few moments like a sort of great snore of the sleeping world. Over the lower ground there was a bit of a mist, but on the hill where we lay the air was clear, and the moon, then in her last quarter, flung a fairly good light on the grass and scattered straw.

'While we lay there Uncle Job amused me by telling me strange stories of the wars he had served in and the wounds he had got. He had already fought the French in the Low Countries, and hoped to fight 'em again. His stories lasted so long that at last I was hardly sure that I was not a soldier myself, and had seen such service as he told of. The wonders of his tales quite bewildered my mind, till I fell asleep and dreamed of battle, smoke, and flying soldiers, all of a kind with the doings he had been bringing up to me.

'How long my nap lasted I am not prepared to say. But some faint sounds over and above the rustle of the ewes in the straw, the bleat of the lambs, and the tinkle of the sheep-bell brought me to my waking senses. Uncle Job was still beside me; but he too had fallen asleep. I looked out from the straw, and saw what it was that had aroused me. Two men, in boat-cloaks, cocked hats, and swords, stood by the hurdles about twenty yards off.

'I turned my ear thitherward to catch what they were saying, but though I heard every word o't, not one did I understand. They spoke in a tongue that was not ours—in French, as I afterward found. But if I could not gain the meaning of a word, I was shrewd boy enough to find out a deal of the talkers' business. By the light o' the moon I could see that one of 'em carried a roll of paper in his hand, while every moment he spoke quick to his comrade, and pointed right and left with the other hand to spots along the shore. There was no doubt that he was explaining to the second gentleman the shapes and features of the coast. What happened soon after made this still clearer to me.

'All this time I had not waked uncle Job, but now I began to be afeared that they might light upon us, because uncle breathed so heavily through's nose. I put my mouth to his ear and whispered, "Uncle Job."

' "What is it, my boy?" he said, just as if he hadn't been asleep at all.

' "Hush!" says I. "Two French generals—"

' "French?" says he.

' "Yes," says I. "Come to see where to land their army!"

'I pointed 'em out; but I could say no more, for the pair were coming at that moment much nearer to where we lay. As soon as they got as near as eight or ten yards, the officer with a roll in his hand stooped down to a slanting hurdle, unfastened his roll upon it, and spread it out. Then suddenly he sprung a dark lantern open on the paper, and showed it to be a map.

' "What be they looking at?" I whispered to Uncle Job.

' "A chart of the Channel," says the sergeant (knowing about such things).

'The other French officer now stooped likewise, and over the map they had a long consultation, as they pointed here and there on the paper, and then hither and thither at places along the shore beneath us. I noticed that the manner of one officer was very respectful toward the other, who seemed much his superior, the second in rank calling him by a sort of title that I did not know the sense of. The head one, on the other hand, was quite familiar with his friend, and more than once clapped him on the shoulder.

'Uncle Job had watched as well as I, but though the map had been in the lantern-light, their faces had always been in shade. But when they rose from stooping over the chart the light flashed upward, and fell smart upon one of 'em's features. No sooner had this happened than Uncle Job gasped, and sank down as if he'd been in a fit.

' "What is it—what is it, Uncle Job?" said I.

' "O good God!" says he, under the straw.

' "What?" says I.

' "Boney!" he groaned out.

' "Who?" says I.

' "Bonaparty," he said. "The Corsican ogre. O that I had got but my new-flinted firelock, that there man should die! But I haven't got my new-flinted firelock, and that there man must live. So lie low, as you value your life!"

'I did lie low, as you mid suppose. But I couldn't help peeping. And then I too, lad as I was, knew that it was the face of Bonaparte. Not know Boney? I should think I did know Boney. I should have known him by the half the light o' that lantern. If I had seen a picture of his features once, I had seen it a hundred times. There was his bullet head, his short neck, his round yaller cheeks and chin, his gloomy face, and his great glowing eyes. He took off his hat to blow himself a bit, and there was the forelock in the middle of his forehead, as in all the draughts of him. In moving, his cloak fell a little open, and I could see for a moment his white-fronted jacket and one of his epaulets.

'But none of this lasted long. In a minute he and his general had rolled up the map, shut the lantern, and turned to go down towards the shore.

'Then Uncle Job came to himself a bit. "Slipped across in the night-time to see how to put his men ashore," he said. "The like o' that man's coolness eyes will never again see! Nephew, I must act in this, and immediate, or England's lost!"

'When they were over the brow, we crope out, and went some little way to look after them. Halfway down they were joined by two others, and six or seven minutes brought them to the shore. Then, from behind a rock, a boat came out into the weak moonlight of the Cove, and they jumped in; it put off instantly, and vanished in a few minutes between the two rocks that stand at the mouth of the Cove as we all know. We climmed back to where we had been before, and I could see, a short way out, a larger vessel, though still not very large. The little boat drew up alongside, was made fast at the stern as I suppose, for the largest sailed away, and we saw no more.

'My uncle Job told his officers as soon as he got back to camp; but what they thought of it I never heard—neither did he. Boney's army never came, and a good job for me; for the Cove below my father's house was where he meant to land, as this secret visit showed. We coast-folk should have been cut down one and all, and I should not have sat here to tell this tale.'

We who listened to old Selby that night have been familiar with his simple grave-stone for these ten years past. Thanks to the incredulity of the age his tale has been seldom repeated. But if anything short of the direct testimony of his own eyes could persuade an auditor that Bonaparte had examined these shores for himself with a view to a practicable landing-place, it would have been Solomon Selby's manner of narrating the adventure which befell him on the down.

Christmas 1882.

Jack London born John Griffith London on 12 January 1876, in San Francisco, the illegitimate son of an Irish vagrant and an American girl, who later married John London. After a childhood of poverty he went to high school when nineteen, and to the University of California for one year. He was, in turn, seaman, tramp, arrested as a vagabond, unsuccessful Klondike gold-rush follower, war correspondent in the Russo-Japanese War of 1904, and prolific novelist, short story writer, and journalist.

'TO BUILD A FIRE' like WHITE FANG and THE CALL OF THE WILD, which sold more than one and a half million copies, is a traditional, direct narrative, relying for effect upon pace, and intense realism of setting, which London achieves by drawing upon his own experiences in the North American wilderness. An additional dimension is added to the narrative not by the characteristic surprise ending of a Maupassant story, but by a subdued, continuous ironic parallel between the events described and the general situation of mankind.

London's life was ended by suicide on 22 November 1916.

TO BUILD A FIRE

Jack London

DAY HAD BROKEN COLD AND GREY, EXCEEDINGLY COLD AND GREY, WHEN the man turned aside from the main Yukon trail and climbed the high earth-bank, where a dim and little-travelled trail led eastward through the fat spruce timberland. It was a steep bank, and he paused for breath at the top, excusing the act to himself by looking at his watch. It was nine o'clock. There was no sun nor hint of sun, though there was not a cloud in the sky. It was a clear day, and yet there seemed an intangible pall over the face of things, a subtle gloom that made the day dark, and that was due to the absence of sun. This fact did not worry the man. He was used to the lack of sun. It had been days since he had seen the sun, and he knew that a few more days must pass before that cheerful orb, due south, would just peep above the sky-line and dip immediately from view.

The man flung a look back along the way he had come. The Yukon lay a mile wide and hidden under three feet of ice. On top of this ice were as many feet of snow. It was all pure white, rolling in gentle undulations where the ice-jams of the freeze-up had formed. North and south, as far as the eye could see, it was unbroken white, save for a dark hair-line that curved and twisted from around the spruce-covered island to the south, and that curved and twisted away into the north, where it disappeared behind another spruce-covered island. This dark hair-line was the trail— the main trail—that led south five hundred miles to the Chilcoot Pass, Dyea, and salt water; and that led north seventy miles to Dawson, and still on to the north a thousand miles to Nulato, and finally to St Michael on Bering Sea, a thousand miles and a half a thousand more.

But all this—the mysterious, far-reaching hair-line trail, the absence of sun from the sky, the tremendous cold, and the strangeness and weirdness of it all—made no impression on the man. It was not because he was long used to it. He was a new-comer in the land, a _chechaquo_, and this was his first winter. The trouble with him was that he was without imagination. He was quick and alert in the things of life, but only in the things, and not in the significances. Fifty degrees below zero meant eighty-odd degrees of frost. Such fact impressed him as being cold and uncomfortable, and that was all. It did not lead him to meditate upon his frailty as a creature of temperature, and upon man's frailty in general, able only to live within certain narrow limits of heat and cold; and from there on it did not lead him to the conjectural field of immortality and man's place in the universe. Fifty degrees below zero stood for a bite of frost that hurt and that must be guarded against by the use of mittens, ear-flaps, warm moccasins, and thick socks. Fifty degrees below zero was to him just precisely fifty degrees below zero. That there should be anything more to it than that was a thought that never entered his head.

As he turned to go on, he spat speculatively. There was a sharp, explosive crackle that startled him. He spat again. And again, in the air, before it could fall to the snow, the spittle crackled. He knew that at fifty below spittle crackled on the snow, but this spittle had crackled in the air. Undoubtedly it was colder than fifty below—how much colder he did not know. But the temperature did not matter. He was bound for the old claim on the left fork of Henderson Creek, where the boys were already. They had come over across the divide from the Indian Creek country, while he had come the roundabout way to take a look at the possibilities of getting out logs in the spring from the islands in the Yukon. He would be in to camp by six o'clock; a bit after dark, it was true, but the boys would be there, a fire would be going, and a hot supper would be ready. As for lunch, he pressed his hand against the protruding bundle under his jacket. It was also under his shirt, wrapped up in a handkerchief, and lying against the naked skin. It was the only way to keep the biscuits from freezing. He smiled agreeably to himself as he thought of those biscuits, each cut open and sopped in bacon grease, and each enclosing a generous slice of fried bacon.

He plunged in among the big spruce trees. The trail was faint. A foot of snow had fallen since the last sled had passed over, and he was glad he was without a sled, travelling light. In fact, he carried nothing but the lunch wrapped in the handkerchief. He was surprised, however, at the cold. It certainly was cold, he concluded, as he rubbed his numbed nose and cheekbones with his mittened hand. He was a warm-whiskered man, but the hair on his face did not protect the high cheek-bones and the eager nose that thrust itself aggressively into the frosty air.

At the man's heels trotted a dog, a big native husky, the proper wolf-dog, grey-coated and without any visible or temperamental difference from its brother, the wild wolf. The animal was depressed by the tremendous cold. It knew that it was no time for travelling. Its instinct told it a truer tale than was told to the man by the man's judgement. In reality, it was not merely colder than fifty below zero; it was colder than sixty below, than seventy below. It was seventy-five below zero. Since the freezing-point is thirty-two above zero it meant that one hundred and seven degrees of frost obtained. The dog did not know anything about thermometers. Possibly in its brain there was no sharp consciousness of a condition of very cold such as was in the man's brain. But the brute had its instinct. It experienced a vague but menacing apprehension that subdued it and made it slink along at the man's heels, and that made it question eagerly every unwonted movement of the man as if expecting him to go into camp or to seek shelter somewhere and build a fire. The dog had learned fire, and it wanted fire, or else to burrow under the snow and cuddle its warmth away from the air.

The frozen moisture of its breathing had settled on its fur in a fine powder of frost, and especially were its jowls, muzzle, and eyelashes whitened by its crystalled breath. The man's red beard and moustache were likewise frosted, but more solidly, the deposit taking the form of ice and increasing with every warm, moist breath he exhaled. Also, the man was chewing tobacco, and the muzzle of ice held his lips so rigidly that he was unable to clear his chin when he expelled the juice. The result was that a crystal beard of the colour and solidity of amber was increasing its length on his chin. If he fell down it would shatter itself, like glass, into brittle fragments. But he did not mind the appendage. It was the penalty all tobacco-chewers paid in that country, and he had been out before in two cold snaps. They had not been so cold as this, he knew, but by the spirit thermometer at Sixty Mile he knew they had been registered at fifty below and at fifty-five.

He held on through the level stretch of woods for several miles, crossed a wide flat of nigger-heads, and dropped down a bank to the frozen bed of a small stream. This was Henderson Creek, and he knew he was ten miles from the forks. He looked at his watch. It was ten o'clock. He was making four miles an hour, and he calculated that he would arrive at the forks at half-past twelve. He decided to celebrate that event by eating his lunch there.

The dog dropped in again at his heels, with a tail drooping discouragement, as the man swung along the creek-bed. The furrow of the old sled-trail was plainly visible, but a dozen inches of snow covered the marks of the last runners. In a month no man had come up or down that silent creek. The man held steadily on. He was not much given to thinking, and just then particularly he had nothing to think about save that he would eat lunch at the forks and that at six o'clock he would be in camp with the boys. There was nobody to talk to; and, had there been, speech would have been impossible because of the ice-muzzle on his mouth. So he continued monotonously to chew tobacco and to increase the length of his amber beard.

Once in a while the thought reiterated itself that it was very cold and that he had never experienced such cold. As he walked along he rubbed his cheek-bones and nose with the back of his mittened hand. He did this automatically, now and again changing hands. But rub as he would, the instant he stopped his cheek-bones went numb, and the following instant the end of his nose went numb. He was sure to frost his cheeks; he knew that, and experienced a pang of regret that he had not devised a nose-strap of the sort Bud wore in cold snaps. Such a strap passed across the cheeks, as well, and saved them. But it didn't matter much, after all. What were frosted cheeks? A bit painful, that was all; they were never serious.

Empty as the man's mind was of thoughts, he was keenly observant, and he noticed the changes in the creek, the curves and bends and timber-jams, and always he sharply noted where he placed his feet. Once, coming around a bend, he shied abruptly, like a startled horse, curved away from the place where he had been walking, and retreated several paces back along the trail. The creek he knew was frozen clear to the bottom—no creek could contain water in that arctic winter—but he knew also that there were springs that bubbled out from the hillsides and ran along under the snow and on top the ice of the creek. He knew that the coldest snaps never froze these springs, and he knew likewise their danger. They were traps. They hid pools of water under the snow that might be three inches deep, or three feet. Sometimes a skin of ice half an inch thick covered them, and in turn was covered by the snow. Sometimes there were alternate layers of water and ice-skin, so that when one broke through he kept on breaking through for a while, sometimes wetting himself to the waist.

That was why he had shied in such panic. He had felt the give under his feet and heard the crackle of a snow-hidden ice-skin. And to get his feet wet in such a temperature meant trouble and danger. At the very least it meant delay, for he would be forced to stop and build a fire, and under its protection to bare his feet while he dried his socks and moccasins. He stood and studied the creek-bed and its banks, and decided that the flow of water came from the right. He reflected awhile, rubbing his nose and cheeks and skirted to the left, stepping gingerly and testing the footing for each step. Once clear of the danger, he took a fresh chew of tobacco and swung along at his four-mile gait.

In the course of the next two hours he came upon several similar traps. Usually the snow above the hidden pools had a sunken, candied appearance that advertised the danger. Once again, however, he had a close call; and once, suspecting danger, he compelled the dog to go on in front. The dog did not want to go. It hung back until the man shoved it forward, and then it went quickly across the white, unbroken surface. Suddenly it broke through, floundered to one side, and got away to firmer footing. It had wet its forefeet and legs and almost immediately the water that clung to it turned to ice. It made quick efforts to lick the ice off its legs, then dropped down in the snow and began to bite out the ice that had formed between the toes. This was a matter of instinct. To permit the ice to remain would mean sore feet. It did not know this. It merely obeyed the mysterious prompting that arose from the deep crypts of its being. But the man knew, having achieved a judgement on the subject, and he removed the mitten from his right hand and helped tear out the ice-particles. He did not expose his fingers more than a minute and was astonished at the swift numbness that smote them. It certainly was cold.

He pulled on the mitten hastily, and beat the hand savagely across his chest.

At twelve o'clock the day was at its brightest. Yet the sun was too far south on its winter journey to clear the horizon. The bulge of the earth intervened between it and Henderson Creek, where the man walked under a clear sky at noon and cast no shadow. At half-past twelve, to the minute, he arrived at the f rks of the creek. He was pleased at the speed he had made. If he kept it up, ie would certainly be with the boys by six. He unbuttoned his jacket and shirt and drew forth his lunch. The action consumed no more than a quarter of a minute, yet in that brief moment the numbness laid hold of the exposed fingers. He did not put the mitten on, but, instead, struck the fingers a dozen sharp smashes against his leg. Then he sat down on a snow-covered log to eat. The sting that followed upon the striking of his fingers against his leg ceased so quickly that he was startled. He had had no chance to take a bite of biscuit. He struck the fingers repeatedly and returned them to the mitten, baring the other hand for the purpose of eating. He tried to take a mouthful but the ice-muzzle prevented. He had forgotten to build a fire and thaw out. He chuckled at his foolishness, and as he chuckled he noted the numbness creeping into the exposed fingers. Also, he noted that the stinging which had first come to his toes when he sat down was already passing away. He wondered whether the toes were warm or numbed. He moved them inside the moccasins and decided that they were numbed.

He pulled the mitten on hurriedly and stood up. He was a bit frightened. He stamped up and down until the stinging returned into the feet. It certainly was cold was his thought. That man from Sulphur Creek had spoken the truth when telling how cold it sometimes got in the country. And he had laughed at him at the time! That showed one must not be too sure of things. There was no mistake about it, it *was* cold. He strode up and down, stamping his feet and threshing his arms, until reassured by the returning warmth. Then he got out matches and proceeded to make a fire. From the undergrowth, where high water of the previous spring had lodged a supply of seasoned twigs, he got his firewood. Working carefully from a small beginning, he soon had a roaring fire, over which he thawed the ice from his face and in the protection of which he ate his biscuits. For the moment the cold of space was outwitted. The dog took satisfaction in the fire, stretching out close enough for warmth and far enough away to escape being singed.

When the man had finished, he filled his pipe and took his comfortable time over a smoke. Then he pulled on his mittens, settled the ear-flaps of his cap firmly about his ears, and took the creek trail up the left fork. The dog was disappointed and yearned back towards the fire. This man did not know cold. Possibly all the generations of his ancestry had been ignorant of cold, of real cold, of cold one hundred and seven degrees below freezing-point. But the dog knew; all its ancestry knew, and it had inherited the knowledge. And it knew that it was not good to walk abroad in such fearful cold. It was the time to lie snug in a hole in the snow and wait for a curtain of cloud to be drawn across the face of outer space whence this cold came. On the other hand, there was no keen intimacy between the dog and the man. The one was the toil-slave of the other, and the only caresses it had ever received were the caresses of the whip-lash and of harsh and menacing throat-sounds that threatened the whip-lash. So the dog made no effort to communicate its apprehension to the man. It was not concerned in the welfare of the man; it was for its own sake that it yearned back towards the fire. But the man whistled, and spoke to it with the sound of whip-lashes, and the dog swung in at the man's heels and followed after.

The man took a chew of tobacco and proceeded to start a new amber beard. Also, his moist breath quickly powdered with white his moustache, eyebrows, and lashes. There did not seem to be so many springs on the left fork of the Henderson, and for half an hour the man saw no signs of any. And then it happened. At the place where there were no signs, where the soft, unbroken snow seemed to advertise solidity beneath, the man broke through. It was not deep. He wet himself halfway to the knees before he floundered out to the firm crust.

He was angry, and cursed his luck aloud. He had hoped to get into camp with the boys at six o'clock, and this would delay him an hour, for he would have to build a fire and dry out his footgear. This was imperative at that low temperature—he knew that much; and he turned aside to the bank, which he climbed. On top, tangled in the underbrush about the trunks of several small spruce trees, was a high-water deposit of dry fire-wood—sticks and twigs, principally, but also larger portions of seasoned branches and fine, dry, last-year's grasses. He threw down several large pieces on top of the snow. This served for a foundation and prevented the young flame from drowning itself in the snow it otherwise would melt. The flame he got by touching a match to a small shred of birch-bark that he took from his pocket. This burned even more readily than paper. Placing it on the foundation, he fed the young flames with wisps of dry grass and with the tiniest dry twigs.

He worked slowly and carefully, keenly aware of his danger. Gradually, as the flame grew stronger, he increased the size of the twigs with which he fed it. He squatted in the snow, pulling the twigs out from their entanglement in the brush and feeding directly to the flame. He knew there must be no failure. When it is seventy-five below zero, a man must not fail in his first attempt to build a fire—that is, if his feet are wet. If his feet are dry, and he fails, he can run along the trail for half a mile and restore his circulation. But the circulation of wet and freezing feet cannot be restored by running when it is seventy-five below. No matter how fast he runs, the wet feet will freeze the harder.

All this the man knew. The old-timer on Sulphur Creek had told him about it the previous fall, and now he was appreciating the advice. Already all sensation had gone out of his feet. To build the fire he had been forced to remove his mittens, and the fingers had quickly gone numb. His pace of four miles an hour had kept his heart pumping blood to the surface of his body and to all the extremities. But the instant he stopped, the action of the pump eased down. The cold of space smote the unprotected tip of the planet, and he, being on that unprotected tip, received the full force of the blow. The blood of his body recoiled before it. The blood was alive, like the dog, and like the dog it wanted to hide away and cover itself up from the fearful cold. So long as he walked four miles an hour, he pumped that blood, willy-nilly, to the surface; but now it ebbed away and sank down into the recesses of his body. The extremities were the first to feel its absence. His wet feet froze the faster, and his exposed fingers numbed the faster, though they had not yet begun to freeze. Nose and cheeks were already freezing, while the skin of all his body chilled as it lost its blood.

But he was safe. Toes and nose and cheeks would be only touched by the frost, for the fire was beginning to burn with strength. He was feeding it with twigs the size of his finger. In another minute he would be able to feed it with branches the size of his wrist and then he could remove his wet footgear, and while it dried he could keep his naked feet warm by the fire, rubbing them at first, of course, with snow. The fire was a success. He was safe. He remembered the advice of the old-timer on Sulphur Creek, and smiled. The old-timer had been very serious in laying down the law that no man must travel alone in the Klondike after fifty below. Well, here he was; he had had an accident; he was alone; and he saved himself. Those old-timers were rather womanish, some of them, he thought. All a man had to do was to keep his head, and he was all right. Any man who was a man could travel alone. But it was surprising, the rapidity with which his cheeks and nose were freezing. And he had not thought his fingers could go lifeless in so short a time. Lifeless they were, for he could scarcely make them move together to grip a twig, and they seemed remote from his body and from him. When he touched a twig, he had to look and see whether or not he had hold of it. The wires were pretty well down between him and his finger-ends.

All of which counted for little. There was the fire, snapping and crackling and promising life with every dancing flame. He started to untie his moccasins. They were coated with ice; the thick German socks were like sheaths of iron halfway to the knees; and the moccasin strings were like rods of steel all twisted and knotted as by some conflagration.

For a moment he tugged with his numbed fingers, then, realizing the folly of it, he drew his sheath-knife.

But before he could cut the strings, it happened. It was his own fault or, rather, his mistake. He should not have built the fire under the spruce tree. He should have built it in the open. But it had been easier to pull the twigs from the brush and drop them directly on the fire. Now the tree under which he had done this carried a weight of snow on its boughs. No wind had blown for weeks, and each bough was fully freighted. Each time he had pulled a twig he had communicated a slight agitation to the tree—an imperceptible agitation, so far as he was concerned, but an agitation sufficient to bring about the disaster. High up in the tree one bough capsized its load of snow. This fell on the boughs beneath, capsizing them. This process continued, spreading out and involving the whole tree. It grew like an avalanche, and it descended without warning upon the man and the fire, and the fire was blotted out! Where it had burned was a mantle of fresh and disordered snow.

The man was shocked. It was as though he had just heard his own sentence of death. For a moment he sat and stared at the spot where the fire had been. Then he grew very calm. Perhaps the old-timer on Sulphur Creek was right. If he had only had a trail-mate he would have been in no danger now. The trail-mate could have built the fire. Well, it was up to him to build the fire over again, and this second time there must be no failure. Even if he succeeded, he would most likely lose some toes. His feet must be badly frozen by now, and there would be some time before the second fire was ready.

Such were his thoughts, but he did not sit and think them. He was busy all the time they were passing through his mind. He made a new foundation for a fire, this time in the open, where no treacherous tree could blot it out. Next, he gathered dry grasses and tiny twigs from the high-water flotsam. He could not bring his fingers together to pull them out, but he was able to gather them by the handful. In this way he got many rotten twigs and bits of green moss that were undesirable, but it was the best he could do. He worked methodically, even collecting an armful of the larger branches to be used later when the fire gathered strength. And all the while the dog sat and watched him, a certain yearning wistfulness in its eyes, for it looked upon him as the fire-provider, and the fire was slow in coming.

When all was ready, the man reached in his pocket for a second piece of birch-bark. He knew the bark was there, and, though he could not feel it with his fingers, he could hear its crisp rustling as he fumbled for it. Try as he would, he could not clutch hold of it. And all the time, in his consciousness, was the knowledge that each instant his feet were freezing. This thought tended to put him in a panic, but he fought against it and kept calm. He pulled on his mittens with his teeth, and threshed his arms back and forth, beating his hands with all his might against his sides. He did this sitting down, and he stood up to do it; and all the while the dog sat in the snow, its wolf-brush of a tail curled around warmly over its forefeet, its sharp wolf-ears pricked forward intently as it watched the man. And the man as he beat and threshed with his arms and hands, felt a great surge of envy as he regarded the creature that was warm and secure in its natural covering.

After a time he was aware of the first far-away signals of sensation in his beaten fingers. The faint tingling grew stronger till it evolved into a stinging ache that was excruciating, but which the man hailed with satisfaction. He stripped the mitten from his right hand and fetched forth the birch-bark. The exposed fingers were quickly going numb again. Next he brought out his bunch of sulphur matches. But the tremendous cold had already driven the life out of his fingers. In his effort to separate one match from the others, the whole bunch fell in the snow. He tried to pick it out of the snow but failed. The dead fingers could neither touch nor clutch. He was very careful. He drove the thought of his freezing feet, and nose, and cheeks out of his mind, devoting his whole soul to the matches. He watched, using the sense of vision in place of that of touch, and when he saw his fingers on each side the bunch, he closed—that is, he willed to close them, for the wires were down, and the fingers did not obey. He pulled the mitten on the right hand, and beat it fiercely against his knee. Then, with both mittened hands, he scooped the bunch of matches, along with much snow, into his lap. Yet he was no better off.

After much manipulation he managed to get the bunch between the heels of his mittened hands. In this fashion he carried it to his mouth. The ice crackled and snapped when by a violent effort he opened his mouth. He drew the lower jaw in, curled the upper lip out of the way, and scraped the bunch with his upper teeth in order to separate a match. He succeeded in getting one, which he dropped on his lap. He was no better off. He could not pick it up. Then he devised a way. He picked it up in his teeth and scratched it on his leg. Twenty times he scratched before he succeeded in lighting it. As it flamed he held it with his teeth to the birch-bark. But the burning brimstone went up his nostrils and into his lungs, causing him to cough spasmodically. The match fell into the snow and went out.

The old-timer on Sulphur Creek was right, he thought in the moment of controlled despair that ensued: after fifty below, a man should travel with a partner. He beat his hands, but failed in exciting any sensation. Suddenly he bared both hands, removing the mittens with his teeth. He caught the whole bunch between the heels of his hands. His arm-muscles not being frozen enabled him to press the hand-heels tightly against the matches. Then he scratched the bunch along his leg. It flared into flame, seventy sulphur matches at once! There was no wind to blow them out. He kept his head to one side to escape the strangling fumes, and held the blazing bunch to the birch-bark. As he so held it, he became aware of sensation in his hand. His flesh was burning. He could smell it. Deep down below the surface he could feel it. The sensation developed into pain that grew acute. And still he endured it, holding the flame of the matches clumsily because his own burning hands were in the way, absorbing most of the flame.

At last, when he could endure no more, he jerked his hands apart. The blazing matches fell sizzling into the snow, but the birch-bark was alight. He began laying dry grasses and the tiniest twigs on the flame. He could not pick and choose, for he had to lift the fuel between the heels of his hands. Small pieces of rotten wood and green moss clung to the twigs, and he bit them off as well as he could with his teeth. He cherished the flame carefully and awkwardly. It meant life, and it must not perish. The withdrawal of blood from the surface of his body now made him begin to shiver, and he grew more awkward. A large piece of moss fell squarely on the little fire. He tried to poke it out with his fingers, but his shivering frame made him poke too far, and he disrupted the nucleus of the little fire, the burning grasses and tiny twigs separated and scattering. He tried to poke them together again, but in spite of the tenseness of the effort, his shivering got away with him, and the twigs were hopelessly scattered. Each twig gushed a puff of smoke and went out. The fire-provider had failed. As he looked apathetically about him, his eyes chanced on the dog, sitting across the ruins of the fire from him, in the snow, making restless, hunching movements, slightly lifting one forefoot and then the other, shifting its weight back and forth on them with wistful eagerness.

The sight of the dog put a wild idea into his head. He remembered the tale of the man, caught in a blizzard, who killed a steer and crawled inside the carcass, and so was saved. He would kill the dog and bury his hands in the warm body until the numbness went out of them. Then he could build another fire. He spoke to the dog, calling it to him; but in his voice was a strange note of fear that frightened the animal, who had never known the man to speak in such a way before. Something was the matter, and its suspicious nature sensed danger—it knew not what danger, but somewhere, somehow, in its brain arose an apprehension of the man. It flattened its ears down at the sound of the man's voice, and its restless, hunching movements and the liftings and shifting of its forefeet became more pronounced; but it would not come to the man. He got on his hands and knees and crawled towards the dog. This unusual posture again excited suspicion, and the animal sidled mincingly away.

The man sat up in the snow for a moment and struggled for calmness.

Then he pulled on his mittens, by means of his teeth, and got upon his feet. He glanced down at first in order to assure himself that he was really standing up, for the absence of sensation in his feet left him unrelated to the earth. His erect position in itself started to drive the webs of suspicion from the dog's mind; and when he spoke peremptorily, with the sound of whip-lashes in his voice, the dog rendered its customary allegiance and came to him. As it came within reaching distance, the man lost his control. His arms flashed out to the dog and he experienced genuine surprise when he discovered that his hands could not clutch, that there was neither bend nor feeling in the fingers. He had forgotten for the moment that they were frozen and that they were freezing more and more. All this happened quickly, and before the animal could get away, he encircled its body with his arms. He sat down in the snow, and in this fashion held the dog, while it snarled and whined and struggled.

But it was all he could do, hold its body encircled in his arms and sit there. He realized that he could not kill the dog. There was no way to do it. With his helpless hands he could neither draw nor hold his sheath knife nor throttle the animal. He released it, and it plunged wildly away, with tail between its legs, and still snarling. It halted forty feet away and surveyed him curiously, with ears sharply pricked forward. The man looked down at his hands in order to locate them, and found them hanging on the ends of his arms. It struck him as curious that one should have to use his eyes in order to find out where his hands were. He began threshing his arms back and forth, beating the mittened hands against his sides. He did this for five minutes, violently, and his heart pumped enough blood up to the surface to put a stop to his shivering. But no sensation was aroused in the hands. He had an impression that they hung like weights on the ends of his arms, but when he tried to run the impression down, he could not find it.

A certain fear of death, dull and oppressive, came to him. This fear quickly became poignant as he realized that it was no longer a mere matter of freezing his fingers and toes, or of his losing hands and feet, but that it was a matter of life and death with the chances against him. This threw him into a panic, and he turned and ran up the creek-bed along the old, dim trail. The dog joined in behind and kept up with him. He ran blindly, without intention, in fear such as he had never known in his life. Slowly, as he ploughed and floundered through the snow, he began to see things again,—the banks of the creek, the old timber-jams the leafless aspens, and the sky. The running made him feel better. He did not shiver. Maybe, if he ran on, his feet would thaw out; and, anyway, if he ran far enough, he would reach camp and the boys. Without doubt he would lose some fingers and toes and some of his face; but the boys would take care of him, and save the rest of him when he got there. And at the same time there was another thought in his mind that said he would never get to the camp and the boys; that it was too many miles away, that the freezing had too great a start on him, and that he would soon be stiff and dead. This thought he kept in the background and refused to consider. Sometimes it pushed itself forward and demanded to be heard, but he thrust it back and strove to think of other things.

It struck him as curious that he could run at all on feet so frozen that he could not feel them when they struck the earth and took the weight of his body. He seemed to himself to skim along above the surface and to have no connection with the earth. Somewhere he had once seen a winged Mercury, and he wondered if Mercury felt as he felt when skimming over the earth.

His theory of running until he reached camp and the boys had one flaw in it; he lacked the endurance. Several times he stumbled, and finally he tottered, crumpled up, and fell. When he tried to rise, he failed. He must sit and rest, he decided, and next time he would merely walk and keep on going. As he sat and regained his breath, he noted that he was feeling quite warm and comfortable. He was not shivering, and it even seemed that a warm glow had come to his chest and trunk. And yet, when he touched his nose or cheeks, there was no sensation. Running would not thaw them out. Nor would it thaw out his hands and feet. Then the thought came to him that the frozen portions of his body must be extending. He tried to keep this thought down, to forget it, to think of something else; he was aware of the panicky feeling that it caused, and he was afraid of the panic. But the thought asserted itself, and peristed, until it produced a vision of his body totally frozen. This was too much, and he made another wild run along the trail. Once he slowed down to a walk, but the thought of the freezing extending itself made him run again.

And all the time the dog ran with him, at his heels. When he fell down a second time, it curled its tail over its forefeet and sat in front of him, facing him, curiously eager and intent. The warmth and security of the animal angered him, and he cursed it till it flattened down its ears appeasingly. This time the shivering came more quickly upon the man. He was losing in his battle with the frost. It was creeping into his body from all sides. The thought of it drove him on, but he ran no more than a hundred feet, when he staggered and pitched headlong. It was his last panic. When he had recovered his breath and control, he sat up and entertained in his mind the conception of meeting death with dignity. However, the conception did not come to him in such terms. His idea of it was that he had been making a fool of himself, running around like a chicken with its head cut off—such was the simile that occurred to him. Well, he was bound to freeze anyway, and he might as well take it decently. With this new-found peace of mind came the first glimmerings of drowsiness. A good idea, he thought, to sleep off to death. It was like taking an anaesthetic. Freezing was not so bad as people thought. There were lots worse ways to die.

He pictured the boys finding his body next day. Suddenly he found himself with them, coming along the trail and looking for himself. And, still with them, he came around a turn in the trail and found himself lying in the snow. He did not belong with himself any more, for even then he was out of himself, standing with the boys and looking at himself in the snow. It certainly was cold, was his thought. When he got back to the States he could tell the folks what real cold was. He drifted on from this to a vision of the old-timer on Sulphur Creek. He could see him quite clearly, warm and comfortable, and smoking a pipe.

'You were right, old hoss; you were right,' the man mumbled to the old-timer of Sulphur Creek.

Then the man drowsed off into what seemed to him the most comfortable and satisfying sleep he had ever known. The dog sat facing him and waiting. The brief day drew to a close in a long, slow twilight. There were no signs of a fire to be made, and, besides, never in the dog's experience had it known a man to sit like that in the snow and make no fire. As the twilight drew on, its eager yearning for the fire mastered it, and with a great lifting and shifting of forefeet, it whined softly, then flattened its ears down in anticipation of being chidden by the man. But the man remained silent. Later, the dog whined loudly. And still later it crept close to the man and caught the scent of death. This made the animal bristle and back away. A little longer it delayed, howling under the stars that leaped and danced and shone brightly in the cold sky. Then it turned and trotted up the trail in the direction of the camp it knew, where were the other food-providers and fire-providers.

Guy de Maupassant born 1850 in Normandy, France, where he spent much of his youth. After education at the seminary at Yvetot and the Lycée Corneille, Rouen, he entered the Civil Service when he had completed his compulsory military service during the Franco-Prussian War. In the later part of his life Maupassant earned his living by writing, producing novels, plays, and about three hundred short stories. It is for the stories he is remembered, and for his influence on other writers all over the world. He was one of the great influences on the modern short story. His observations of life are sharp and accurate, realistic. His stories vary in form, and often exploit the effect of a surprise ending. He claimed that for himself 'psychology in a novel or story consists in this: to show the inner man by his life.' Hence his stories are often clear observations of an incident, objective, without explanations or long passages which reveal the characters' thoughts or feelings.

His stories are collected in many editions, BOULE DE SUIF AND OTHER STORIES is in a Penguin edition.

Maupassant died in 1893.

THE PIECE OF STRING

Guy de Maupassant

ON ALL THE ROADS ROUND GODERVILLE THE PEASANTS AND THEIR WIVES were making their way in towards the little town, for it was market day. The men were plodding along stolidly, their bodies thrust forward with every movement of their long bandy legs; they were misshapen from their heavy work and all the tedious, back-breaking tasks that make up the life of the agricultural labourer; for the downward pressure on the plough raises the left shoulder and so twists the spine, while the firm stance necessary for reaping makes for bandy legs. Their blue starched smocks, as glossy as patent-leather, were relieved round the collar and wrists with fine white embroidery; they bellied out round the men's bony frames like inflated balloons, with a head, two arms and two legs sticking out.

Some were leading a cow or a calf on a rope, while their wives urged the animal on from behind with branches still covered with leaves. The women were carrying on their arms large baskets, from which protruded the heads of chickens or ducks. They walked with a shorter, brisker step than their menfolk; their spare, erect figures were wrapped in skimpy little shawls, pinned across their flat chests, and their hair was covered by a tight-fitting coif with a cap on top.

From time to time a farm-cart would pass, drawn at a jog-trot by an old pony; in it two men, seated side by side, and a woman at the back holding on to the sides against the violent jolting bobbed up and down grotesquely.

On the square at Goderville there was a confused jostling mass of animals and human beings. The horns of the bullocks and the tall beaver hats of the better-off peasants and the caps of their wives stood out above the crush. And the shrill, piercing, high-pitched voices made a harsh, unceasing babel, above which from time to time rose a great, deep-chested roar of laughter from some cheery soul, or the mooing of a cow tied up to the wall of a house.

Everywhere there was the smell of cowhouses and milk and manure, of hay and sweat, the rank, powerful reek of men and animals, characteristic of those who work on the land.

Master Hauchecorne, of Bréauté, had just reached Goderville and was making his way towards the market square, when he caught sight of a small piece of string on the ground. Master Hauchecorne, thrifty, like all true Normans, reflected that it was always worth while picking up anything that might come in useful; so he bent down, with some difficulty, for he suffered from rheumatism. He picked up the bit of thin string off the ground and was preparing to roll it up carefully, when he caught sight of Master Malandain, the saddler, at his shop-door watching him. They had had a difference of opinion in the past over a head-stall, and had been on bad terms ever since, being both of an unforgiving disposition.

Master Hauchecorne felt somehow ashamed at being seen by his enemy like this, looking for a bit of string in the muck. He quickly concealed his treasure trove under his smock, slipping it into his trouser pocket; then he pretended to look for something which he couldn't find, and presently he went on towards the square, leaning forward, bent double with his rheumatism.

He was immediately lost in the shrill-voiced, slow-moving crowd, where everyone was bargaining keenly. The peasants were prodding the cows; they went away and came back again, hesitating, always afraid of being taken in, unable to make up their minds; they watched the seller's expression, trying to fathom his cunning or spot the defects of the animal.

The women, having put down their big baskets at their feet, had taken out the fowls, which now lay on the ground, tied by the legs, with terror in their eyes and their combs scarlet. They listened to the bids, refused to come down, hard-faced and impassive, or else, suddenly making up their minds to accept the lower price offered, shouted after the purchaser, who was slowly walking away:

'Right you are, Master Anthime; you can have it.'

Then gradually the crowd in the square thinned, and, as the midday Angelus rang, those who lived too far away to go home scattered to the inns.

At Jourdain's the big room was as full of diners as the courtyard was of vehicles of every kind—farm-carts large and small, gigs and traps, shandrydans of nameless varieties, brown with dung, shapeless, patched up, raising their shafts to heaven like arms, or tilted forward with their tail-boards in the air.

Quite close to the diners as they sat at table, the vast fireplace, in which a bright fire was blazing, threw out its heat on to the backs of the row on the right. Three spits were turning, laden with chickens, pigeons, and legs of mutton; and an appetizing smell of meat roasting and gravy trickling over the browning flesh issued from the fireplace, raised everyone's spirits and made every mouth water.

All the aristocracy of the plough took its meals at Master Jourdain's, innkeeper and horse-dealer, a crafty fellow, who had made his pile. Dishes were brought in and carried out again as empty as the jugs of golden cider. Everybody was talking about the business done, what each had bought and sold. Questions were asked about the prospects for the harvest. The weather was good for the green crops, but rather damp for the wheat.

Suddenly the roll of a drum was heard in the courtyard in front of the house. All the diners got up at once, except for a few who were not interested, and ran to the door or the windows, with their mouths still full and their napkins in their hands.

When he had finished his roll on the drum, the town-crier read out his notice in a series of jerks, with pauses in the wrong places, so that it made nonsense:

'Notice is hereby given to the inhabitants of Goderville and in general to all—those present at the market that there has been lost this morning on the Beuzeville road between—nine and ten o'clock a black leather wallet containing five hundred francs and some business papers. Anyone finding the same is requested to bring it—without delay to the Town Hall or to Master Fortuné Houlbrèque, of Manneville. A reward of twenty francs is offered.'

Then the man continued his round. The deep notes of the drum and the town-crier's announcement, now only faintly audible, were repeated a second time in the distance.

Everyone began discussing the occurrence, speculating on Master Houlbrèque's chances of recovering his wallet or the reverse.

At last the meal came to an end.

They were finishing their coffee, when the police sergeant appeared at the door and enquired:

'Is Master Hauchecorne here?'

Master Hauchecorne, who was sitting at the far end of the table, replied:

'Yes, I'm here.'

The sergeant went on:

'Master Hauchecorne, will you be so good as to come with me to the Town Hall? The Mayor would like to speak to you.'

The peasant, surprised and worried, hurriedly swallowed his brandy, got up, and, even more bent than in the morning, for the first few steps after a rest were particularly painful, started off in the wake of the sergeant, repeating:

'I'm here, I'm here.'

The Mayor was waiting for him, sitting in an armchair. He was the local solicitor—a stout, important man, fond of pompous language.

'Master Hauchecorne,' he said, 'you were seen this morning to pick up the wallet lost by Master Houlbrèque, of Manneville, on the Beuzeville road.'

The peasant, taken aback, looked at the Mayor; he was already frightened at the suspicion that had fallen upon him, without quite knowing why.

'Me? I picked up the wallet, did I?'

'Yes, you.'

'On my honour, I knows nought about it.'

'You were seen.'

'I were seen; who seen me?'

'Master Malandain, the saddler.'

Then the old man remembered, understood, and, flushing with anger cried:

'So, 'e's seen me, 'as 'e, the scoundrel? This is what 'e seen me pick up, this 'ere piece of string; look, Sir!'

And, rummaging in the depths of his pocket, he pulled out the little bit of string.

But the Mayor shook his head incredulously:

'You'll never persuade me, Master Hauchecorne, that Master Malandain, who is a reliable man, mistook a piece of string for a wallet.'

The peasant, now in a furious temper, raised his hand and spat on the floor as evidence of his good faith, repeating:

'But it's God's truth, all the same; it's the whole truth and nothing but the truth, s'welp me God!'

The mayor went on:

'After picking up the object, you even went on searching in the mud for some time, in case any coin might have fallen out.'

The old fellow was speechless with anger and fright:

'Some folks'll say any damned thing at all; fancy telling lies like that to discredit an honest man; some folks'll say anything.'

His protestations were unavailing; the Mayor didn't believe him.

He was confronted with Master Malandain, who repeated and upheld his accusation. They abused one another for an hour. At his own request, Master Hauchecorne was searched and nothing was found on him.

Finally, the Mayor, not knowing what to do, sent him away, warning him that he was going to report the matter to higher authority and ask for instructions.

The news had spread. As he left the Town Hall, the old fellow was surrounded and questioned with a curiosity sometimes genuine, sometimes ironical, but always good-natured. And he began to tell the story of the piece of string. No one believed him; they all merely laughed.

As he walked on, everybody stopped him, and he stopped his acquaintances, beginning his story over and over again, repeating his protestations of innocence, turning out his pockets to show that he had got nothing.

But everybody said: 'Go on, you cunning old devil!'

And he lost his temper, working himself up into a fever of nervous exasperation, because no one would believe him; he didn't know what to do and merely went on repeating his story.

It was getting dark and time to be going home. He set out with three neighbours, to whom he pointed out the spot where he had picked up the piece of string. And all the way home he enlarged on the incident.

In the evening he took a turn round the village of Bréauté in order to tell everyone. He met with nothing but incredulity.

He couldn't sleep all night for the worry of it.

Next day, about one o'clock in the afternoon, Marius Paumelle, one of Master Breton's farm hands at Ymauville brought back the wallet with its contents intact to Master Houlbrèque at Manneville.

The man stated that he had actually found the wallet on the road, but, not knowing how to read, had taken it home with him and given it to his employer.

The news soon spread. Master Hauchecorne heard about it. He immediately went round repeating his story, with the sequel. He was vindicated.

'What got my goat,' he would say, 'wasn't so much the thing itself, if you understand what I mean, but the lies. There's nothing 'urts so much as to be blamed because somebody has told a lie.'

He talked all day about his adventure; he told the story to people he passed on the road, to those who dropped into the local for a drink, and to the congregation, as they came out of church the following Sunday. He stopped total strangers to tell them. His mind was now at rest, but something nevertheless still worried him without his knowing exactly what it was. People seemed amused as they listened to him; they didn't seem convinced, and he was conscious of whispering behind his back.

The following Tuesday he went to the Goderville market, simply in order to tell his story.

Malandain, standing at his door, burst out laughing as he passed. He wondered why.

He accosted a farmer from Criquetot, who didn't let him finish his story, and, digging him in the ribs, shouted at him:

'Go on, you cunning old devil!' and turned on his heel.

Master Hauchecorne was still puzzled and was getting more and more worried. Why did they call him 'a cunning old devil'?

At dinner in Jourdain's inn he began again explaining what had happened.

A horse-dealer from Montivilliers shouted at him:

'Get along, you old scoundrel! I know all about your little games with your string.'

Hauchecorne stammered:

'But the wallet has been found.'

The other retorted:

'Shut your mouth, old man; the man who returns a thing isn't always the one who found it. Nobody's any the wiser. Now I've got you guessing!'

The peasant was flabbergasted; at last he understood. He was being accused of having had the wallet returned by a confederate, an accomplice. He tried to protest, but the whole table roared with laughter.

He couldn't finish his meal, and went out amid general mocking laughter.

He went home ashamed and indignant, choking with impotent rage, all the more distressed because, with his typical Norman cunning, he was quite capable of doing what he was accused of having done, and even of boasting of it as a clever trick. His duplicity being so well known, he realized dimly that he would never be able to establish his innocence. And the injustice of the suspicion wounded him deeply.

Then he began telling the story all over again, making it longer every day, adding fresh arguments at every telling, more emphatic protestations, more solemn oaths, which he thought out and elaborated, when he was alone, for he could never get the incident of the piece of string out of his mind. The more involved his defence became, the more closely reasoned his arguments, the less did people believe him.

'That's just the sort of argument a fellow uses when he's lying,' people were saying behind his back.

He felt it, and was eating his heart out, exhausting himself in vain attempts to establish his innocence.

He began to fail visibly.

The local wits now used to get him to tell the story of the string for a joke, as people egg on an old soldier to tell the story of his campaigns.

His mind, seriously affected, was giving way.

Towards the end of December, he took to his bed.

He died early in January, and in his last delirium he kept on protesting his innocence, repeating over and over again:

'A little piece of string . . . just a little piece of string, Sir, . . . look, 'ere it is!'

Ambrose Bierce born in Chester, Ohio, in 1842. He received little formal education, but became a skilled columnist, short story writer, poet, and satirist. His first stories were written in England. He returned to America in 1876 and wrote a satirical column in W. R. Hearst's EXAMINER, in San Francisco. For fifteen years he attacked politicians and business men whom he considered to be corrupt. He became highly unpopular, and much of his work was either rejected by publishers, or unsold. In 1913 he left Washington for Mexico, and was said to have been killed in the war between Villa and Carranza, in 1914.

Although a prolific writer, most of his best work is to be found in one book of short stories, IN THE MIDST OF LIFE, 1891.

AN OCCURRENCE AT
OWL CREEK BRIDGE

Ambrose Bierce

A MAN STOOD UPON A RAILROAD BRIDGE IN NORTHERN ALABAMA, LOOKING down into the swift water twenty feet below. The man's hands were behind his back, the wrists bound with a cord. A rope loosely encircled his neck. It was attached to a stout cross-timber above his head, and the slack fell to the level of his knees. Some loose boards laid upon the sleepers supporting the metals of the railway supplied a footing for him and his executioners—two private soldiers of the Federal army, directed by a sergeant who in civil life may have been a deputy sheriff. At a short remove upon the same temporary platform was an officer in the uniform of his rank, armed. He was a captain. A sentinel at each end of the bridge stood with his rifle in the position known as 'support', that is to say, vertical in front of the left shoulder, the hammer resting on the forearm thrown straight across the chest—a formal and unnatural position, enforcing an erect carriage of the body. It did not appear to be the duty of these two men to know what was occurring at the centre of the bridge; they merely blockaded the two ends of the foot plank which traversed it.

Beyond one of the sentinels, nobody was in sight; the railroad ran straight away into a forest for a hundred yards then, curving, was lost to view. Doubtless there was an outpost farther along .The other bank of the stream was open ground—a gentle acclivity topped with a stockade of vertical tree trunks, loopholed for rifles, with a single embrasure through which protruded the muzzle of a brass cannon commanding the bridge. Midway of the slope between bridge and fort were the spectators—a single company of infantry in line, at 'parade rest,' the butts of the rifles on the ground, the barrels inclining slightly backward against the right shoulder, the hands crossed upon the stock. A lieutenant stood at the right of the line, the point of his sword upon the ground, his left hand resting upon his right. Excepting the group of four at the centre of the bridge, not a man moved. The company faced the bridge, staring stonily, motionless. The sentinels, facing the banks of the stream, might have been statues to adorn the bridge. The captain stood with folded arms, silent, observing the work of his subordinates, but making no sign. Death is a dignitary who when he comes announced is to be received with formal manifestations of respect, even by those most familiar with him. In the code of military etiquette silence and fixity are forms of deference.

The man who was engaged in being hanged was apparently about thirty-five years of age. He was a civilian, if one might judge from his habit, which was that of a planter. His features were good—a straight nose, firm mouth, broad forehead, from which his long, dark hair was combed straight back, falling behind his ears to the collar of his well-fitting frock coat. He wore a mustache and pointed beard, but no whiskers; his eyes were large and dark grey, and had a kindly expression which one would hardly have expected in one whose neck was in the hemp. Evidently this was no vulgar assassin. The liberal military code makes provision for hanging many kinds of persons, and gentlemen are not excluded.

The preparations being complete, the two private soldiers stepped aside and each drew away the plank upon which he had been standing. The sergeant turned to the captain, saluted, and placed himself immediately behind that officer, who in turn moved apart one pace. These movements left the condemned man and the sergeant standing on the two ends of the same plank, which spanned three of the crossties of the bridge. The end upon which the civilian stood almost, but not quite, reached a fourth. This plank had been held in place by the weight of the captain; it was now held by that of the sergeant. At a signal from the former, the latter would step aside, the plank would tilt, and the condemned man go down between two ties. The arrangement commended itself to his judgment as simple and effective. His face had not been covered nor his eyes bandaged. He looked a moment at his 'unsteadfast footing,' then let his gaze wander to the swirling water of the stream racing madly beneath his feet. A piece of dancing driftwood caught his attention and his eyes followed it down the current. How slowly it appeared to move! What a sluggish stream!

He closed his eyes in order to fix his last thoughts upon his wife and children. The water, touched to gold by the early sun, the brooding mists under the banks at some distance down the stream, the fort, the soldiers, the piece of drift—all had distracted him. And now he became conscious of a new disturbance. Striking through the thought of his dear ones was a sound which he could neither ignore nor understand, a sharp, distinct, metallic percussion like the stroke of a blacksmith's hammer upon the anvil; it had the same ringing quality. He wondered what it was, and whether immeasurably distant or near by—it seemed both. Its recurrence was regular, but as slow as the tolling of a death knell. He awaited each stroke with impatience and—he knew not why—apprehension. The intervals of silence grew progressively longer; the delays became maddening. With their greater infrequency the sounds increased in strength and sharpness. They hurt his ear like the thrust of a knife; he feared he would shriek. What he heard was the ticking of his watch.

He unclosed his eyes and saw again the water below him. 'If I could free my hands,' he thought, 'I might throw off the noose and spring into the stream. By diving I could evade the bullets and, swimming vigorously, reach the bank, take to the woods, and get away home. My home, thank

God, is as yet outside their lines; my wife and little ones are still beyond the invader's farthest advance.'

As these thoughts, which have here to be set down in words, were flashed into the doomed man's brain rather than evolved from it, the captain nodded to the sergeant. The sergeant stepped aside.

II

Peyton Farquhar was a well-to-do planter of an old and highly respected Alabama family. Being a slave owner and like other slave owners a politician, he was naturally an original secessionist and ardently devoted to the Southern cause. Circumstances of an imperious nature, which it is unnecessary to relate here, had prevented him from taking service with the gallant army which had fought the disastrous campaigns ending with the fall of Corinth, and he chafed under the inglorious restraint, longing for the release of his energies, the larger life of the soldier, the opportunity for distinction. That opportunity, he felt, would come, as it comes to all in war time. Meanwhile he did what he could. No service was too humble for him to perform in aid of the South, no adventure too perilous for him to undertake if consistent with the character of a civilian who was at heart a soldier, and who in good faith and without too much qualification assented to at least a part of the frankly villainous dictum that all is fair in love and war.

One evening while Farquhar and his wife were sitting on a rustic bench near the entrance to his grounds, a grey-clad soldier rode up to the gate and asked for a drink of water. Mrs Farquhar was only too happy to serve him with her own white hands. While she was fetching the water her husband approached the dusty horseman and inquired eagerly for news from the front.

'The Yanks are repairing the railroads,' said the man, 'and are getting ready for another advance. They have reached the Owl Creek bridge, put it in order, and built a stockade on the north bank. The commandant has issued an order, which is posted everywhere, declaring that any civilian caught interfering with the railroad, its bridges, tunnels, or trains will be summarily hanged. I saw the order.'

'How far is it to the Owl Creek bridge?' Farquhar asked.

'About thirty miles.'

'Is there no force on this side the creek?'

'Only a picket post half a mile out, on the railroad, and a single sentinel at this end of the bridge.'

'Suppose a man—a civilian and student of hanging—should elude the picket post and perhaps get the better of the sentinel,' said Farquhar, smiling, 'what could he accomplish?'

The soldier reflected. 'I was there a month ago,' he replied. 'I observed that the flood of last winter had lodged a great quantity of driftwood against the wooden pier at this end of the bridge. It is now dry and would burn like tow.'

The lady had now brought the water, which the soldier drank. He thanked her ceremoniously, bowed to her husband, and rode away. An hour later, after nightfall, he repassed the plantation, going northward in the direction from which he had come. He was a Federal scout.

III

As Peyton Farquhar fell straight downward through the bridge he lost consciousness and was as one already dead. From this state he was awakened—ages later, it seemed to him—by the pain of a sharp pressure upon his throat, followed by a sense of suffocation. Keen, poignant agonies seemed to shoot from his neck downward through every fiber of his body and limbs. These pains appeared to flash along well-defined lines of ramification and to beat with an inconceivably rapid periodicity. They seemed like streams of pulsating fire heating him to an intolerable temperature. As to his head, he was conscious of nothing but a feeling of fullness—of congestion. These sensations were unaccompanied by thought. The intellectual part of his nature was already effaced; he had power only to feel, and feeling was torment. He was conscious of motion. Encompassed in a luminous cloud, of which he was now merely the fiery heart, without material substance, he swung through unthinkable arcs of oscillation, like a vast pendulum. Then all at once, with terrible suddenness, the light about him shot upward with the noise of a loud splash; a frightful roaring was in his ears, and all was cold and dark. The power of thought was restored; he knew that the rope had broken and he had fallen into the stream. There was no additional strangulation; the noose about his neck was already suffocating him and kept the water from his lungs. To die of hanging at the bottom of a river!—the idea seemed to him ludicrous. He opened his eyes in the darkness and saw above him a gleam of light, but how distant, how inaccessible! He was still sinking, for the light became fainter and fainter until it was a mere glimmer. Then it began to grow and brighten, and he knew that he was rising toward the surface—knew it with reluctance, for he was now very comfortable. 'To be hanged and drowned,' he thought, 'that is not so bad; but I do not wish to be shot. No; I will not be shot; that is not fair.'

He was not conscious of an effort, but a sharp pain in his wrist apprised him that he was trying to free his hands. He gave the struggle his attention, as an idler might observe the feat of a juggler, without interest in the outcome. What splendid effort!—what magnificent, what superhuman strength! Ah, that was a fine endeavor! Bravo! The cord fell away; his arms parted and floated upward, the hands dimly seen on each side in the growing light. He watched them with a new interest as first one and then the other pounced upon the noose at his neck. They tore it away and thrust it fiercely aside, its undulations resembling those of a water snake. 'Put it back, put it back!' He thought he shouted these words to his hands, for the undoing of the noose had been succeeded by the direst pang that he had yet experienced. His neck ached horribly; his brain was on fire; his heart, which had been fluttering faintly, gave a great leap, trying to force itself out at his mouth. His whole body was racked and wrenched with an insupportable anguish! But his disobedient hands gave no heed to the command. They beat the water vigorously with quick, downward strokes, forcing him to the surface. He felt his head emerge; his eyes were blinded by the sunlight; his chest expanded convulsively, and with a supreme and crowning agony his lungs engulfed a great draught of air, which instantly he expelled in a shriek!

He was now in full possession of his physical senses. They were, indeed, preternaturally keen and alert. Something in the awful disturbances of his organic system had so exalted and refined them that they made record of things never before perceived. He felt the ripples upon his face and heard their separate sounds as they struck. He looked at the forest on the bank of the stream, saw the individual trees, the leaves and the veining of each leaf—saw the very insects upon them: the locusts, the brilliant-bodied flies, the grey spiders stretching their webs from twig to twig. He noted the prismatic colours in all the dewdrops upon a million blades of grass. The humming of the gnats that danced above the eddies of the stream, the beating of the dragonflies' wings, the strokes of the water spiders' legs, like oars which had lifted their boat—all these made audible music. A fish slid along beneath his eyes and he heard the rush of its body parting the water.

He had come to the surface facing down the stream; in a moment the visible world seemed to wheel slowly round, himself the pivotal point, and he saw the bridge, the fort, the soldiers upon the bridge, the captain, the sergeant, the two privates, his executioners. They were in silhouette against the blue sky. They shouted and gesticulated, pointing at him. The captain had drawn his pistol, but did not fire; the others were unarmed. Their movements were grotesque and horrible, their forms gigantic.

Suddenly he heard a sharp report and something struck the water smartly within a few inches of his head, spattering his face with spray. He heard a second report, and saw one of the sentinels with his rifle at his shoulder, a light cloud of blue smoke rising from the muzzle. The man in the water saw the eye of the man on the bridge gazing into his own through the sights of the rifle. He observed that it was a grey eye and remembered having read that grey eyes were keenest, and that all famous marksmen had them. Nevertheless, this one had missed.

A counterswirl had caught Farquhar and turned him half round; he was again looking into the forest on the bank opposite the fort. The sound of a clear, high voice in a monotonous singsong now rang out behind him and came across the water with a distinctness that pierced and subdued all other sounds, even the beating of the ripples in his ears. Although no soldier, he had frequented camps enough to know the dread significance of that deliberate, drawling, aspirated chant; the lieutenant on shore was taking a part in the morning's work. How coldly and pitilessly—with what an even, calm intonation, presaging and enforcing tranquillity in the men—with what accurately measured intervals fell those cruel words:

'Attention, company! . . . Shoulder arms! . . . Ready! . . . Aim! . . . Fire!'

Farquhar dived—dived as deeply as he could. The water roared in his ears like the voice of Niagara, yet he heard the dulled thunder of the volley and, rising again toward the surface, met shining bits of metal, singularly flattened, oscillating slowly downward. Some of them touched him on the face and hands, then fell away, continuing their descent. One lodged between his collar and neck; it was uncomfortably warm and he snatched it out.

As he rose to the surface, gasping for breath, he saw that he had been a long time under water; he was perceptibly farther downstream—nearer to safety. The soldiers had almost finished reloading; the metal ramrods flashed all at once in the sunshine as they were drawn from the barrels, turned in the air, and thrust into their sockets. The two sentinels fired again, independently and ineffectually.

The hunted man saw all this over his shoulder; he was now swimming vigorously with the current. His brain was as energetic as his arms and legs; he thought with the rapidity of lightning.

'The officer,' he reasoned, 'will not make that martinet's error a second time. It is as easy to dodge a volley as a single shot. He has probably already given the command to fire at will. God help me, I cannot dodge them all!'

An appalling splash within two yards of him was followed by a loud, rushing sound, *diminuendo*, which seemed to travel back through the air to the fort and died in an explosion which stirred the very river to its deeps! A rising sheet of water, which curved over him, fell down upon him, blinded him, strangled him! The cannon had taken a hand in the game. As he shook his head free from the commotion of the smitten water, he heard the deflected shot humming through the air ahead, and in an instant it was cracking and smashing the branches in the forest beyond.

'They will not do that again,' he thought; 'the next time they will use a charge of grape. I must keep my eye upon the gun; the smoke will apprise me—the report arrives too late; it lags behind the missile. That is a good gun.'

Suddenly he felt himself whirled round and round—spinning like a top. The water, the banks, the forests, the now distant bridge, fort, and men— all were commingled and blurred. Objects were represented by their colours only; circular horizontal streaks of colour—that was all he saw. He had been caught in a vortex and was being whirled on with a velocity of advance and gyration which made him giddy and sick. In a few moments he was flung upon the gravel at the foot of the left bank of the stream—the southern bank—and behind a projecting point which con- cealed him from his enemies. The sudden arrest of his motion, the abrasion of one of his hands on the gravel, restored him, and he wept with delight. He dug his fingers into the sand, threw it over himself in handfuls, and audibly blessed it. It looked like diamonds, rubies, emeralds; he could think of nothing beautiful which it did not resemble. The trees upon the bank were giant garden plants; he noted a definite order in their arrange- ment, inhaled the fragrance of their blooms. A strange, roseate light shone through the spaces among their trunks and the wind made in their branches the music of aeolian harps. He had no wish to perfect his escape —was content to remain in that enchanting spot until retaken.

A whiz and rattle of grapeshot among the branches high above his head roused him from his dream. The baffled cannoneer had fired him a random farewell. He sprang to his feet, rushed up the sloping bank, and plunged into the forest.

All that day he travelled, laying his course by the rounding sun. The forest seemed interminable; nowhere did he discover a break in it, not even a woodman's road. He had not known that he lived in so wild a region. There was something uncanny in the revelation.

By nightfall he was fatigued, footsore, famishing. The thought of his wife and children urged him on. At last he found a road which led him in what he knew to be the right direction. It was as wide and straight as a city street, yet it seemed untravelled. No fields bordered it, no dwelling anywhere. Not so much as the barking of a dog suggested human habitation. The black bodies of the trees formed a straight wall on both sides, terminating on the horizon in a point, like a diagram in a lesson in perspective. Overhead, as he looked up through this rift in the wood, shone great golden stars looking unfamiliar and grouped in strange constellations. He was sure they were arranged in some order which had a secret and malign significance. The wood on either side was full of singular noises, among which—once, twice, and again—he distinctly heard whispers in an unknown tongue.

His neck was in pain and lifting his hand to it he found it horribly swollen. He knew that it had a circle of black where the rope had bruised it. His eyes felt congested; he could no longer close them. His tongue was swollen with thirst; he relieved its fever by thrusting it forward from between his teeth into the cold air. How softly the turf had carpeted the untravelled avenue—he could no longer feel the roadway beneath his feet!

Doubtless, despite his suffering, he had fallen asleep while walking, for now he sees another scene—perhaps he has merely recovered from a delirium. He stands at the gate of his own home. All is as he left it, and all bright and beautiful in the morning sunshine. He must have travelled the entire night. As he pushes open the gate passes and up the wide white walk, he sees a flutter of female garments; his wife, looking fresh and cool and sweet, steps down from the veranda to meet him. At the bottom of the steps she stands waiting, with a smile of ineffable joy, an attitude of matchless grace and dignity. Ah, how beautiful she is! He springs forward with extended arms. As he is about to clasp her, he feels a stunning blow upon the back of his neck; a blinding white light blazes all about him with a sound like the shock of a cannon—then all is darkness and silence!

Peyton Farquhar was dead; his body, with a broken neck, swung gently from side to side beneath the timbers of the Owl Creek bridge.

Stephen Crane born 1871 in Newark, New Jersey. He lived only until 1900, and most of his writing was produced in the 1890's. He was a newspaper reporter, and war correspondent in Cuba and in Greece. Like Hemingway later, much of his work dealt with the violence he found in the life around him. His realistic attitude had much in common with the new naturalism of the great French writers of the period. In 1895 Crane travelled in the far West of America, and from this came his story 'THE BRIDE COMES TO YELLOW SKY', lighter in tone than most of his stories. Crane is probably best known for his novel of war, THE RED BADGE OF COURAGE, 1895, and it is worth contrasting this novel with his longer stories such as 'THE OPEN BOAT', or 'MAGGIE: A GIRL OF THE STREETS', 1896.

THE BRIDE COMES TO YELLOW SKY

Stephen Crane

I

THE GREAT PULLMAN WAS WHIRLING ONWARD WITH SUCH DIGNITY OF motion that a glance from the window seemed simply to prove that the plains of Texas were pouring eastward. Vast flats of green grass, dull-hued spaces of mesquit and cactus, little groups of frame houses, woods of light and tender trees, all were sweeping into the east, sweeping over the horizon, a precipice.

A newly married pair had boarded this coach at San Antonio. The man's face was reddened from many days in the wind and sun, and a direct result of his new black clothes was that his brick-coloured hands were constantly performing in a most conscious fashion. From time to time he looked down respectfully at his attire. He sat with a hand on each knee, like a man waiting in a barber's shop. The glances he devoted to other passengers were furtive and shy.

The bride was not pretty, nor was she very young. She wore a dress of blue cashmere, with small reservations of velvet here and there, and with steel buttons abounding. She continually twisted her head to regard her puff sleeves, very stiff, straight, and high. They embarrassed her. It was quite apparent that she had cooked, and that she expected to cook, dutifully. The blushes caused by the careless scrutiny of some passengers as she had entered the car were strange to see upon this plain, under-class countenance, which was drawn in placid, almost emotionless lines.

They were evidently very happy. 'Ever been in a parlour-car before?' he asked, smiling with delight.

'No,' she answered; 'I never was. It's fine, ain't it?'

'Great! And then after a while we'll go forward to the diner, and get a big lay-out. Finest meal in the world. Charge a dollar.'

'Oh, do they?' cried the bride. 'Charge a dollar? Why, that's too much —for us—ain't it, Jack?'

'Not this trip, anyhow,' he answered bravely. 'We're going to go the whole thing.'

Later he explained to her about the trains. 'You see, it's a thousand miles from one end of Texas to the other; and this train runs right across it, and never stops but four times.' He had the pride of an owner. He pointed out to her the dazzling fittings of the coach; and in truth her eyes opened wider as she contemplated the sea-green figured velvet, the shining brass, silver, and glass, the wood that gleamed as darkly brilliant as the surface of a pool of oil. At one end a bronze figure sturdily held a support for a separated chamber, and at convenient places on the ceiling were frescos in olive and silver.

To the minds of the pair, their surroundings reflected the glory of their marriage that morning in San Antonio; this was the environment of their new estate; and the man's face in particular beamed with an elation that made him appear ridiculous to the negro porter. This individual at times surveyed them from afar with an amused and superior grin. On other occasions he bullied them with skill in ways that did not make it exactly plain to them that they were being bullied. He subtly used all the manners of the most unconquerable kind of snobbery. He oppressed them; but of this oppression they had small knowledge, and they speedily forgot that infrequently a number of travellers covered them with stares of derisive enjoyment. Historically there was supposed to be something infinitely humorous in their situation.

'We are due in Yellow Sky at 3:42,' he said, looking tenderly into her eyes.

'Oh, are we?' she said, as if she had not been aware of it. To evince surprise of her husband's statement was part of her wifely amiability. She took from a pocket a little silver watch: and as she held it before her, and stared at it with a frown of attention, the new husband's face shone.

'I bought it in San Anton' from a friend of mine,' he told her gleefully.

'It's seventeen minutes past twelve,' she said, looking up at him with a kind of shy and clumsy coquetry. A passenger, noting this play, grew excessively sardonic, and winked at himself in one of the numerous mirrors.

At last they went to the dining-car. Two rows of negro waiters, in glowing white suits, surveyed their entrance with the interest, and also the equanimity, of men who had been forewarned. The pair fell to the lot of a waiter who happened to feel pleasure in steering them through their meal. He viewed them with the manner of a fatherly pilot, his countenance radiant with benevolence. The patronage, entwined with the ordinary deference, was not plain to them. And yet, as they returned to their coach, they showed in their faces a sense of escape.

To the left, miles down a long purple slope, was a little ribbon of mist where moved the keening Rio Grande. The train was approaching it at an angle, and the apex was Yellow Sky. Presently it was apparent that, as the distance from Yellow Sky grew shorter, the husband became commensurately restless. His brick-red hands were more insistent in their prominence. Occasionally he was even rather absent-minded and far-away when the bride leaned forward and addressed him.

As a matter of truth, Jack Potter was beginning to find the shadow of a deed weigh upon him like a leaden slab. He, the town marshal of Yellow Sky, a man known, liked, and feared in his corner, a prominent person, had gone to San Antonio to meet a girl he believed he loved, and there, after the usual prayers, had actually induced her to marry him, without consulting Yellow Sky for any part of the transaction. He was now bringing his bride before an innocent and unsuspecting community.

Of course people in Yellow Sky married as it pleased them, in accordance with a general custom; but such was Potter's thought of his duty to his friends, or of their idea of his duty, or of an unspoken form which does not control men in these matters, that he felt he was heinous. He had committed an extraordinary crime. Face to face with this girl in San Antonio, and spurred by his sharp impulse, he had gone headlong over all the social hedges. At San Antonio he was like a man hidden in the dark. A knife to sever any friendly duty, any form, was easy to his hand in that remote city. But the hour of Yellow Sky—the hour of daylight—was approaching.

He knew full well that his marriage was an important thing to his town. It could only be exceeded by the burning of the new hotel. His friends could not forgive him. Frequently he had reflected on the advisability of telling them by telegraph, but a new cowardice had been upon him. He feared to do it. And now the train was hurrying him toward a scene of amazement, glee, and reproach. He glanced out of the window at the line of haze swinging slowly in toward the train.

Yellow Sky had a kind of brass band, which played painfully, to the delight of the populace. He laughed without heart as he thought of it. If the citizens could dream of his prospective arrival with his bride, they would parade the band at the station and escort them, amid cheers and laughing congratulations, to his adobe home.

He resolved that he would use all the devices of speed and planscraft in making the journey from the station to his house. Once within that safe citadel, he could issue some sort of vocal bulletin, and then not go among the citizens until they had time to wear off a little of their enthusiasm.

The bride looked anxiously at him. 'What's worrying you, Jack?'

He laughed again. 'I'm not worrying, girl; I'm only thinking of Yellow Sky.'

She flushed in comprehension.

A sense of mutual guilt invaded their minds and developed a finer tenderness. They looked at each other with eyes softly aglow. But Potter often laughed the same nervous laugh; the flush upon the bride's face seemed quite permanent.

The traitor to the feelings of Yellow Sky narrowly watched the speeding landscape. 'We're nearly there,' he said.

Presently the porter came and announced the proximity of Potter's home. He held a brush in his hand, and, with all his airy superiority gone, he brushed Potter's new clothes as the latter slowly turned this way and that way. Potter fumbled out a coin and gave it to the porter, as he had seen others do. It was a heavy and muscle-bound business, as that of a man shoeing his first horse.

The porter took their bag, and as the train began to slow they moved forward to the hooded platform of the car. Presently the two engines and their long string of coaches rushed into the station of Yellow Sky.

'They have to take water here,' said Potter, from a constricted throat and in mournful cadence, as one announcing death. Before the train stopped his eye had swept the length of the platform, and he was glad and astonished to see there was none upon it but the station-agent, who, with a slightly hurried and anxious air, was walking toward the water-tanks. When the train had halted, the porter alighted first, and placed in position a little temporary step.

'Come on, girl,' said Potter, hoarsely. As he helped her down they each laughed on a false note. He took the bag from the negro, and bade his wife cling to his arm. As they slunk rapidly away, his hang-dog glance perceived that they were unloading the two trunks, and also that the station-agent, far ahead near the baggage-car, had turned and was running toward him, making gestures. He laughed, and groaned as he laughed, when he noted the first effect of his marital bliss upon Yellow Sky. He gripped his wife's arm firmly to his side, and they fled. Behind them the porter stood, chuckling fatuously.

II

The California express on the Southern Railway was due at Yellow Sky in twenty-one minutes. There were six men at the bar of the Weary Gentleman saloon. One was a drummer who talked a great deal and rapidly; three were Texans who did not care to talk at that time; and two were Mexican sheep-herders, who did not talk as a general practice in the Weary Gentleman saloon. The barkeeper's dog lay on the board walk that crossed in front of the door. His head was on his paws, and he glanced drowsily here and there with the constant vigilance of a dog that is kicked on occasion. Across the sandy street were some vivid green grass-plots, so wonderful in appearance, amid the sands that burned near them in a blazing sun, that they caused a doubt in the mind. They exactly resembled the grass mats used to represent lawns on the stage. At the cooler end of the railway station, a man without a coat sat in a tilted chair and smoked his pipe. The fresh-cut bank of the Rio Grande circled near the town, and there could be seen beyond it a great plum-coloured plain of mesquit.

Save for the busy drummer and his companions in the saloon, Yellow Sky was dozing. The new-comer leaned gracefully upon the bar, and recited many tales with the confidence of a bard who has come upon a new field.

'—and at the moment that the old man fell downstairs with the bureau in his arms, the old woman was coming up with two scuttles of coal, and of course—'

The drummer's tale was interrupted by a young man who suddenly appeared in the open door. He cried: 'Scratchy Wilson's drunk, and has turned loose with both hands.' The two Mexicans at once set down their glasses and faded out of the rear entrance of the saloon.

The drummer, innocent and jocular, answered: 'All right, old man. S'pose he has? Come in and have a drink, anyhow.'

But the information had made such an obvious cleft in every skull in the room that the drummer was obliged to see its importance. All had become instantly solemn. 'Say,' said he, mystified, 'what is this?' His three companions made the introductory gesture of eloquent speech; but the young man at the door forestalled them.

'It means, my friend,' he answered, as he came into the saloon, 'that for the next two hours this town won't be a health resort.'

The barkeeper went to the door, and locked and barred it; reaching out of the window, he pulled in heavy wooden shutters, and barred them. Immediately a solemn, chapel-like gloom was upon the place. The drummer was looking from one to another.

'But say,' he cried, 'what is this, anyhow? You don't mean there is going to be a gun-fight?'

'Don't know whether there'll be a fight or not,' answered one man, grimly; 'but there'll be some shootin'—some good shootin'.'

The young man who had warned them waved his hand. 'Oh, there'll be a fight fast enough, if any one wants it. Anybody can get a fight out there in the street. There's a fight just waiting.'

The drummer seemed to be swayed between the interest of a foreigner and a perception of personal danger.

'What did you say his name was?' he asked.

'Scratchy Wilson,' they answered in chorus.

'And will he kill anybody? What are you going to do? Does this happen often? Does he rampage around like this once a week or so? Can he break in that door?'

'No; he can't break down that door,' replied the barkeeper. 'He's tried it three times. But when he comes you'd better lay down on the floor, stranger. He's dead sure to shoot at it, and a bullet may come through.'

Thereafter the drummer kept a strict eye upon the door. The time had not yet been called for him to hug the floor, but, as a minor precaution, he sidled near to the wall. 'Will he kill anybody?' he said again.

The men laughed low and scornfully at the question.

'He's out to shoot, and he's out for trouble. Don't see any good in experimentin' with him.'

'But what do you do in a case like this? What do you do?'

A man responded: 'Why, he and Jack Potter—'

'But,' in chorus the other men interrupted, 'Jack Potter's in San Anton'.'

'Well, who is he? What's he got to do with it?'

'Oh, he's the town marshal. He goes out and fights Scratchy when he gets on one of these tears.'

'Wow!' said the drummer, mopping his brow. 'Nice job he's got.'

The voices had toned away to mere whisperings. The drummer wished to ask further questions, which were born of an increasing anxiety and bewilderment; but when he attempted them, the men merely looked at him in irritation and motioned him to remain silent. A tense waiting hush was upon them. In the deep shadows of the room their eyes shone as they listened for sounds from the street. One man made three gestures at the barkeeper; and the latter, moving like a ghost, handed him a glass and a bottle. The man poured a full glass of whisky, and set down the bottle noiselessly. He gulped the whisky in a swallow, and turned again toward the door in immovable silence. The drummer saw that the barkeeper, without a sound, had taken a Winchester from beneath the bar. Later he saw this individual beckoning to him, so he tiptoed across the room.

'You better come with me back of the bar.'

'No, thanks,' said the drummer, perspiring; 'I'd rather be where I can make a break for the back door.'

Whereupon the man of bottles made a kindly but peremptory gesture. The drummer obeyed it, and, finding himself seated on a box with his head below the level of the bar, balm was laid upon his soul at sight of various zinc and copper fittings that bore a resemblance to armour-plate. The barkeeper took a seat comfortably upon an adjacent box.

'You see,' he whispered, 'this here Scratchy Wilson is a wonder with a gun—a perfect wonder; and when he goes on the war-trail, we hunt our holes—naturally. He's about the last one of the old gang that used to hang out along the river here. He's a terror when he's drunk. When he's sober he's all right—kind of simple—wouldn't hurt a fly—nicest fellow in town. But when he's drunk—whoo!'

There were periods of stillness. 'I wish Jack Potter was back from San Anton',' said the barkeeper. 'He shot Wilson up once—in the leg—and he would sail in and pull out the kinks in this thing.'

Presently they heard from a distance the sound of a shot, followed by three wild yowls. It instantly removed a bond from the men in the darkened saloon. There was a shuffling of feet. They looked at each other. 'Here he comes,' they said.

III

A man in a maroon-coloured flannel shirt, which had been purchased for purposes of decoration, and made principally by some Jewish women on the East Side of New York, rounded a corner and walked into the middle of the main street of Yellow Sky. In either hand the man held a long, heavy blue-black revolver. Often he yelled, and these cries rang through a semblance of a deserted village, shrilly flying over the roofs in a volume that seemed to have no relation to the ordinary vocal strength of a man. It was as if the surrounding stillness formed the arch of a tomb over him. These cries of ferocious challenge rang against walls of silence. And his boots had red tops with gilded imprints, of the kind beloved in winter by little sledding boys on the hillsides of New England.

The man's face flamed in a rage begot of whisky. His eyes, rolling, and yet keen for ambush, hunted the still doorways and windows. He walked with the creeping movement of the midnight cat. As it occurred to him, he roared menacing information. The long revolvers in his hands were as easy as straws; they were moved with an electric swiftness. The little fingers of each hand played sometimes in a musician's way. Plain from the low collar of the shirt, the cords of his neck straightened and sank, straightened and sank, as passion moved him. The only sounds were his terrible invitations. The calm adobes preserved their demeanour at the passing of this small thing in the middle of the street.

There was no offer of fight—no offer of fight. The man called to the sky. There were no attractions. He bellowed and fumed and swayed his revolvers here and everywhere.

The dog of the barkeeper of the Weary Gentleman saloon had not appreciated the advance of events. He yet lay dozing in front of his master's door. At sight of the dog, the man paused and raised his revolver humorously. At sight of the man, the dog sprang up and walked diagonally away, with a sullen head, and growling. The man yelled, and the dog broke into a gallop. As it was about to enter an alley, there was a loud noise, a whistling, and something spat the ground directly before it. The dog screamed, and, wheeling in terror, galloped headlong in a new direction. Again there was a noise, a whistling, and sand was kicked viciously before it. Fear-stricken, the dog turned and flurried like an animal in a pen. The man stood laughing, his weapons at his hips.

Ultimately the man was attracted by the closed door of the Weary Gentleman saloon. He went to it and, hammering with a revolver, demanded drink.

The door remaining imperturbable, he picked a bit of paper from the walk, and nailed it to the framework with a knife. He then turned his back contemptuously upon this popular resort and, walking to the opposite side of the street and spinning there on his heel quickly and lithely, fired at the bit of paper. He missed it by a half-inch. He swore at himself, and went away. Later he comfortably fusilladed the windows of his most intimate friend. The man was playing with this town; it was a toy for him.

But still there was no offer of fight. The name of Jack Potter, his ancient antagonist, entered his mind, and he concluded that it would be a glad thing if he should go to Potter's house, and by bombardment induce him to come out and fight. He moved in the direction of his desire, chanting Apache scalp-music.

When he arrived at it, Potter's house presented the same still front as had the other adobes. Taking up a strategic position, the man howled a challenge. But this house regarded him as might a great stone god. It gave no sign. After a decent wait, the man howled further challenges, mingling with them wonderful epithets.

Presently there came the spectacle of a man churning himself into deepest rage over the immobility of a house. He fumed at it as the winter wind attacks a prairie cabin in the North. To the distance there should have gone the sound of a tumult like the fighting of two hundred Mexicans. As necessity bade him, he paused for breath or to reload his revolvers.

IV

Potter and his bride walked sheepishly and with speed. Sometimes they laughed together shamefacedly and low.

'Next corner, dear,' he said finally.

They put forth the efforts of a pair walking bowed against a strong wind. Potter was about to raise a finger to point the first appearance of the new home when, as they circled the corner, they came face to face with a man in a maroon-coloured shirt, who was feverishly pushing cartridges into a large revolver. Upon the instant the man dropped his revolver to the ground and, like lightning, whipped another from its holster. The second weapon was aimed at the bridegroom's chest.

There was a silence. Potter's mouth seemed to be merely a grave for his tongue. He exhibited an instinct to at once loosen his arm from the woman's grip, and he dropped the bag to the sand. As for the bride, her face had gone as yellow as old cloth. She was a slave to hideous rites, gazing at the apparitional snake.

The two men faced each other at a distance of three paces. He of the revolver smiled with a new and quiet ferocity.

'Tried to sneak up on me,' he said. 'Tried to sneak up on me!' His eyes grew more baleful. As Potter made a slight movement, the man thrust his revolver venomously forward. 'No; don't you do it, Jack Potter. Don't you move a finger toward a gun just yet. Don't you move an eyelash. The time has come for me to settle with you, and I'm goin' to do it my own way, and loaf along with no interferin'. So if you don't want a gun bent on you, just mind what I tell you.'

Potter looked at his enemy. 'I ain't got a gun on me, Scratchy,' he said. 'Honest, I ain't.' He was stiffening and steadying, but yet somewhere at the back of his mind a vision of the Pullman floated: the sea-green figured velvet, the shining brass, silver, and glass, the wood that gleamed as darkly brilliant as the surface of a pool of oil—all the glory of the marriage, the environment of the new estate. 'You know I fight when it comes to fighting, Scratchy Wilson; but I ain't got a gun on me. You'll have to do all the shootin' yourself.'

His enemy's face went livid. He stepped forward, and lashed his weapon to and fro before Potter's chest. 'Don't you tell me you ain't got no gun on you, you whelp. Don't tell me no lie like that. There ain't a man in Texas ever seen you without no gun. Don't take me for no kid.' His eyes blazed with light, and his throat worked like a pump.

'I ain't takin' you for no kid,' answered Potter. His heels had not moved an inch backward. 'I'm takin' you for a damn fool. I tell you I ain't got a gun, and I ain't. If you're goin' to shoot me up, you better begin now; you'll never get a chance like this again.'

So much enforced reasoning had told on Wilson's rage; he was calmer. 'If you ain't got a gun, why ain't you got a gun?' he sneered. 'Been to Sunday-school?'

'I ain't got a gun because I've just come from San Anton' with my wife. I'm married,' said Potter. 'And if I'd thought there was going to be any galoots like you prowling around when I brought my wife home, I'd had a gun, and don't you forget it.'

'Married!' said Scratchy, not at all comprehending.

'Yes, married. I'm married,' said Potter, distinctly.

'Married?' said Scratchy. Seemingly for the first time, he saw the drooping, drowning woman at the other man's side. 'No!' he said. He was like a creature allowed a glimpse of another world. He moved a pace backward, and his arm, with the revolver, dropped to his side. 'Is this the lady?' he asked.

'Yes; this is the lady,' answered Potter.

There was another period of silence.

'Well,' said Wilson at last, slowly, 'I s'pose it's all off now.'

'It's all off if you say so, Scratchy. You know I didn't make the trouble.' Potter lifted his valise.

'Well, I 'low it's off, Jack,' said Wilson. He was looking at the ground. 'Married!' He was not a student of chivalry; it was merely that in the presence of this foreign condition he was a simple child of the earlier plains. He picked up his starboard revolver, and, placing both weapons in their holsters, he went away. His feet made funnel-shaped tracks in the heavy sand.

Sherwood Anderson born 1876 in Camden, Ohio. His father, who worked in the saddlery and harness business, moved from town to town, and Sherwood Anderson had little regular schooling. As a boy he worked at odd jobs, as stable boy, and on racecourses, and in factories. His stories reflect often this background of his early life. Later he worked at advertising, his first book of stories WINESBURG, OHIO, in 1919, brought him a reputation as a writer.

His stories have a realism consistent with his claim that 'the business of the story teller is with life, in his own time, life as he feels it, smells it, tastes it'. He was impatient with the stricter form and conventional patterns of earlier stories, and though his own stories often seem deliberately loose and formless they are closely constructed. He was concerned to give expression to the lives and emotions of ordinary, often inarticulate people. In style he worked towards brief sentences, an avoidance of literary diction, and towards the use of colloquial language. His prose used rhythms and repetitions, and was an influence on younger American writers. Many of his stories illustrate a first person method of narration particularly suited to his subject and style.

Short stories: THE TRIUMPH OF THE EGG, 1921, DEATH IN THE WOODS, 1933. Autobiography: A STORY TELLER'S STORY, 1924.

Sherwood Anderson died in 1941.

I'M A FOOL

Sherwood Anderson

IT WAS A HARD JOLT FOR ME, ONE OF THE MOST BITTEREST I EVER HAD TO face. And it all came about through my own foolishness, too. Even yet sometimes, when I think of it, I want to cry or swear or kick myself. Perhaps, even now, after all this time, there will be a kind of satisfaction in making myself look cheap by telling of it.

It began at three o'clock one October afternoon as I sat in the grand stand at the fall trotting and pacing meet at Sandusky, Ohio.

To tell the truth, I felt a little foolish that I should be sitting in the grand stand at all. During the summer before I had left my home town with Harry Whitehead and, with a nigger named Burt, had taken a job as swipe with one of the two horses Harry was campaigning through the fall race meets that year. Mother cried and my sister Mildred, who wanted to get a job as a school teacher in our town that fall, stormed and scolded about the house all during the week before I left. They both thought it something disgraceful that one of our family should take a place as a swipe with race horses. I've an idea Mildred thought my taking the place would stand in the way of her getting the job she'd been working so long for.

But after all I had to work, and there was no other work to be got. A big lumbering fellow of nineteen couldn't just hang around the house and I had got too big to mow people's lawns and sell newspapers. Little chaps who could get next to people's sympathies by their sizes were always getting jobs away from me. There was one fellow who kept saying to everyone who wanted a lawn mowed or a cistern cleaned, that he was saving money to work his way through college, and I used to lay awake nights thinking up ways to injure him without being found out. I kept thinking of wagons running over him and bricks falling on his head as he walked along the street. But never mind him.

I got the place with Harry and I liked Burt fine. We got along splendid together. He was a big nigger with a lazy sprawling body and soft, kind eyes, and when it came to a fight he could hit like Jack Johnson. He had Bucephalus, a big black pacing stallion that could do 2.09 or 2.10, if he had to, and I had a little gelding named Doctor Fritz that never lost a race all fall when Harry wanted him to win.

We set out from home late in July in a box car with the two horses and after that, until late November, we kept moving along to the race meets and the fairs. It was a peachy time for me, I'll say that. Sometimes now I think that boys who are raised regular in houses, and never have a fine nigger like Burt for best friend, and go to high schools and college, and never steal anything, or get drunk a little, or learn to swear from fellows who know how, or come walking up in front of a grand stand in their shirt sleeves and with dirty horsey pants on when the races are going on and the grand stand is full of people all dressed up—What's the use of talking about it? Such fellows don't know nothing at all. They've never had no opportunity.

But I did. Burt taught me how to rub down a horse and put the bandages on after a race and steam a horse out and a lot of valuable things for any man to know. He could wrap a bandage on a horse's leg so smooth that if it had been the same colour you would think it was his skin, and I guess he'd have been a big driver, too, and got to the top like Murphy and Walter Cox and the others if he hadn't been black.

Gee whizz, it was fun. You got to a county seat town, maybe say on a Saturday or Sunday, and the fair began the next Tuesday and lasted until Friday afternoon. Doctor Fritz would be, say in the 2.25 trot on Tuesday afternoon and on Thursday afternoon Bucephalus would knock 'em cold in the 'free-for-all' pace. It left you a lot of time to hang around and listen to horse talk, and see Burt knock some yap cold that got too gay, and you'd find out about horses and men and pick up a lot of stuff you could use all the rest of your life, if you had some sense and salted down what you heard and felt and saw.

And then at the end of the week when the race meet was over, and Harry had run home to tend up to his livery stable business, you and Burt hitched the two horses to carts and drove slow and steady across country, to the place for the next meeting, so as to not over-heat the horses, etc., etc., you know.

Gee whizz, Gosh amighty, the nice hickorynut and beechnut and oaks and other kinds of trees along the roads, all brown and red, and the good smells, and Burt singing a song that was called Deep River, and the country girls at the windows of houses and everything. You can stick your colleges up your nose for all me. I guess I know where I got my education.

Why, one of those little burgs of towns you come to on the way, say now on a Saturday afternoon, and Burt says, 'let's lay up here.' And you did.

And you took the horses to a livery stable and fed them, and you got your good clothes out of a box and put them on.

And the town was full of farmers gaping, because they could see you were race horse people, and the kids maybe never see a nigger before and was afraid and run away when the two of us walked down their main street.

And that was before prohibition and all that foolishness, and so you went into a saloon, the two of you, and all the yaps come and stood around, and there was always someone pretended he was horsey and knew things and spoke up and began asking questions, and all you did was to lie and lie all you could about what horses you had, and I said I owned them, and then some fellow said 'will you have a drink of whiskey' and Burt knocked his eye out the way he could say, off-hand like, 'Oh well, all right, I'm agreeable to a little nip. I'll split a quart with you.' Gee whizz.

But that isn't what I want to tell my story about. We got home late in November and I promised mother I'd quit the race horses for good. There's a lot of things you've got to promise a mother because she don't know any better.

And so, there not being any work in our town any more than when I left there to go to the races, I went off to Sandusky and got a pretty good place taking care of horses for a man who owned a teaming and delivery and storage and coal and real estate business there. It was a pretty good place with good eats, and a day off each week, and sleeping on a cot in a big barn, and mostly just shovelling in hay and oats to a lot of big good-enough skates of horses, that couldn't have trotted a race with a toad. I wasn't dissatisfied and I could send money home.

And then, as I started to tell you, the fall races come to Sandusky and I got the day off and I went. I left the job at noon and had on my good clothes and my new brown derby hat, I'd just bought the Saturday before, and a stand-up collar.

First of all I went down-town and walked about with the dudes. I've always thought to myself, 'put up a good front' and so I did it. I had forty dollars in my pocket and so I went into the West House, a big hotel, and walked up to the cigar stand. 'Give me three twenty-five cent cigars,' I said. There was a lot of horsemen and strangers and dressed-up people from other towns standing around in the lobby and in the bar, and I mingled amongst them. In the bar there was a fellow with a cane and a Windsor tie on, that it made me sick to look at him. I like a man to be a man and dress up, but not to go put on that kind of airs. So I pushed him aside, kind of rough, and had me a drink of whiskey. And then he looked at me, as though he thought maybe he'd get gay, but he changed his mind and didn't say anything. And then I had another drink of whiskey, just to show him something, and went out and had a hack out to the races, all to myself, and when I got there I bought myself the best seat I could get up in the grand stand, but didn't go in for any of these boxes. That's putting on too many airs.

And so there I was, sitting up in the grand stand as gay as you please and looking down on the swipes coming out with their horses, and with their dirty horsey pants on and the horse blankets swung over their shoulders, same as I had been doing all the year before. I liked one thing about the same as the other, sitting up there and feeling grand and being down there and looking up at the yaps and feeling grander and more important, too.

One thing's about as good as another, if you take it just right. I've often said that.

Well, right in front of me, in the grand stand that day, there was a fellow with a couple of girls and they was about my age. The young fellow was a nice guy all right. He was the kind maybe that goes to college and then comes to be a lawyer or maybe a newspaper editor or something like that, but he wasn't stuck on himself. There are some of that kind are all right and he was one of the ones.

He had his sister with him and another girl and the sister looked around over his shoulder, accidental at first, not intending to start anything—she wasn't that kind—and her eyes and mine happened to meet.

You know how it is. Gee, she was a peach! She had on a soft dress, kind of blue stuff and it looked carelessly made, but was well sewed and made and everything. I knew that much. I blushed when she looked right at me and so did she. She was the nicest girl I've ever seen in my life. She wasn't stuck on herself and she could talk proper grammar without being like a school teacher or something like that. What I mean is, she was O.K. I think maybe her father was well-to-do, but not rich to make her chesty because she was his daughter, as some are. Maybe he owned a drug store or a drygoods store in their home town, or something like that. She never told me and I never asked.

My own people are all O.K. too, when you come to that. My grandfather was Welsh and over in the old country, in Wales he was—But never mind that.

The first heat of the first race come off and the young fellow setting there with the two girls left them and went down to make a bet. I knew what he was up to, but he didn't talk big and noisy and let everyone around know he was a sport, as some do. He wasn't that kind. Well, he come back and I heard him tell the two girls what horse he'd bet on, and when the heat was trotted they all half got to their feet and acted in the excited, sweaty way people do when they've got money down on a race, and the horse they bet on is up there pretty close at the end, and they think maybe he'll come on with a rush, but he never does because he hasn't got the old juice in him, come right down to it.

And then, pretty soon, the horses came out for the 2.18 pace and there was a horse in it I knew. He was a horse Bob French had in his string but Bob didn't own him. He was a horse owned by a Mr Mathers down at Marietta, Ohio.

This Mr Mathers had a lot of money and owned some coal mines or something, and he had a swell place out in the country, and he was stuck on race horses, but was a Presbyterian or something, and I think more than likely his wife was one, too, maybe a stiffer one than himself. So he never raced his horses hisself, and the story round the Ohio race tracks was that when one of his horses got ready to go to the races he turned him over to Bob French and pretended to his wife he was sold.

So Bob had the horses and he did pretty much as he pleased and you can't blame Bob, at least, I never did. Sometimes he was out to win and sometimes he wasn't. I never cared much about that when I was swiping a horse. What I did want to know was that my horse had the speed and could go out in front, if you wanted him to.

And, as I'm telling you, there was Bob in this race with one of Mr Mathers' horses, was named 'About Ben Ahem' or something like that, and was fast as a streak. He was a gelding and had a mark of 2.21, but could step in .08 or .09.

Because when Burt and I were out, as I've told you, the year before, there was a nigger, Burt knew, worked for Mr Mathers and we went out there one day when we didn't have no race on at the Marietta Fair and our boss Harry was gone home.

And so everyone was gone to the fair but just this one nigger and he took us all through Mr Mathers' swell house and he and Burt tapped a bottle of wine Mr Mathers had hid in his bedroom, back in a closet, without his wife knowing, and he showed us this Ahem horse. Burt was always stuck on being a driver but didn't have much chance to get to the top, being a nigger, and he and the other nigger gulped that whole bottle of wine and Burt got a little lit up.

So the nigger let Burt take this About Ben Ahem and step him a mile in a track Mr Mathers had all to himself, right there on the farm. And Mr Mathers had one child, a daughter, kinda sick and not very good looking, and she came home and we had to hustle and get About Ben Ahem stuck back in the barn.

I'm only telling you to get everything straight. At Sandusky, that afternoon I was at the fair, this young fellow with the two girls was fussed, being with the girls and losing his bet. You know how a fellow is that way. One of them was his girl and the other his sister. I had figured that out.

'Gee whizz,' I says to myself, 'I'm going to give him the dope.'

He was mighty nice when I touched him on the shoulder. He and the girls were nice to me right from the start and clear to the end. I'm not blaming them.

And so he leaned back and I gave him the dope on About Ben Ahem. 'Don't bet a cent on this first heat because he'll go like an oxen hitched to a plow, but when the first heat is over go right down and lay on your pile.' That's what I told him.

Well, I never saw a fellow treat any one sweller. There was a fat man sitting beside the little girl, that had looked at me twice by this time, and I at her, and both blushing, and what did he do but have the nerve to turn and ask the fat man to get up and change places with me so I could set with his crowd.

Gee whizz, craps amighty. There I was. What a chump I was to go and get gay up there in the West House bar, and just because that dude was standing there with a cane and that kind of a necktie on, to go and get all balled up and drink that whiskey, just to show off.

Of course she would know, me setting right beside her and letting her smell of my breath. I could have kicked myself right down out of that grand stand and all around that race track and made a faster record than most of the skates of horses they had there that year.

Because that girl wasn't any mutt of a girl. What wouldn't I have give right then for a stick of chewing gum to chew, or a lozenger, or some liquorice, or most anything. I was glad I had those twenty-five cent cigars in my pocket and right away I give that fellow one and lit one myself. Then the fat man got up and we changed places and there I was, plunked right down beside her.

They introduced themselves and the fellow's best girl, he had with him, was named Miss Elinor Woodbury, and her father was a manufacturer of barrels from a place called Tiffin, Ohio. And the fellow himself was named Wilbur Wessen and his sister was Miss Lucy Wessen.

I suppose it was their having such swell names got me off my trolley. A fellow, just because he has been a swipe with a race horse, and works taking care of horses for a man in the teaming, delivery, and storage business, isn't any better or worse than any one else. I've often thought that, and said it too.

But you know how a fellow is. There's something in that kind of nice clothes, and the kind of nice eyes she had, and the way she had looked at me, awhile before, over her brother's shoulder, and me looking back at her, and both of us blushing.

I couldn't show her up for a boob, could I?

I made a fool of myself, that's what I did. I said my name was Walter Mathers from Marietta, Ohio, and then I told all three of them the smashingest lie you ever heard. What I said was that my father owned the horse. About Ben Ahem and that he had let him out to this Bob French for racing purposes, because our family was proud and had never gone into racing that way, in our own name, I mean. Then I had got started and they were all leaning over and listening, and Miss Lucy Wessen's eyes were shining, and I went the whole hog.

I told about our place down at Marietta, and about the big stables and the grand brick house we had on a hill, up above the Ohio River, but I knew enouth not to do it in no bragging way. What I did was to start things and then let them drag the rest out of me. I acted just as reluctant to tell as I could. Our family hasn't got any barrel factory, and, since I've known us, we've always been pretty poor, but not asking anything of any one at that, and my grandfather, over in Wales—but never mind that.

We set there talking like we had known each other for years and years, and I went and told them that my father had been expecting maybe this Bob French wasn't on the square, and had sent me up to Sandusky on the sly to find out what I could.

And I bluffed it through I had found out all about the 2.18 pace, in which About Ben Ahem was to start.

I said he would lose the first heat by pacing like a lame cow and then he would come back and skin 'em alive after that. And to back up what I said I took thirty dollars out of my pocket and handed it to Mr Wilbur Wessen and asked him, would he mind, after the first heat, to go down and place it on About Ben Ahem for whatever odds he could get. What I said was that I didn't want Bob French to see me and none of the swipes.

Sure enough the first heat come off and About Ben Ahem went off his stride, up the back stretch, and looked like a wooden horse or a sick one, and come in to be last. Then this Wilbur Wessen went down to the betting place under the grand stand and there I was with the two girls, and when that Miss Woodbury was looking the other way once, Lucy Wessen kinda, with her shoulder you know, kinda touched me. Not just tucking down, I don't mean. You know how a woman can do. They get close, but not getting gay either. You know what they do. Gee whizz.

And then they give me a jolt. What they had done, when I didn't know, was to get together, and they had decided Wilbur Wessen would bet fifty dollars, and the two girls had gone and put in ten dollars each, of their own money, too. I was sick then, but I was sicker later.

About the gelding, About Ben Ahem, and their winning their money, I wasn't worried a lot about that. It come out O.K. Ahem stepped the next three heats like a bushel of spoiled eggs going to market before they could be found out, and Wilbur Wessen had got nine to two for the money. There was something else eating at me.

Because Wilbur come back, after he had bet the money, and after that he spent most of his time talking to that Miss Woodbury, and Lucy Wessen and I was left alone together like on a desert island. Gee, if I'd only been on the square or if there had been any way of getting myself on the square. There ain't any Walter Mathers, like I said to her and them, and there hasn't ever been one, but if there was, I bet I'd go to Marietta, Ohio, and shoot him to-morrow.

There I was, big boob that I am. Pretty soon the race was over, and Wilbur had gone down and collected our money, and we had a hack down-town, and he stood us a swell supper at the West House, and a bottle of champagne beside.

And I was with that girl and she wasn't saying much, and I wasn't saying much either. One thing I know. She wasn't stuck on me because of the lie about my father being rich and all that. There's a way you know. . . . Craps amighty. There's a kind of girl, you see just once in your life, and if you don't get busy and make hay, then you're gone for good and all, and might as well go jump off a bridge. They give you a look from inside of them somewhere, and it ain't no vamping, and what it means is —you want that girl to be your wife, and you want nice things around her like flowers and swell clothes, and you want her to have the kids you're going to have, and you want good music played and no rag time. Gee whizz.

There's a place over near Sandusky, across a kind of bay, and it's called Cedar Point. And after we had supper we went over to it in a launch, all by ourselves. Wilbur and Miss Lucy and that Miss Woodbury had to catch a ten o'clock train back to Tiffin, Ohio, because, when you're out with girls like that you can't get careless and miss any trains and stay out all night, like you can with some kinds of Janes.

And Wilbur blowed himself to the launch and it cost him fifteen cold plunks, but I wouldn't never have knew if I hadn't listened. He wasn't no tin horn kind of a sport.

Over at the Cedar Point place, we didn't stay around where there was a gang of common kind of cattle at all.

There was big dance halls and dining places for yaps, and there was a beach you could walk along and get where it was dark, and we went there.

She didn't talk hardly at all and neither did I, and I was thinking how glad I was my mother was all right, and always made us kids learn to eat with a fork at table, and not swill soup, and not be noisy and rough like a gang you see around a race track that way.

Then Wilbur and his girl went away up the beach and Lucy and I sat down in a dark place, where there was some roots of old trees, the water had washed up, and after that the time, till we had to go back in the launch and they had to catch their trains, wasn't nothing at all. It went like winking your eye.

Here's how it was. The place we were setting in was dark, like I said, and there was the roots from that old stump sticking up like arms, and there was a watery smell, and the night was like—as if you could put your hand out and feel it—so warm and soft and dark and sweet like an orange.

I most cried and I most swore and I most jumped up and danced, I was so mad and happy and sad.

When Wilbur come back from being alone with his girl, and she saw him coming, Lucy she says, 'we got to go to the train now,' and she was most crying too, but she never knew nothing I knew, and she couldn't be so all busted up. And then, before Wilbur and Miss Woodbury got up to where we was, she put her face up and kissed me quick and put her head up against me and she was all quivering and—Gee whizz.

Sometimes I hope I have cancer and die. I guess you know what I mean. We went in the launch across the bay to the train like that, and it was dark, too. She whispered and said it was like she and I could get out of the boat and walk on the water, and it sounded foolish, but I knew what she meant.

And then quick we were right at the depot, and there was a big gang of yaps, the kind that goes to the fairs, and crowded and milling around like cattle, and how could I tell her? 'It won't be long because you'll write and I'll write to you!' That's all she said.

I got a chance like a hay barn afire. A swell chance I got.

And maybe she would write me, down at Marietta that way, and the letter would come back, and stamped on the front of it by the U.S.A. 'there ain't any such guy,' or something like that, whatever they stamp on a letter that way and me trying to pass myself off for a big bug and a swell—to her, as decent a little body as God ever made. Craps almighty—a swell chance I got!

And then the train come in, and she got on it, and Wilbur Wessen he come and shook hands with me, and that Miss Woodbury was nice too and bowed to me, and I at her, and the train went and I busted out and cried like a kid.

Gee, I could have run after that train and made Dan Patch look like a freight train after a wreck but, socks amighty, what was the use? Did you ever see such a fool?

I'll bet you what—if I had an arm broke right now or a train had run over my foot—I wouldn't go to no doctor at all. I'd go set down and let her hurt and hurt—that's what I'd do.

I'll bet you what—if I hadn't a drunk that booze I'd a never been such a boob as to go tell such a lie—that couldn't never be made straight to a lady like her.

I wish I had that fellow right here that had on a Windsor tie and carried a cane. I'd smash him for fair. Gosh darn his eyes. He's a big fool—that's what he is.

And if I'm not another you just go find me one and I'll quit working and be a bum and give him my job. I don't care nothing for working, and earning money, and saving it for no such boob as myself.

Doris Lessing born on a farm in Southern Rhodesia in 1919. She spent her childhood there, leaving for England at the age of thirty. By that time, she had written her first novel, THE GRASS IS SINGING, which was published soon after her arrival in England, with considerable success. She followed this with a collection of short stories called THIS WAS THE OLD CHIEF'S COUNTRY, many of which describe African tribal ways of life with compassion and understanding. Miss Lessing's critical attitude towards apartheid, which she describes as 'white supremacy', has resulted in her exclusion from South Africa and Rhodesia. She lives in London.

In 1952 MARTHA QUEST was published, the first of a series of five novels with the title figure of the first as central character in each novel. Her attitude to writing can be summarised in her own words: 'Novels, stories, plays, can convey the truth about personal relations, emotions, and attitudes of which the people subject to them are perhaps unaware.'

'THROUGH THE TUNNEL' is taken from her collection entitled THE HABIT OF LOVING, published in 1957. It follows a classic pattern of the narrative short story, moving from conflict through a series of testing situations to a climax and a resolution of the conflict. The writer here shows her understanding of human psychology, together with a skilful control of suspense.

Suggested further reading: NINE AFRICAN STORIES, Longman.

THROUGH THE TUNNEL

Doris Lessing

GOING TO THE SHORE ON THE FIRST MORNING OF THE HOLIDAY, THE YOUNG English boy stopped at a turning of the path and looked down at a wild and rocky bay, and then over to the crowded beach he knew so well from other years. His mother walked on in front of him, carrying a bright striped bag in one hand. Her other arm, swinging loose, was very white in the sun.

The boy watched that white, naked arm, and turned his eyes, which had a frown behind them, toward the bay and back again to his mother. When she felt he was not with her, she swung around.

'Oh, there you are Jerry!' she said. She looked impatient, then smiled. 'Why, darling, would you rather not come with me? Would you rather—' she frowned, conscientiously worrying over what amusements he might secretly be longing for which she had been too busy to imagine.

He was very familiar with that anxious, apologetic smile. Contrition sent him running after her. And yet, as he ran, he looked back over his shoulder at the wild bay; and all morning, as he played on the safe beach, he was thinking of it.

Next morning, when it was time for the routine of swimming and sunbathing, his mother said, 'Are you tired of the usual beach, Jerry? Would you like to go somewhere else?'

'Oh, no!' he said quickly, smiling at her out of that unfailing impulse of contrition—a sort of chivalry. Yet, walking down the path with her, he blurted out, 'I'd like to go and have a look at those rocks down there.'

She gave the idea her attention. It was a wild-looking place, and there was no one there, but she said, 'Of course, Jerry. When you've had enough, come to the big beach. Or just go straight back to the villa, if you like.'

She walked away, that bare arm, now slightly reddened from yesterday's sun, swinging. And he almost ran after her again, feeling it unbearable that she should go by herself, but he did not.

She was thinking. Of course he's old enough to be safe without me. Have I been keeping him too close? He mustn't feel he ought to be with me. I must be careful.

He was an only child. . . . She was a widow. She was determined to be neither possessive nor lacking in devotion. She went worrying off to her beach.

As for Jerry, once he saw that his mother had gained her beach, he began the steep descent to the bay. From where he was, high up among redbrown rocks, it was a scoop of moving bluish green fringed with white.

As he went lower, he saw that it spread among small promontories and inlets of rough, sharp rock, and the crisping, lapping surface showed

61

stains of purple and darker blue. Finally, as he ran sliding and scraping down the last few yards, he saw an edge of white surf, and the shallow, luminous movement of water over white sand, and, beyond that, a solid, heavy blue.

He ran straight into the water and began swimming. He was a good swimmer. He went out fast over the gleaming sand, over a middle region where rocks lay like discolored monsters under the surface, and then he was in the real sea—a warm sea where irregular cold currents from the deep water shocked his limbs.

When he was so far out that he could look back not only on the little bay but past the promontory that was between it and the big beach, he floated on the buoyant surface and looked for his mother. There she was, a speck of yellow under an umbrella that looked like a slice of orange peel. He swam back to shore, relieved at being sure she was there, but all at once very lonely.

On the edge of a small cape that marked the side of the bay away from the promontory was a loose scatter of rocks. Above them, some boys were stripping off their clothes. They came running, naked, down to the rocks.

The English boy swam toward them, and kept his distance at a stone's throw. They were of that coast, all of them burned smooth dark brown, and speaking a language he did not understand. To be with them, of them, was a craving that filled his whole body. He swam a little closer; they turned and watched him with narrowed, alert dark eyes.

Then one smiled and waved. It was enough. In a minute, he had swum in and was on the rocks beside them, smiling with a desperate, nervous supplication. They shouted cheerful greetings at him, and then, as he preserved his nervous, uncomprehending smile, they understood that he was a foreigner strayed from his own beach, and they proceeded to forget him. But he was happy. He was with them.

They began diving again and again from a high point into a well of blue sea between rough, pointed rocks. After they had dived and come up, they swam around, hauled themselves up, and waited their turn to dive again.

They were big boys—men to Jerry. He dived, and they watched him, and when he swam around to take his place, they made way for him. He felt he was accepted, and he dived again, carefully, proud of himself.

Soon the biggest of the boys poised himself, shot down into the water, and did not come up. The others stood about watching. Jerry, after waiting for the sleek brown head to appear, let out a yell of warning; they looked at him idly and turned their eyes back toward the water.

After a long time, the boy came up on the other side of a big dark rock, letting the air out of his lungs in a spluttering gasp and a shout of triumph.

Immediately, the rest of them dived in. One moment, the morning seemed full of chattering boys; the next, the air and the surface of the water were empty. But through the heavy blue, dark shapes could be seen moving and groping.

Jerry dived, shot past the school of underwater swimmers, saw a black wall of rock looming at him, touched it, and bobbed up at once to the surface, where the wall was a low barrier he could see across. There was no one visible; under him, in the water, the dim shapes of the swimmers had disappeared. Then one, and then another of the boys came up on the far side of the barrier of rock, and he understood that they had swum through some gap or hole in it. He plunged down again.

He could see nothing through the stinging salt water but the blank rock. When he came up, the boys were all on the diving rock, preparing to attempt the feat again. And now, in a panic of failure, he yelled up, in English, 'Look at me! Look!' and he began splashing and kicking in the water like a foolish dog.

They looked down gravely, frowning. He knew the frown. At moments of failure, when he clowned to claim his mother's attention, it was with just this grave embarrassed inspection that she rewarded him.

Through his hot shame, feeling the pleading grin on his face like a scar that he could never remove, he looked up at the group of big brown boys on the rock and shouted 'Bonjour! Merci! Au revoir! Monsieur, monsieur!' while he hooked his fingers round his ears and waggled them.

Water surged into his mouth; he choked, sank, came up. The rock, lately weighted with the boys, seemed to rear up out of the water as their weight was removed. They were flying down past him, now, into the water; the air was full of falling bodies. Then the rock was empty in the hot sunlight. He counted one, two, three. . . .

At fifty, he was terrified. They must all be drowning beneath him, in the watery caves of the rock! At a hundred, he stared around him at the empty hillside, wondering if he should yell for help.

He counted faster, faster, to hurry them up, to bring them to the surface quickly, to drown them quickly—anything rather than the terror of counting on and on into the blue emptiness of the morning. And then, at a hundred and sixty, the water beyond the rock was full of boys blowing like brown whales. They swam back to the shore without a look at him.

He climbed back to the diving rock and sat down, feeling the hot roughness of it under his thighs. The boys were gathering up their bits of clothing and running off along the shore to another promontory.

They were leaving to get away from him. He cried openly, fists in his eyes. There was no one to see him, and he cried himself out.

It seemed to him that a long time had passed and he swam out to where he could see his mother. Yes, she was still there, a yellow spot under an orange umbrella. He swam back to the big rock, climbed up, and dived into the blue pool among the fanged and angry boulders. Down he went, until he touched the wall of rock again. But the salt was so painful in his eyes that he could not see.

He came to the surface, swam to shore and went back to the villa to wait for his mother. Soon she walked slowly up the path, swinging her striped bag, the flushed, naked arm dangling beside her. 'I want some swimming goggles,' he panted, defiant and beseeching.

She gave him a patient, inquisitive look as she said casually, 'Well, of course, darling.'

But now, now, now! He must have them this minute, and no other time. He nagged and pestered until she went with him to a shop. As soon as she had bought the goggles, he grabbed them from her hand as if she were going to claim them for herself, and was off, running down the steep path to the bay.

Jerry swam out to the big barrier rock, adjusted the goggles, and dived. The impact of the water broke the rubber-enclosed vacuum, and the goggles came loose.

He understood that he must swim down to the base of the rock from the surface of the water. He fixed the goggles tight and firm, filled his lungs, and floated, face down on the water.

Now he could see. It was as if he had eyes of a different kind—fish-eyes that showed everything clear and delicate and wavering in the bright water.

Under him, six or seven feet down, was a floor of perfectly clean, shining white sand, rippled firm and hard by the tides. Two grayish shapes steered there, like long, rounded pieces of wood or slate.

They were fish. He saw them nose toward each other, poise motionless, make a dart forward, swerve off, and come around again. It was like a water dance.

A few inches above them, the water sparkled as if sequins were dropping through it. Fish again—myriads of minute fish, the length of his fingernail, were drifting through the water, and in a moment he could feel the innumerable tiny touches of them, against his limbs. It was like swimming in flaked silver.

The great rock the big boys had swum through rose sheer out of the white sand, black, tufted lightly with greenish weed. He could see no gap in it. He swam down to its base.

Again and again he rose, took a big chestful of air, and went down. Again and again he groped over the surface of the rock, feeling it, almost hugging it in the desperate need to find the entrance.

And then, once, while he was clinging to the black wall, his knees came up and he shot his feet out forward and they met no obstacle. He had found the hole.

He gained the surface, clambered about the stones that littered the barrier rock until he found a big one, and, with this in his arms, let himself down over the side of the rock. He dropped, with the weight, to the sandy floor.

Clinging tight to the anchor of the stone, he lay on his side and looked in under the dark shelf at the place where his feet had gone. He could see the hole.

It was an irregular, dark gap, but he could not see deep into it. He let go of his anchor, clung with his hands to the edges of the hole, and tried to push himself in.

He got his head in, found his shoulders jammed, moved them in sidewise, and was inside as far as his waist. He could see nothing ahead.

Something soft and clammy touched his mouth. He saw a dark frond moving against the grayish rock, and panic filled him. He thought of octopuses, or clinging weed.

He pushed himself out backward and caught a glimpse, as he retreated, of a harmless tentacle of seaweed drifting in the mouth of the tunnel. But it was enough.

He reached the sunlight, swam to shore, and lay on the diving rock. He looked down into the blue well of water. He knew he must find his way through that cave, or hole, or tunnel, and out the other side.

First, he thought, he must learn to control his breathing. He let himself down into the water with another big stone in his arms, so that he could lie effortlessly on the bottom.

One, two, three. He counted steadily. He could hear the movement of blood in his head. Fifty-one, fifty-two. . . .

His chest was hurting. He let go of the rock and went up into the air. He saw that the sun was low. He rushed to the villa and found his mother at her supper. She said only, 'Did you enjoy yourself?' and he said, 'Yes.'

All night, the boy dreamed of the water-filled cave in the rock, and as soon as breakfast was over he went to the bay.

That night, his nose bled badly. For hours he had been underwater, learning to hold his breath, and now he felt weak and dizzy. His mother said, 'I shouldn't overdo things, darling, if I were you.'

That day and the next, Jerry exercised his lungs as if everything, the whole of his life, all that he would become, depended upon it. Again his nose bled at night, and his mother insisted on his coming with her the next day.

It was a torment to him to waste a day of his careful self-training, but he stayed with her on that other beach, which now seemed a place for small children, a place where his mother might lie safe in the sun. It was not his beach.

He did not ask for permission, on the following day, to go to his beach.

He went, before his mother could consider the complicated rights and wrongs of the matter.

A day's rest, he discovered, had improved his count by ten. The big boys had made the passage while he counted a hundred and sixty. He had been counting fast, in his fright. Probably now, if he tried, he could get through that long tunnel, but he was not going to try yet.

A curious, most unchildlike persistence, a controlled impatience, made him wait. In the meantime, he lay underwater on the white sand, littered now by stones he had brought down from the upper air, and studied the entrance to the tunnel. He knew every jut and corner of it, as far as it was possible to see. It was as if he already felt its sharpness about his shoulders.

He sat by the clock in the villa, when his mother was not near, and checked his time. He was incredulous and then proud to find he could hold his breath without strain for two minutes. The words 'two minutes,' authorized by the clock, brought the adventure that was so necessary to him close.

In another four days, his mother said casually one morning, they must go home. On the day before they left, he would do it. He would do it if it killed him, he said defiantly to himself. But two days before they were to leave—a day of triumph when he increased his count by fifteen—his nose bled so badly that he turned dizzy and had to lie limply over the big rock like a bit of seaweed, watching the thick red blood flow onto the rock and trickle slowly down to the sea. He was frightened.

Supposing he turned dizzy in the tunnel? Supposing he died there, trapped? Supposing—his head went around in the hot sun, and he almost gave up. He thought he would return to the house and lie down, and next summer, perhaps, when he had another year's growth in him—then he would go through the hole.

But even after he had made the decision, or thought he had, he found himself sitting up on the rock and looking down into the water, and he knew that now, this moment, when his nose had only just stopped bleeding, when his head was still sore and throbbing—this was the moment when he would try. If he did not do it now, he never would.

He was trembling with fear that he would not go, and he was trembling with horror at that long, long tunnel under the rock, under the sea. Even in the open sunlight, the barrier rock seemed very wide and very heavy; tons of rock pressed down on where he would go. If he died there he would lie until one day—perhaps not before next year—those big boys would swim into it and find it blocked.

He put on his goggles, fitted them tight, tested the vacuum. His hands were shaking. Then he chose the biggest stone he could carry and slipped over the edge of the rock until half of him was in the cool, enclosing water and half in the hot sun.

He looked up once at the empty sky, filled his lungs once, twice, and then sank fast to the bottom with the stone. He let it go and began to count. He took the edges of the hole in his hands and drew himself into it, wriggling his shoulders in sidewise as he remembered he must.

Soon he was clear inside. He was in a small rock-bound hole filled with yellowish-gray water. The water was pushing him up against the roof. The roof was sharp and pained his back. He pulled himself along with his hands—fast, fast—and used his legs as levers.

His head knocked against something; a sharp pain dizzied him. Fifty, fifty-one, fifty-two. . . . He was without light, and the water seemed to press upon him with the weight of rock. Seventy-one, seventy-two. . . . There was no strain on his lungs. He felt like an inflated balloon, his lungs were so light and easy, but his head was pulsing.

He was being continually pressed against the sharp roof, which felt slimy as well as sharp. Again he thought of octopuses, and wondered if the tunnel might be filled with weed that could tangle him. He gave himself a panicky, convulsive kick forward, ducked his head, and swam.

His feet and hands moved freely, as if in open water. The hole must have widened out. He thought he must be swimming fast, and he was frightened of banging his head if the tunnel narrowed.

A hundred, a hundred and one. . . . The water paled. Victory filled him. His lungs were beginning to hurt. A few more strokes and he would be out. He was counting wildly; he said a hundred and fifteen, and then, a long time later, a hundred and fifteen again. The water was a clear jewel-green all around him. Then he saw, above his head, a crack running up through the rock. Sunlight was falling through it, showing the clean dark rock of the tunnel, a single mussel shell, and darkness ahead.

He was at the end of what he could do. He looked up at the crack as if it were filled with air and not water, as if he could put his mouth to it to draw in air. A hundred and fifteen, he heard himself say inside his head—but he had said that long ago.

He must go on into the blackness ahead, or he would drown. His head was swelling, his lungs cracking. A hundred and fifteen, a hundred and fifteen pounded through his head, and he feebly clutched at rocks in the dark, pulling himself forward, leaving the brief space of sunlit water behind.

He felt he was dying. He was no longer quite conscious. He struggled on in the darkness between lapses into unconsciousness. An immense, swelling pain filled his head, and then the darkness cracked with an explosion of green light. His hands, groping forward, met nothing, and his feet, kicking back, propelled him out into the open sea.

He drifted to the surface, his face turned up to the air. He was gasping like a fish. He felt he would sink now and drown; he could not swim the few feet back to the rock. Then he was clutching it and pulling himself up onto it.

He lay face down, gasping. He could see nothing but a red-veined clotted dark. His eyes must have burst, he thought; they were full of blood. He tore off his goggles and a gout of blood went into the sea. His nose was bleeding, and the blood had filled the goggles.

He scooped up handfuls of water from the cool, salty sea, to splash on his face, and did not know whether it was blood or salt water he tasted. After a time, his heart quieted, his eyes cleared, and he sat up.

He could see the local boys diving and playing half a mile away. He did not want them. He wanted nothing but to get back home and lie down.

In a short while, Jerry swam to shore and climbed slowly up the path to the villa. He flung himself on his bed and slept, waking at the sound of feet on the path outside. His mother was coming back. He rushed to the bathroom, thinking she must not see his face with bloodstains, or tearstains, on it. He came out of the bathroom and met her as she walked into the villa.

'Have a nice morning?' she asked, laying her hand on his warm brown shoulder a moment.

'Oh, yes, thank you,' he said.

'You look a bit pale.' And then, sharp and anxious, 'How did you bang your head?'

'Oh, just banged it,' he told her.

She looked at him closely. He was stained. His eyes were glazed-looking. She was worried. And then she said to herself, 'Oh, don't fuss! Nothing can happen. He can swim like a fish.'

They sat down to lunch together.

'Mummy,' he said, 'I can stay under water for two minutes—three minutes, at least.' It came bursting out of him.

'Can you, darling?' she said. 'Well, I shouldn't overdo it. I don't think you ought to swim any more today.'

She was ready for a battle of wills, but he gave in at once. It was no longer of the least importance to go to the bay.

H. E. Bates born in Rushden, Northamptonshire, in 1905, and educated at Kettering Grammar School. At nineteen, then working as a warehouse attendant, he wrote his first short story. His first novel was written the following year, when he had become a clerk-journalist on a provincial newspaper. During his prolific writing career he had more than thirty volumes published, including novels, short stories, essays on the countryside, and a critical study of the short story. Many of his stories are set in the English countryside.

During the Second World War he was commissioned to write Air Force stories under the pseudonym of Flying Officer X. Bates described 'THE BLACK BOXER' as a transition 'between the dreamy world of the subjective, seen in my early writings, in which mood was more important than character, and a wider, harder, more objective world in which character was of great importance.' Realism of setting and language is preferred to careful plot manipulation. 'I have never from the first', he said, 'had the slightest interest in plots.'

'THE BLACK BOXER' is found in COUNTRY TALES, 1938, together with many of his best short stories.

THE BLACK BOXER

H. E. Bates

THE MORNING SUN WAS BEATING HOT OVER PETERSON'S FAIR-GROUND. THE big coloured awnings shrouding the shows and roundabouts hung heavy and still, and the rings of little gay triangular flags on the roofs of the roundabouts and on the helter-skelter tower flapped senselessly in the summer air.

Perched on a ladder outside the entrance to Sullivan's boxing show a figure in blue dungarees was polishing the big copper bell hanging before the gold and scarlet curtains. In the intervals between polishing the bell and staring lazily over the fair he sometimes spat and dreamily watched the spittle make its arc in the bright sunlight and settle in the hot dust below. Sometimes he seemed to take languid aim at the specks of confetti scattered in the dusty grass like handfuls of gay coloured seeds.

He was a small, sharp-faced man, like a little terrier. His yellowish face was peppered with pock-marks and he was slightly deformed in his left shoulder so that he looked by turns pathetic and sinister. His name was Waite but Sullivan's boxers called him Dutchy. He helped to clean up the show and he often towelled the sweat off the boxers and rubbed them over with the flesh-gloves after the fights.

He gave the bell a final polish and descended the ladder and lit the fag-end of a cigarette and slouched off across the fair-ground. Men in dungarees and red check shirts and woollen jerseys were busy polishing the brass spirals of the roundabouts and women were hurrying to and fro with pails of water. The smoke of cooking-fires was rising in soft bluish-white clouds from behind the caravans. A workman kneeling high up on the roof of the highest roundabout was hammering and screwing behind a figure of Venus, naked and shining gold in the sunlight. At every tap of his hammer the Venus trembled in all her limbs.

Dutchy stopped and looked up at the man and whistled him softly.

'Seen Zeke?' he called.

The man raised his oily face and looked over the fair-ground and called down.

'Some chaps round at the back of Cappo's.'

'See Zeke?'

'Can I see through a bloody shooting-gallery?'

He bent down again and tapped behind the Venus, so that she trembled again. Dutchy threw away his cigarette and flashed out a remark about the Venus and the man.

'Aw, go to bed!' the other bawled. He put his arm about the naked

Venus in order to steady the figure. Dutchy flashed another remark and walked away.

He slouched lazily through the fair towards Cappo's shooting-gallery. On reaching the shooting-gallery he slipped through a gangway between the awnings and walked across a space of grass and skirted a group of caravans. Beyond the caravans a line of Peterson's great yellow-and-scarlet trailing vans was drawn up, making a little secluded space of clean grass out of reach of the black and white ponies grazing in the field beyond them. He saw at once that something was happening: a group of show-hands had formed in a ring and were laughing and clapping their hands and shouting noisily. Dutchy slouched from behind the caravans and leaned against the wheel of a water-cart and looked at them.

In the middle of the ring a big negro was dancing a curious dance, alone. He was dressed in a pair of old grey flapping trousers and a grey sweater tucked in at the top of his trousers, which he kept up with a big bandanna handkerchief printed with great spots of yellow. He was six feet tall, powerful, with magnificent shoulders; the arch of his massive chest looked formidable and superb. He was dancing with a curious flowing negro rhythm, swaying his big hips with an arrogant invitation, brandishing his long arms above his head and letting them droop and swing senselessly with the rhythm of his body. Sometimes he clapped his black hands above his head and on his thighs and his big haunches, and sometimes he let them rest with light grace on the folds of the bandanna handkerchief. He bent his knees and twisted his feet and slithered backward over the grass and then worked forward again, comically slipping and pitching head-first like a man on a sheet of ice. He arched his whole body backward and began to work his feet furiously, as though the grass were moving from beneath him. The show-hands roared at him. He curled and twisted himself and worked the patter of his feet to a mad crescendo and let them fall as suddenly into a solemn, melancholy step again. As his big arms dropped to his side and the dance died down he suddenly began to fling wild cart-wheels, scattering the show-hands in all directions. His wild calls mingled with the shouts and laughter of the show-hands, who all applauded. At the noise a young girl came to the door of a green-and-gold caravan carrying a copper jug which flashed in the sunshine. She set down the jug on the topmost step of the van and clapped her hands. Dutchy spat in the grass and grinned at her and applauded too.

When the dance had finished and the applause had died away the show-hands closed in about the negro again and he began explaining the steps of the dance. He danced each step slowly again, talking above the murmurs of the men in a clear bass voice. There was something fine and superior about the quality of his deep voice, his perfect accent and the slow, meditative choice of his words. He had a habit of throwing back his head and smiling richly as he talked. His head was massive, the nose flat and broad and the left ear was wrinkled like a cauliflower. The skin of his face was a deep gleaming black, but it was softened by a strange blush of rose. His thick hair was black and dull as soot, and his eyes were bright and sharp as jet against the whites. He looked invincibly strong and as though he gloried in his strength, and at moments there was something about his face solemnly noble, marvellously dignified and sad.

Someone came up behind Dutchy and tapped him on the shoulder and whispered:

'Zeke busy?'

Dutchy jerked back his head and discovered O'Brien, a young light-weight of Sullivan's.

'See for yourself,' he said.

'He's wanted,' O'Brien said.

'Who wants him?'

'Sullivan. He's down at the booth with Sandy.'

Dutchy took his hands out of his pockets and spat.

'I'll go over and tell him. I want to see him myself,' he said.

He walked across the grass and broke the ring of showmen and touched the negro on the shoulder and whispered something to him.

'I'll come,' said the negro.

Dutchy waited aside. The negro slowly put on his jacket. The show-hands were dancing about the grass, practising the steps he had shown them. The negro kept smiling broadly. Finally he walked away with Dutchy past the caravans and by the shooting-gallery and across the fair-ground. 'You know what Sullivan wants,' said Dutchy, as they walked along.

The negro did not speak. They passed beneath the workman tapping at the gilded Venus.

'It's about this training,' said Dutchy.

'There's nothing wrong with me,' said the negro.

'But you're going to fight this Harrison boy Friday and I ain't seen you doing a skip or a bit of shadow for a hell of a while.'

'When you've done as much shadow-boxing as I have,' said the negro, 'you won't be in a travelling-show.'

He suddenly thrust out his arm as they walked along. 'Feel that,' he said.

Dutchy pinched the flesh of the negro's forearm: it seemed as hard as the foreleg of a horse. He nodded and was silent.

'If I train too much I go stale,' said the negro. 'You know that.'

'Tell that to Sullivan,' said Dutchy.

'I hate Sullivan,' said the negro.

They came within sight of the long scarlet, gold-tasselled tent of Sullivan's boxing-show. The ladder was standing at the head of the entrance-steps where Dutchy had left it, and in the hot sunshine the copper bell flashed brightly against the red curtains behind. The sun-baked awnings, the painted yellow pay-box and the immense pictures of the world's boxing champions painted crudely across the whole width of the show all looked cheap and tawdry.

Dutchy and the negro stopped before the steps of the show. The air was hot and breathless and the negro's skin gleamed like rose-black silk in the sunshine.

'Go in and tell him you're doing a bit with the ball this afternoon,' said Dutchy. 'We can play pontoon for a bit when you're done.'

The negro shook his head.

'I'm going to sleep this afternoon.'

He turned abruptly on his heel and walked away behind the long red show-tent. He walked without haste, gracefully and lightly.

Coming to the rear of the tent he turned the corner. Sullivan's vans were drawn up behind the tent and outside Sullivan's own van stood a young red-haired boxer talking to Sullivan himself. Sullivan was resting one foot on the steps of the van. His elbow was crooked on his knee and he was fingering his black chin with his hand. He was a small, thin-faced, unshaven, dirty man with narrow eyes and weedy black hair. His mother had been a dancer from Belfast and his father, a Pole, had been a conjurer in a travelling-show. Sullivan had inherited his mother's name and her dirty tongue. From his father he had learned inexhaustible trickeries. He had been in the show-business for longer than he could remember and had run the boxing-show for twenty years.

He looked up at the negro quickly and searchingly. There was something mean and shifty and subtle about the continual flickering of his small black eyes.

'Hello, Zeke,' he said.

The negro nodded.

'Been training, I see,' said Sullivan. 'Yes?'

The negro shook his head.

'Ain't it time you trained a bit?' said Sullivan.

The negro showed his white teeth and said, 'I'm all right. I don't want to go stale.'

Sullivan sprang off the steps of the van and in a flash of angry temper thrust his face up towards the negro's. 'Stale? You know the rules of this bloody show as well as I do.'

The negro looked down at his quivering face impassively, without a word.

'You know the rules of this show!' shouted Sullivan. 'You train and keep yourself in proper nick. I've run this show for twenty years and if you can tell me anything I don't know about boxing I'd be bloody glad to hear

it. Bloody glad. You never fought a round last week—not a damn round!
And you talk to me about going stale. While I keep you in this show you
keep yourself fit like any other man.'

The red-haired boxer walked quietly away. Sullivan's hands were
quivering with temper. The negro held out his right arm and said with
perfect calm:

'Feel that. I am as fit as any man you ever had in your show.'

Sullivan knocked the arm aside impatiently.

'You know as well as I do you don't need to worry about your arms!'
he half shouted. 'Nor your head. It's here, my old cock'—he pressed his
two hands on the negro's stomach and screwed up his eyes ominously and
lowered his voice—'You niggers are all alike. Your guts are like a sponge.'

The negro, impassive and tolerant and composed, did not speak.

'Ain't forgot you're fighting this Harrison boy Friday?' said Sullivan
quickly.

'I know.'

'I want you to beat him. If you beat him he'll want to come back before
the show goes and fight you again. See that? That means another house—
means money. I'm putting up ten pounds in this bout—seven and three.
That's money. Ain't that worth training for? Ain't it? I want to see you
win, Zeke, I want to see you win this fight.' Sullivan spat. 'You ain't
been winning so many fights lately,' he added slowly.

'I have won plenty of fights for you,' said the negro.

'Not lately—you're getting soft—I don't like it!' Sullivan paused and
scratched his unshaven chin and squinted up into the negro's face. His eyes
were narrow and inquisitive.

'How old are you, Zeke?' he said.

For the first time uneasiness came into the negro's face. He hesitated.

'I am thirty-four,' he said.

Sullivan whistled very softly.

'Good age for a boxer,' he said.

'For a white man.'

'It's a good age for any boxer—I don't care who he is,' said Sullivan.
'If a boxer ain't careful that's when he begins to lay the fat on. And that's
what you'll do—that's what I don't like. Look at your guts. You better do
a bit with the ball before the sun gets too hot.'

'I will train this afternoon,' said the negro.

'You'll train now! Do I run this show or do you?'

'I don't feel the heat so much.'

'You'll do it now!' shouted Sullivan. 'You'll do it now or get out of
this show!'

They stood looking at each other for one moment antagonistically, in
perfect silence. Sullivan's little eyes, bloodshot in the whites, were dilating

with anger and his hands were unsteady with temper. The negro gave one long look at him and then without a word or a change of expression he turned and strode away, imperturbable, solemn and dignified, and vanished into the boxing caravan, a long red wagon painted with Sullivan's name in big yellow letters down both sides, before Sullivan himself could move or speak again.

II

On Friday evening Sullivan and his four boxers were displaying themselves in the blazing light of the big electric lamps hanging over the platform outside the show. The fair was flashing and whirling and quivering with light. Between the shows moved a dark flock of people. There was an air of gaiety and great excitement in the shrieking and laughing and shouting of voices, the brassy music of the big roundabout, the crack of rifle shots and the thunder of switchback cars, which never seemed to rest. The night was sultry, without wind, and above the electric lights the summer darkness, freckled with tiny stars, was coming down a soft dark blue.

The four boxers, in dressing-gowns, stood in an imposing line, their arms folded, facing the crowd. Sullivan stood before them in his shirt-sleeves, shouting and gesticulating with a megaphone. His voice was thin and hoarse and he kept striking his fist with the palm of his hand, like an orator.

'The greatest array of real fighters any generation ever saw in any one show at any time! I'm telling you. I ain't asking you if these men look like fighters. Look at 'em! You know what a boxer looks like. You don't want me to tell you that these men ain't milk-sops! You're sportsmen! You come here because you're sportsmen. Now take a look at that young feller in the blue dressing-gown. Take a look at him! Dan O'Brien—nine stone ten—nineteen years old—and he'll fight a six-round exhibition bout with any jack-man in this crowd, any jack-man two stone above his own weight. Any jack-man you like to name!'

Sullivan seized a pair of boxing gloves and flourished them before the crowd and searched it fiercely. A hand went up among the white faces and Sullivan tossed the gloves among the crowd.

'There's a sportsman!' he yelled. 'Now another? Where's another? Any man like a six-round exhibition bout with Sandy Hack, from Dunkirk, twenty-three years old, eleven stone six? Hack will fight any man in the fourteen stone class! Thank you!'

Sullivan leapt nimbly across the platform and stood before a huge, sardonic-faced heavy-weight, dark and glowering as a Russian, and yelled:

'Dado Flowers! Twelve stone ten! Flowers has fought in America, and

76

it would be an honour for any boy to beat him in a six-round bout! An honour! What will he give away? He'll fight an elephant!'

Someone at the back of the crowd threw up his hand and Sullivan tossed the gloves away and clapped his hands. 'And now, gentlemen.' He leaned forward confidentially and spread out his hands in caricature of a Jew, and spoke in a harsh deliberate whisper.

'Half a crown. See!'

There was a flash of silver in his dirty fingers, he smiled, and the coin vanished. He stepped across the platform and twisted the ear of the huge sardonic heavy-weight and the coin dropped neatly into his hands from the boxer's nose. He tossed the coin in the air and caught it again and washed his hands of it. It reappeared in Hack's red hair. Sullivan made a joke about the Scottish people. It was an old joke. The spectators laughed, and then Sullivan pointed his fingers at them and whispered dramatically: 'Wait!' The crowd, fascinated, watched him without a murmur as he crossed the platform and stood by the huge, impassive figure of the negro.

There was a moment's pause. Suddenly the negro opened his mouth and the coin flashed bright against his black skin and seem to disappear between his red lips. When his mouth closed he stood immobile, staring over the crowd without a change in his expression of superb dignity, as though nothing had happened.

Dramatically Sullivan waved his arms and sent his fingers rippling through the negro's thick black hair and disentangled the coin. He grinned cleverly at the crowd and shouted hoarsely:

'Zeke Pinto! The coloured man! The American coloured boxer! Pinto will fight a special ten-round bout for a purse of ten pound with Dan Harrison, your own man!'

The faded red curtains behind the boxers parted and Harrison himself, not yet stripped for boxing, slouched forward on the platform for the crowd to applaud him. His thick, loose body, his half-crouching walk and the heavy-browed, glowering expression of his blond, small-eyed face contrasted strangely with the perfect repose, the superb pride and the blackness of the negro. While Sullivan continued to shout hoarsely the details of the contest between them, they stood side by side without moving or looking at each other, incongruous and indifferent to one another to the point of contempt.

The crowd were beginning to throng towards the pay-boxes and vanish through the openings in the red curtains on either side of the booth. Sullivan seized the megaphone and began to yell a frenzy of speech over the crowd, cajoling and demanding vociferously like some desperate orator. Between his more impassioned speeches O'Brien clanged arresting notes on the copper bell. The big Russian-looking heavy-weight began working on the punch-ball hanging up outside the curtains, fisting it grimly with light fascinating punches and watching it perpetually with a sardonic, half-smiling grin. Harrison slouched through the curtains and disappeared.

The negro did not change his expression of impassive dignity, and suddenly, as though incensed by it, Sullivan took the megaphone from his lips and whispered to him in a voice of sneering impatience:

'Wake up. Do something. Get round to the van and get Dutchy to give you a rub-down. You look as if you're having a bad dream.'

The negro turned and vanished through the curtains without a word. He elbowed his way through the waiting crowd inside the booth and walked out of the booth across the grass between the show-vans towards the boxers' dressing-van. He hated Sullivan. He had hated him bitterly since morning for his meanness, his bad temper, his sneers, the insult of the word nigger. He had ached to knock Sullivan senseless. He had hated so much the craftiness in his sudden question 'How old are you, Zeke?' that it had given him a curious sense of pleasure to tell him that he was only thirty-four. But the pleasure had quickly vanished again. During the hot afternoon, sitting gambling with Dutchy in the shade of one of Peterson's vans, he had often reminded himself that he was older than Sullivan dreamed. He was past forty. At forty a boxer was an old man. Until lately it had been easy to deceive Sullivan; but lately he had begun to feel slower in the ring and had lost fights which he ought to have won. When he lost the money went out of the show, so that Sullivan also lost. That was bad business. He saw the significance of Sullivan's question: he was growing old and he was bad business. There were younger boxers. He knew already what to expect if he lost the fight with Harrison.

He walked across the dark grass and up the steps of the dressing-van slowly, realizing for one moment what it all meant to him. He opened the door of the van. A paraffin-lamp was burning, there was a powerful smell of liniment, and he saw Dutchy sitting on a box, smoking a cigarette and reading a pink comic-newspaper. He stepped into the van and shut the door with his back. It seemed every moment more than ever imperative that he should win the fight with Harrison.

At the sound of the door Dutchy dropped the pink newspaper as though startled and jumped to his feet.

'All right?' he said quickly.

'Sullivan sent me to you for a rub-down.'

'You don't want a rub-down before you fight, do you?'

The negro sat down on the box.

'In this show you do what Sullivan tells you.'

Dutchy spat a shred of tobacco from his mouth with a sound of disgust and took a penny from his pocket and spun it in the air. He caught it deftly on the back of his left hand and covered it with his right. He had a passion for gambling. The smoke of his cigarette burned straight upward into his eyes, so that his face was wrinkled and squinting as he turned it to the negro.

'Heads,' said Pinto.

Dutchy looked at the coin and put it back into his pocket.

'Again,' said the negro. 'What I lose I'll square up later.'

Dutchy tossed the coin and the negro called 'Heads' again, wrongly. Too lazy to take the cigarette from his mouth Dutchy blew away the ash with a snort of his nose. The negro, dreamily watching the grey ash float in the air and settle again, seemed oblivious for a moment of Dutchy and the toss of the coin. He murmured 'Heads' again.

'Your luck's out,' said Dutchy.

They went on alternately tossing and calling the coin for what seemed to the negro a long time. The repeated spin of the coin became like the everlasting revolution of the thought that he must win the fight with Harrison. He felt himself filled by an oppressive gloomy determination to win.

Dutchy was in the act of tossing the coin when footsteps ran up the ladder of the van and Sullivan burst in. He immediately began to speak to the negro.

'I want you to win this fight, Zeke,' he said. 'And I want you to win it fair—straight—no monkey business. See that?'

'What sort of a house?' drawled Dutchy.

'Packed. D'ye hear me, Zeke?'

The negro was staring at the photographs of boxers pinned everywhere on the walls of the van.

'D'ye hear me, Zeke? I want you to win this fight—and clean. This boy can box. But you beat him clean and it'll be credit to you. Box him and beat him clean. You hear me?'

'Don't I always fight clean?' said the negro.

'I know, I know you do. Don't get your rag out. I want you to win, that's all. I'll treat you square. Trust me. I'll get back now and watch Dado finishing, and you can come over and show yourself in a minute or two. I'll treat you square.'

He left the van quickly, but before Dutchy or the negro could move the door opened again and Sullivan thrust in his head. He delivered an urgent last whisper:

'Box him and beat him clean, that's all. That's all. I'll treat you square. Trust me.'

He vanished.

There was a moment of silence. The negro slowly unloosened his dressing-gown and stood on the box on which he had been sitting. Dutchy spat out his cigarette in disgust. 'Trust me,' he sneered softly. 'Trust a bloody snake.'

With quick light fingers he began loosening the negro's muscles, first on the calves, then the thighs, and finally on the body. The black skin was supple and fine as satin in his fingers. The air was sultry and little yellow balls of sweat stood on his face before he had finished.

'You'll win,' he kept saying to the negro between little panting noises. 'Any money. Easy.'

The negro stood utterly immobile, not speaking, staring at the rows of boxing photographs with something sceptical and philosophical in his eyes. Dutchy worked over the muscles just above the belt-line, kneading them gently. The muscles yielded, flabbier than the rest of his body.

'You'll win,' said Dutchy. 'Keep him off your guts, that's all.'

The negro nodded. Presently he knotted up his dressing-gown and they walked together out of the van and across the grass among the show-vans and entered the boxing-booth. The tent, brilliantly lighted, was thronged with spectators surging backwards and forwards about the ropes of the ring like a flock of sheep penned between the ropes and the red canvas. There was a low, continuous murmur of voices. The white light of electric lamps poured down on Flowers and a bony young boxer in red drawers, sparring out their last round. Flowers was ambling carelessly about the ring, flickering and tapping his man with sardonic friendliness. Sometimes the young boxer would aim fierce unhappy blows at Flowers, making the loose boards creak under his clumsy feet, and the crowd would break into laughter. Flowers was smiling and there was a smear of blood across the young boxer's mouth as the round ended and the crowd applauded the men.

The negro elbowed his way through the crowd and the ring had been empty a second or two when he climbed over the ropes and sat down in the corner. Almost at the same moment Harrison climbed into the ring too, and sat in the corner opposite him. The crowd cat-called and applauded and broke into a hum of conversation at the sight of Harrison, who sat staring across the ring from under his blond surly brows. The negro looked at the crowd calmly. It was a big house. Two of Sullivan's men climbed a ladder and rolled back a sheet of the canvas roof and let in a current of fresh air. Dutchy climbed into the ring and began to put on the negro's gloves.

'Keep him off your guts,' he whispered. 'Let him wear hisself out. He's a madhead. Let him gallop for three rounds and you'll have him taped.'

Without speaking or even nodding in answer the negro leaned back his head and let it rest against the ropes. Staring upward he could see through the gap in the roof a sprinkle of stars shining against the darkness of the summer sky.

Dutchy was putting on his second glove when Sullivan crawled into the ring under the bottom rope. Standing in the centre of the ring he held up his hand and called for order. The negro did not look at him and he heard only vaguely the speech he began to bawl at the crowd. He felt tired and he did not want to fight.

Sullivan was repeating the old formula. 'You come to this show to see a fight! You come to see fair play! And you shall have 'em! If you have any remarks to pass I ask you to pass them afterwards—not while the rounds are in progress. Be fair to these boys and they will give you a good fight. A good, honest fight! That's straight, ain't it! No love-tapping! You know what I mean by no love-tapping! The boys are out to win. I tell you on my oath, my solid oath, and God strike me dead if I tell a lie—there never has been a squared fight in this show—and never will be!'

His voice rose to a shout and the crowd applauded vigorously.

'Now I shall present a ten-round contest between Dan Harrison—'

Harrison stood up and the crowd began to cheer for him.

'Dan Harrison, of your own town, and Zeke Pinto, the American coloured boxer. A ten-round fight for a purse of ten pounds!' The negro stood up and nodded his head, and Sullivan appealed to the spectators:

'Give the coloured man a clap. A man's a man and a boxer a boxer, whether he's coloured or not. Pinto will fight fair and clean, and if he wins I hope you will acknowledge him like the sportsmen I know you are. Give the coloured man a clap, gentlemen, give the coloured man a clap.'

The negro half rose to his feet again, making a slight bow. He was conscious vaguely of the noise of applause, the quivering of the many white pairs of hands under the bright lights, and of Harrison arching back his thick neck, drinking something from a dark wine bottle and spitting it over the side of the ring again.

A moment later Sullivan, who was to referee the fight himself, took off his jacket and called the two boxers to the centre of the ring and spoke with them. Conscious merely of the harsh voice repeating the old formula again, the negro did not listen. By turns there would come over him the strange feeling that he did not want to fight, and the gloomy oppressive thought that he must fight and win. 'And keep your tempers,' said Sullivan. 'Like good boys. That's all.'

The negro returned to his corner. He took off his dressing-gown and putting his hands on the ropes, worked his body to and fro, loosening his muscles. Against his bright yellow drawers his naked skin gleamed very black, the fine lights suffused with rose, as though the blackness had been smeared with a soft pink oil. He took one long deep breath; Dutchy whispered something to him; and he heard the stroke of the gong.

He stood upright, turned about, walked towards the centre of the ring and touched gloves with Harrison. His pose was quiet, unstooping and unexaggerated. His huge black form was splendid and intimidating in its dignity. His face was marvellously calm. Harrison came forward with a low crouch of his shoulders, his surly blond head thrust forward aggressively, his guard very close. They worked away and round each other for a second or two, watchfully. The crowd was silent.

Suddenly Harrison made a lead with his left to the negro's face and followed up swiftly. The negro took the punches on his gloves. Harrison led again and the negro fought back, grazing Harrison's face. They closed with each other, and Harrison began peppering the negro's body with short jabs which fell on his ribs and the soft flesh just above the belt. The negro tried to cover himself and step away but the blows were unexpected and quick and he took the punishment of them unguarded. When he finally broke away he was panting and there was a dull throbbing in his body where the punches had fallen. As he stepped away Harrison forced him to the ropes and attacked him viciously, hooking his right. The negro saw the blow coming and waited for what seemed a complete second, and then side-stepped swiftly. It was a beautiful movement. He heard the crowd murmur in admiration. Experiencing a moment of satisfaction and feeling fresh and cool again he worked away from the corner before Harrison could recover. Harrison followed and they began fighting close in again, and again a shower of quick jabbing blows fell on the negro's body. The punches were short, stinging and powerful. The negro felt shaken and winded. He covered his body with his arms and ducked his head, taking the blows on his arms and shoulders until he had recovered his breath. Harrison came to a clinch at last and Sullivan broke them away. A little excited, Harrison left his hands loose after the clinch had been broken and the negro stepped across and found his jaw with a quick hook of his right. Harrison went down, panting and resting on his elbow while Sullivan counted to nine, bawling the counts in order to make himself heard above the babble of the crowd. At nine Harrison was on his feet again. He rushed straight for the negro, his head low and aggressive. They closed, and they were chest to chest, struggling for an opening, as the gong rang.

In the interval the negro sat with his arms limp on the ropes, his head back and his eyes closed. The fanning of the towel sent waves of cooler air on his face. He nodded when Dutchy gave him the old advice: 'Keep him off your guts,' and sometimes he felt the muscles of his body flutter just above the belt, where Harrison had jabbed him. He knew that Harrison had found his weakness.

The second round began as though Harrison had conceived a violent hatred for the negro. He was younger than the negro by twenty years. He had a fast, powerful, fearless style, and he was warm with resentment at having taken a count of nine. He led quickly for the negro's face but Pinto stepped aside and struck his left ear with the heel of the glove. It was as though the punch had released a whirlwind: the short jabbing blows began to rain on the negro's body before he could cover up again. Crooking his arms and lowering his head, he staggered against Harrison and tried to fend him off, but the punches had sickened him. He had backed away to the ropes, and this time when Harrison attacked again he was too slow to duck away. He took a fresh onslaught of body blows that sickened him from his knees upward. He felt strange and stunned and the shouts of the crowd were like a great drumming in his head. The crowd was shouting for Harrison. He staggered drunkenly and recovered and then crouched and staggered against Harrison, keeping his head low. For the rest of the round he did nothing but try desperately to keep out of Harrison's reach and he was lying on the boards when the gong rang.

During the interval Dutchy worked on his stomach and freshened him with the towel and urged the old advice upon him. He nodded vaguely. The whole pandemonium of the fair seemed to clamour in his head, the shouting of the crowd, the tunes of the hurdy-gurdy, the snap of rifle-shots, the thunder of switchbacks and the silly shrieking of young girls. He could not gather his thoughts.

During the third round and again in the fourth Harrison knocked him down. Each time he took a count of nine, resting on his elbow. At every count the crowd shouted wildly. He knew that he was losing, and he knew that no one wanted him to win. After every punch he felt slower, and behind Harrison's big menancing face the white faces of the crowd seemed to surge up to him and ebb away in a babbling tide.

In the intervals his arms felt leaden, his legs fluttered with sickness, and his body felt old and sore. He knew that he was looked upon as beaten already. He could see the unpleasantness in Sullivan's face as he leaned in the corner and noted the points on a scrap of paper.

When the gong rang for the fifth round Harrison rushed across the ring and met him with a wild attack on his body. He was flushed and sweating, and his eyes were glowing with an eagerness to finish off the negro. He hooked wildly but the blow missed and the negro, full of a sudden despairing calmness, gathered himself and swung heavily at Harrison's jaw. The punch connected, Harrison went down, and then leapt to his feet again before Sullivan had time to count. The crowd cheered him. He rushed at the negro madly again, without success. The negro felt strangely calm, his fears lessened. Harrison seemed suddenly baffled and angry. He repeated his attack and the crowd clamoured madly for the knockout. He came and attacked again, angry and distressed by his failure to hit the negro. The negro, for the first time impassive and unharassed, struck Harrison's jaw with a short, straight punch. Harrison tottered and fell on one knee, hanging to the rope with his left hand. The booth was like a madhouse, the crowd yelling for Harrison to stand up. He rose slowly, holding to the ropes, panting heavily. The ropes were very loose and as he trusted his weight to them they sagged and he pitched forward drunkenly. The negro followed up with his right. Harrison gloved off the blow but staggered and pitched forward again, like a boomerang. Something like a primitive frenzy came over the negro. He leapt forward and hit Harrison madly as he was falling. The blow struck hard below the belt and Harrison quivered and pitched upward through the ropes and dropped heavily into the crowd.

The negro stood utterly still in the ring. It was all over. He was conscious vaguely of Harrison being counted out and of the crowd yelling angrily for a foul. He knew that he had fouled Harrison, and he knew that the crowd hated him.

Sullivan finished the count and seizing the negro's arm held it above his head and shouted:

'Pinto!'

The crowd hooted the negro, who stood statuesque and bewildered, as though not understanding what had happened. His arm dropped listlessly. Dutchy came into the ring and flung the dressing-gown over his shoulders. Sullivan walked round the ring holding up his hands and trying to quieten the pandemonium, but the crowd called derisively 'Go to Hell! Shut your bloody mouth!' Harrison crawled back through the ropes, holding his stomach, dazed and reeling. The crowd cheered and clamoured for him. His seconds began a furious altercation with Sullivan, thrusting their faces close up to him, livid with temper. Flowers and Hack leapt into the ring and pushed away the seconds, elbowing them away like policemen. The booth was full of a shouting, quarrelling pandemonium.

Dutchy kept close to the negro. 'All right,' he kept repeating. 'All right. Didn't I tell you you'd win?'

The negro, dazed and despondent, never moved. He looked like a solemn black statue. He stared apathetically from the crowd to Harrison and from Harrison to Sullivan. He saw Sullivan waving some paper money in his hand and he saw Harrison take the money and count it. There were three pounds. After that he vaguely understood that Sullivan was appealing to the crowd, who were beginning to listen to his hoarse insinuating voice.

'You know that in this show or any other show the referee's word must stand. Ain't that so? If the referee gives way to the crowd what happens? You know what happens! He's no more good! He's finished. He's done. Napoo! I've refereed more fights than any man in this show has ever seen. And if any other man will come up here in my place I shall welcome him gladly! Gladly! Harrison's a good fighter—a game feller—and when he was knocked out he was leading on points, let me tell you that. He's a game feller.'

The crowd began to cheer again.

'But he was knocked out! Knocked out! And fair. And no man in this crowd will make me change my opinion that he was knocked out! But to show that I think he's a game feller and a good fighter—'

The negro saw Sullivan flourish another pound note in the air. He saw Harrison come forward and accept the money while Sullivan patted his back. The crowd cheered and clapped and stamped its feet for Harrison.

Sullivan held up his hands and quietened the crowd.

'And now give the coloured man a clap,' he shouted; 'and now give the coloured man a clap!'

The crowd gave the negro a round of applause.

The negro knotted the cord of his dressing-gown. He saw Sullivan looking at him closely, his shifty eyes filled with impatience and contempt. He felt humiliated and dazed, and he hated Sullivan bitterly for awarding him the fight. He climbed under the ropes and leapt softly down on the grass and began to elbow his way through the crowd, back to the dressing-room. Dutchy, following him, threw a towel about his neck. The crowd murmured a little as it parted to let him through.

He went into the dressing-van and sat down on a box. There was an odour of sweat and liniment and the oil from the lamp burning on the table. He stared vaguely at the flame burning steady and yellow behind the smoky lamp-glass, and then at the rows of boxing photographs lit up by the orange light of the lamp. His legs were unsteady and fluttering, as though he had been running very hard and for a long time. His stomach and his ribs were bruised and sore. His arms seemed heavy and wooden and his whole body felt old and feeble and empty, like the husk of something.

'You won,' said Dutchy. 'Didn't I tell you you'd win?'

The negro lifted his hands listlessly for Dutchy to take off the gloves. He was thinking of Sullivan, the foul, and the way the crowd had hooted him. The mad frenzy in which he had fouled Harrison had left him tired and stupefied and ashamed.

Dutchy slipped off first one glove and then the other. The negro opened his hot damp hands and was too listless to shut them again.

Dutchy unknotted the cord of his dressing-gown and threw the gown back over the black shoulders, warm and shining dark with sweat, and began to rub the shoulders gently. The negro slowly stood up. His dressing-gown slipped to the floor and he stood motionless, solemn and mute, staring straight at the boxing pictures pinned on the wall before him.

'Feeling all right?' Dutchy asked. 'Didn't I tell you you'd win? You'll be all right. Didn't I tell you? Easy! You'll be all right.'

He threw the towel aside and drew the flesh gloves on his hands. The negro slowly bent his back. There was a strange expression of sadness on his face and an air of weariness about his whole body, and he was not listening to Dutchy's words.

'Easy,' said Dutchy. 'You'll be all right. Didn't I tell you?'

John Steinbeck born 1902 at Salinas, California, of German descent. After studying science at Stanford University, he worked as labourer, chemist, caretaker, fruit picker, and surveyor. He has lived in many places, principally California, Mexico, Europe. Steinbeck's first novel, CUP OF GOLD, 1929, was about Morgan the pirate. THE GRAPES OF WRATH, his most popular book, tells of a migratory family seeking work in California. It was awarded the Pulitzer Prize and has been compared in influence to UNCLE TOM'S CABIN. His work shows an intense interest in poverty-stricken minority groups, particularly in California, his home state, of which he writes with a mixture of love, poetry, cynicism, and outright bitterness.

During the Second World War, Steinbeck did special writing assignments for the U.S. Army Air Forces. In 1943 he went to Europe as a correspondent for the New York HERALD TRIBUNE. After the war he travelled extensively and reported on his travels for several newspapers and magazines. His most success-ful post-war novels have been THE PEARL, his retelling of an old Mexican folktale, and EAST OF EDEN, which was also successful as a film.

'FLIGHT' was published in the collection THE LONG VALLEY in 1938.

He died in 1968.

FLIGHT

John Steinbeck

ABOUT FIFTEEN MILES BELOW MONTEREY, ON THE WILD COAST, THE TORRES family had their farm, a few sloping acres above a cliff that dropped to the brown reefs and on to the hissing white waters of the ocean. Behind the farm the stone mountains stood up against the sky. The farm buildings huddled like little clinging aphids on the mountain skirts, crouched low to the ground as though the wind might blow them into the sea. The little shack, the rattling, rotting barn were gray-bitten with sea salt, beaten by the damp wind until they had taken on the color of the granite hills. Two horses, a red cow and a red calf, half a dozen pigs and a flock of lean, multi-colored chickens stocked the place. A little corn was raised on the sterile slope, and it grew short and thick under the wind, and all the cobs formed on the landward sides of the stalks.

Mama Torres, a lean, dry woman with ancient eyes, had ruled the farm for ten years, ever since her husband tripped over a stone in the field one day and fell full length on a rattlesnake. When one is bitten on the chest there is not much that can be done.

Mama Torres had three children, two undersized black ones of twelve and fourteen, Emilio and Rosy, whom Mama kept fishing on the rocks below the farm when the sea was kind and when the truant officer was in some distant part of Monterey County. And there was Pepé, the tall smiling son of nineteen, a gentle, affectionate boy, but very lazy. Pepé had a tall head, pointed at the top, and from its peak, coarse black hair grew down like a thatch all around. Over his smiling little eyes Mama cut a straight bang so he could see. Pepé had sharp Indian cheekbones and an eagle nose, but his mouth was as sweet and shapely as a girl's mouth, and his chin was fragile and chiseled. He was loose and gangling, all legs and feet and wrists, and he was very lazy. Mama thought him fine and brave, but she never told him so. She said, 'Some lazy cow must have got into thy father's family, else how could I have a son like thee.' And she said, 'When I carried thee, a sneaking lazy coyote came out of the brush and looked at me one day. That must have made thee so.'

Pepé smiled sheepishly and stabbed at the ground with his knife to keep the blade sharp and free from rust. It was his inheritance, that knife, his father's knife. The long heavy blade folded back into the black handle. There was a button on the handle. When Pepé pressed the button, the blade leaped out ready for use. The knife was with Pepé always, for it had been his father's knife.

One sunny morning when the sea below the cliff was glinting and blue and the white surf creamed on the reef, when even the stone mountains looked kindly, Mama Torres called out the door of the shack, 'Pepé, I have a labor for thee.'

There was no answer. Mama listened. From behind the barn she heard a burst of laughter. She lifted her full long skirt and walked in the direction of the noise.

Pepé was sitting on the ground with his back against a box. His white teeth glistened. On either side of him stood the two black ones, tense and expectant. Fifteen feet away a redwood post was set in the ground. Pepé's right hand lay limply in his lap, and in the palm the big black knife rested. The blade was closed back into the handle. Pepé looked smiling at the sky.

Suddenly Emilio cried, 'Ya!'

Pepé's wrist flicked like the head of a snake. The blade seemed to fly open in mid-air, and with a thump the point dug into the redwood post, and the black handle quivered. The three burst into excited laughter. Rosy ran to the post and pulled out the knife and brought it back to Pepé. He closed the blade and settled the knife carefully in his listless palm again. He grinned self-consciously at the sky.

'Ya!'

The heavy knife lanced out and sunk into the post again. Mama moved forward like a ship and scattered the play.

'All day you do foolish things with the knife, like a toy-baby,' she stormed. 'Get up on thy huge feet that eat up shoes. Get up!' She took him by one loose shoulder and hoisted at him. Pepé grinned sheepishly and came half-heartedly to his feet. 'Look!' Mama cried. 'Big lazy, you must catch the horse and put on him thy father's saddle. You must ride to Monterey. The medicine bottle is empty. There is no salt. Go thou now, Peanut! Catch the horse.'

A revolution took place in the relaxed figure of Pepé. 'To Monterey, me? Alone? *Sí*, Mama.'

She scowled at him. 'Do not think, big sheep, that you will buy candy. No, I will give you only enough for the medicine and the salt.'

Pepé smiled. 'Mama, you will put the hatband on the hat?'

She relented then. 'Yes, Pepé. You may wear the hatband.'

His voice grew insinuating, 'And the green handkerchief, Mama?'

'Yes, if you go quickly and return with no trouble, the silk green handkerchief will go. If you make sure to take off the handkerchief when you eat so no spot may fall on it. . . .'

'*Sí*, Mama. I will be careful. I am a man.'

'Thou? A man? Thou art a peanut.'

He went into the rickety barn and brought out a rope, and he walked agilely enough up the hill to catch the horse.

When he was ready and mounted before the door, mounted on his father's saddle that was so old that the oaken frame showed through torn leather in many places, then Mama brought out the round black hat with the tooled leather band, and she reached up and knotted the green silk handkerchief about his neck. Pepé's blue denim coat was much darker than his jeans, for it had been washed much less often.

Mama handed up the big medicine bottle and the silver coins. 'That for the medicine,' she said, ' and that for the salt. That for a candle to burn for the papa. That for *dulces* for the little ones. Our friend Mrs Rodriguez will give you dinner and maybe a bed for the night. When you go to the church say only ten Paternosters and only twenty-five Ave Marias. Oh! I know, big coyote. You would sit there flapping your mouth over Aves all day while you looked at the candles and the holy pictures. That is not good devotion to stare at the pretty things.'

The black hat, covering the high pointed head and black thatched hair of Pepé, gave him dignity and age. He sat the rangy horse well. Mama thought how handsome he was, dark and lean and tall. 'I would not send thee now alone, thou little one, except for the medicine,' she said softly. 'It is not good to have no medicine, for who knows when the toothache will come, or the sadness of the stomach. These things are.'

'Adios, Mama,' Pepé cried. 'I will come back soon. You may send me often alone. I am a man.'

'Thou art a foolish chicken.'

He straightened his shoulders, flipped the reins against the horse's shoulder and rode away. He turned once and saw that they still watched him, Emilio and Rosy and Mama. Pepé grinned with pride and gladness and lifted the tough buckskin horse to a trot.

When he had dropped out of sight over a little dip in the road, Mama turned to the black ones, but she spoke to herself. 'He is nearly a man now,' she said. 'It will be a nice thing to have a man in the house again.' Her eyes sharpened on the children. 'Go to the rocks now. The tide is going out. There will be abalones to be found.' She put the iron hooks into their hands and saw them down the steep trail to the reefs. She brought the smooth stone *metate* to the doorway and sat grinding her corn to flour and looking occasionally at the road over which Pepé had gone. The noonday came and then the afternoon, when the little ones beat the abalones on a rock to make them tender and Mama patted the tortillas to make them thin. They ate their dinner as the red sun was plunging down toward the ocean. They sat on the doorsteps and watched the big white moon come over the mountain tops.

Mama said, 'He is now at the house of our friend Mrs Rodriguez. She will give him nice things to eat and maybe a present.'

Emilio said, 'Some day I too will ride to Monterey for medicine. Did Pepé come to be a man today?'

Mama said wisely, 'A boy gets to be a man when a man is needed.

Remember this thing. I have known boys forty years old because there was no need for a man.'

Soon afterwards they retired, Mama in her big oak bed on one side of the room, Emilio and Rosy in their boxes full of straw and sheepskins on the other side of the room.

The moon went over the sky and the surf roared on the rocks. The roosters crowed the first call. The surf subsided to a whispering surge against the reef. The moon dropped toward the sea. The roosters crowed again.

The moon was near down to the water when Pepé rode on a winded horse to his home flat. His dog bounced out and circled the horse yelping with pleasure. Pepé slid off the saddle to the ground. The weathered little shack was silver in the moonlight and the square shadow of it was black to the north and east. Against the east the piling mountains were misty with light; their tops melted into the sky.

Pepé walked wearily up the three steps and into the house. It was dark inside. There was a rustle in the corner.

Mama cried out from her bed. 'Who comes? Pepé, is it thou?'

'*Sí*, Mama.'

'Did you get the medicine?'

'*Sí*, Mama.'

'Well, go to sleep, then. I thought you would be sleeping at the house of Mrs Rodriguez.' Pepé stood silently in the dark room. 'Why do you stand there, Pepé? Did you drink wine?'

'*Sí*, Mama.'

'Well, go to bed then and sleep out the wine.'

His voice was tired and patient, but very firm. 'Light the candle, Mama. I must go away into the mountains.'

'What is this, Pepé? You are crazy.' Mama struck a sulphur match and held the little blue burr until the flame spread up the stick. She set light to the candle on the floor beside her bed. 'Now, Pepé, what is this you say?' She looked anxiously into his face.

He was changed. The fragile quality seemed to have gone from his chin. His mouth was less full than it had been, the lines of the lips were straighter, but in his eyes the greatest change had taken place. There was no laughter in them any more nor any bashfulness. They were sharp and bright and purposeful.

He told her in a tired monotone, told her everything just as it had happened. A few people came into the kitchen of Mrs Rodriguez. There was wine to drink. Pepé drank wine. The little quarrel—the man started toward Pepé and then the knife—it went almost by itself. It flew, it darted before Pepé knew it. As he talked, Mama's face grew stern, and it seemed to grow more lean. Pepé finished. 'I am a man now, Mama. The man said names to me I could not allow.'

Mama nodded. 'Yes, thou art a man, my poor little Pepé. Thou art a man. I have seen it coming on thee. I have watched you throwing the knife into the post, and I have been afraid.' For a moment her face had softened, but now it grew stern again. 'Come! We must get you ready. Go. Awaken Emilio and Rosy. Go quickly.'

Pepé stepped over to the corner where his brother and sister slept among the sheepskins. He leaned down and shook them gently. 'Come, Rosy! Come, Emilio! The mama says you must arise.'

The little black ones sat up and rubbed their eyes in the candlelight. Mama was out of bed now, her long black skirt over her nightgown. 'Emilio,' she cried. 'Go up and catch the other horse for Pepé. Quickly now! Quickly.' Emilio put his legs in his overalls and stumbled sleepily out the door.

'You heard no one behind you on the road?' Mama demanded.

'No, Mama. I listened carefully. No one was on the road.'

Mama darted like a bird about the room. From a nail on the wall she took a canvas water bag and threw it on the floor. She stripped a blanket from her bed and rolled it into a tight tube and tied the ends with string. From a box beside the stove she lifted a flour sack half full of black stringy jerky. 'Your father's black coat, Pepé. Here, put it on.'

Pepé stood in the middle of the floor watching her activity. She reached behind the door and brought out the rifle, a long 38-56, worn shiny the whole length of the barrel. Pepé took it from her and held it in the crook of his elbow. Mama brought a little leather bag and counted the cartridges into his hand. 'Only ten left,' she warned. 'You must not waste them.'

Emilio put his head in the door. '*Qui 'st 'l caballo*, Mama.'

'Put on the saddle from the other horse. Tie on the blanket. Here, tie the jerky to the saddle horn.'

Still Pepé stood silently watching his mother's frantic activity. His chin looked hard, and his sweet mouth was drawn and thin. His little eyes followed Mama about the room almost suspiciously.

Rosy asked softly. 'Where goes Pepé?'

Mama's eyes were fierce. 'Pepé goes on a journey. Pepé is a man now. He has a man's thing to do.'

Pepé straightened his shoulders. His mouth changed until he looked very much like Mama.

At last the preparation was finished. The loaded horse stood outside the door. The water bag dripped a line of moisture down the bay shoulder.

The moonlight was being thinned by the dawn and the big white moon was near down to the sea. The family stood by the shack. Mama confronted Pepé. 'Look, my son! Do not stop until it is dark again. Do not sleep even though you are tired. Take care of the horse in order that he may not stop of weariness. Remember to be careful with the bullets— there are only ten. Do not fill thy stomach with jerky or it will make thee sick. Eat a little jerky and fill thy stomach with grass. When thou comest to the high mountains, if thou seest any of the dark watching men, go not near to them nor try to speak to them. And forget not thy prayers.' She put her lean hands on Pepé's shoulders, stood on her toes and kissed him formally on both cheeks, and Pepé kissed her on both cheeks. Then he went to Emilio and Rosy and kissed both of their cheeks.

Pepé turned back to Mama. He seemed to look for a little softness, a little weakness in her. His eyes were searching, but Mama's face remained fierce. 'Go now,' she said. 'Do not wait to be caught like a chicken.'

Pepé pulled himself into the saddle. 'I am a man,' he said.

It was the first dawn when he rode up the hill towards the little canyon which let a trail into the mountains. Moonlight and daylight fought with each other, and the two warring qualities made it difficult to see. Before Pepé had gone a hundred yards, the outlines of his figure were misty; and long before he entered the canyon, he had become a gray, indefinite shadow.

Mama stood stiffly in front of her doorstep, and on either side of her stood Emilio and Rosy. They cast furtive glances at Mama now and then.

When the gray shape of Pepé melted into the hillside and disappeared, Mama relaxed. She began the high, whining keen of the death wail. 'Our beautiful—our brave,' she cried. 'Our protector, our son is gone.' Emilio and Rosy moaned beside her. 'Our beautiful—our brave, he is gone.' It was the formal wail. It rose to a high piercing whine and subsided to a moan. Mama raised it three times and then she turned and went into the house and shut the door.

Emilio and Rosy stood wondering in the dawn. They heard Mama whimpering in the house. They went out to sit on the cliff above the ocean. They touched shoulders. 'When did Pepé come to be a man?' Emilio asked.

'Last night,' said Rosy. 'Last night in Monterey.' The ocean clouds turned red with the sun that was behind the mountains.

'We will have no breakfast,' said Emilio. 'Mama will not want to cook.' Rosy did not answer him. 'Where is Pepé gone?' he asked.

Rosy looked around at him. She drew her knowledge from the quiet air. 'He has gone on a journey. He will never come back.'

'Is he dead? Do you think he is dead?'

Rosy looked back at the ocean again. A little steamer, drawing a line of smoke, sat on the edge of the horizon. 'He is not dead,' Rosy explained. 'Not yet.'

Pepé rested the big rifle across the saddle in front of him. He let the horse walk up the hill and he didn't look back. The stony slope took on a coat of short brush so that Pepé found the entrance to a trail and entered it.

When he came to the canyon opening, he swung once in his saddle and looked back, but the houses were swallowed in the misty light. Pepé jerked forward again. The high shoulder of the canyon closed in on him. His horse stretched out its neck and sighed and settled to the trail.

It was a well-worn path, dark soft leaf-mold earth strewn with broken pieces of sandstone. The trail rounded the shoulder of the canyon and dropped steeply into the bed of the stream. In the shallows the water ran smoothly, glinting in the first morning sun. Small round stones on the bottom were as brown as rust with sun moss. In the sand along the edges of the stream the tall, rich wild mint grew, while in the water itself the cress, old and tough, had gone to heavy seed.

The path went into the stream and emerged on the other side. The horse sloshed into the water and stopped. Pepé dropped his bridle and let the beast drink of the running water.

Soon the canyon sides became steep and the first giant sentinel redwoods guarded the trail, great round red trunks bearing foliage as green and lacy as ferns. Once Pepé was among the trees, the sun was lost. A perfumed and purple light lay in the pale green of the underbush. Gooseberry bushes and blackberries and tall ferns lined the stream, and overhead the branches of the redwoods met and cut off the sky.

Pepé drank from the water bag, and he reached into the flour sack and brought out a black string of jerky. His white teeth gnawed at the string until the tough meat parted. He chewed slowly and drank occasionally from the water bag. His little eyes were slumberous and tired, but the muscles of his face were hard set. The earth of the trail was black now. It gave up a hollow sound under the walking hoofbeats.

The stream fell more sharply. Little waterfalls splashed on the stones. Five-fingered ferns hung over the water and dripped spray from their fingertips. Pepé rode half over in his saddle, dangling one leg loosely. He picked a bay leaf from a tree beside the way and put it into his mouth for a moment to flavor the dry jerky. He held the gun loosely across the pommel.

Suddenly he squared in his saddle, swung the horse from the trail and kicked it hurriedly up behind a big redwood tree. He pulled up the reins tight against the bit to keep the horse from whinnying. His face was intent and his nostrils quivered a little.

A hollow pounding came down the trail, and a horseman rode by, a fat man with red cheeks and a white stubble beard. His horse put down its head and blubbered at the trail when it came to the place where Pepé had turned off. 'Hold up!' said the man and he pulled up his horse's head.

When the last sound of the hoofs died away, Pepé came back into the trail again. He did not relax in the saddle any more. He lifted the big rifle and swung the lever to throw a shell into the chamber, and then he let down the hammer to half cock.

The trail grew very steep. Now the redwood trees were smaller and their tops were dead, bitten dead where the wind reached them. The horse plodded on; the sun went slowly overhead and started down toward the afternoon.

Where the stream came out of a side canyon, the trail left it. Pepé dismounted and watered his horse and filled up his water bag. As soon as the trail had parted from the stream, the trees were gone and only the thick brittle sage and manzanita and chaparral edged the trail. And the soft black earth was gone, too, leaving only the light tan broken rock for the trail bed. Lizards scampered away into the brush as the horse rattled over the little stones.

Pepé turned in his saddle and looked back. He was in the open now: he could be seen from a distance. As he ascended the trail the country grew more rough and terrible and dry. The way wound about the bases of great square rocks. Little gray rabbits skittered in the brush. A bird made a monotonous high creaking. Eastward the bare rock mountain-tops were were pale and powder-dry under the dropping sun. The horse plodded up and up the trail toward a little V in the ridge which was the pass.

Pepé looked suspiciously back every minute or so, and his eyes sought the tops of the ridges ahead. Once, on a white barren spur, he saw a black figure for a moment, but he looked quickly away, for it was one of the dark watchers. No one knew who the watchers were, nor where they lived, but it was better to ignore them and never to show interest in them. They did not bother one who stayed on the trail and minded his own business.

The air was parched and full of light dust blown by the breeze from the eroding mountains. Pepé drank sparingly from his bag and corked it tightly and hung it on the horn again. The trail moved up the dry shale hillside, avoiding rocks, dropping under clefts, climbing in and out of old water scars. When he arrived at the little pass he stopped and looked back for a long time. No dark watchers were to be seen now. The trail behind was empty. Only the high tops of the redwoods indicated where the stream flowed.

Pepé rode on through the pass. His little eyes were nearly closed with weariness, but his face was stern, relentless and manly. The high mountain wind coasted sighing through the pass and whistled on the edges of the big blocks of broken granite. In the air, a red-tailed hawk sailed over close to the ridge and screamed angrily. Pepé went slowly through the broken jagged pass and looked down on the other side.

The trail dropped quickly, staggering among broken rock. At the bottom of the slope there was a dark crease, thick with brush, and on the other side of the crease a little flat, in which a grove of oak trees grew. A scar of green grass cut across the flat. And behind the flat another mountain rose, desolate with dead rocks and starving little black bushes. Pepé drank from the bag again for the air was so dry that it encrusted his nostrils and burned his lips. He put the horse down the trail. The hooves slipped and struggled on the steep way, starting little stones that rolled off into the brush. The sun was gone behind the westward mountain now, but still it glowed brilliantly on the oaks and on the grassy flat. The rocks and the hillsides still sent up waves of the heat they had gathered from the day's sun.

Pepé looked up to the top of the next dry withered ridge. He saw a dark form against the sky, a man's figure standing on top of a rock, and he glanced away quickly not to appear curious. When a moment later he looked up again, the figure was gone.

Downward the trail was quickly covered. Sometimes the horse floundered for footing, sometimes set his feet and slid a little way. They came at last to the bottom where the dark chaparral was higher than Pepé's head. He held up his rifle on one side and his arm on the other to shield his face from the sharp brittle fingers of the brush.

Up and out of the crease he rode, and up a little cliff. The grassy flat was before him, and the round comfortable oaks. For a moment he studied the trail down which he had come, but there was no movement and no sound from it. Finally he rode out over the flat, to the green streak, and at the upper end of the damp he found a little spring welling out of the earth and dropping into a dug basin before it seeped out over the flat.

Pepé filled his bag first, and then he let the thirsty horse drink out of the pool. He led the horse to the clump of oaks, and in the middle of the grove, fairly protected from sight on all sides, he took off the saddle and the bridle and laid them on the ground. The horse stretched his jaws sideways and yawned. Pepé knotted the lead rope about the horse's neck and tied him to a sapling among the oaks, where he could graze in a fairly large circle.

When the horse was gnawing hungrily at the dry grass. Pepé went to the saddle and took a black string of jerky from the sack and strolled to an oak tree on the edge of the grove, from under which he could watch the trail. He sat down in the crisp dry oak leaves and automatically felt for his big black knife to cut the jerky, but he had no knife. He leaned back on his elbow and gnawed at the tough strong meat. His face was blank, but it was a man's face.

The bright evening light washed the eastern ridge, but the valley was darkening. Doves flew down from the hills to the spring, and the quail came running out of the brush and joined them, calling clearly to one another.

Out of the corner of his eye Pepé saw a shadow grow out of the bushy crease. He turned his head slowly. A big spotted wildcat was creeping toward the spring, belly to the ground, moving like thought.

Pepé cocked his rifle and edged the muzzle slowly around. Then he looked apprehensively up the trail and dropped the hammer again. From the ground beside him he picked an oak twig and threw it toward the spring. The quail flew up with a roar and the doves whistled away. The big cat stood up: for a long moment he looked at Pepé with cold yellow eyes, and then fearlessly walked back into the gulch.

The dusk gathered quickly in the deep valley. Pepé muttered his prayers, put his head down on his arm and went instantly to sleep.

The moon came up and filled the valley with cold blue light, and the wind swept rustling down from the peaks. The owls worked up and down the slopes looking for rabbits. Down in the brush of the gulch a coyote gabbled. The oak trees whispered softly in the night breeze.

Pepé started up, listening. His horse had whinnied. The moon was just slipping behind the western ridge, leaving the valley in darkness behind it. Pepé sat tensely gripping his rifle. From far up the trail he heard an answering whinny and the crash of shod hooves on the broken rock. He jumped to his feet, ran to his horse and led it under the trees. He threw on the saddle and cinched it tight for the steep trail, caught the unwilling head and forced the bit into the mouth. He felt the saddle to make sure the water bag and the sack of jerky was there. Then he mounted and turned up the hill.

It was velvet dark. The horse found the entrance to the trail where it left the flat, and started up, stumbling and slipping on the rocks. Pepé's hand rose up to his head. His hat was gone. He had left it under the oak tree.

The horse had struggled far up the trail when the first change of dawn came into the air, a steel grayness as light mixed thoroughly with dark. Gradually the sharp snaggled edge of the ridge stood out above them, rotten granite tortured and eaten by the winds of time. Pepé had dropped his reins on the horn, leaving direction to the horse. The brush grabbed at his legs in the dark until one knee of his jeans was ripped.

Gradually the light flowed down over the ridge. The starved brush and rocks stood out in the half light, strange and lonely in high perspective. Then there came warmth into the light. Pepé drew up and looked back, but he could see nothing in the darker valley below. The sky turned blue over the coming sun. In the waste of the mountainside, the poor dry brush grew only three feet high. Here and there, big outcroppings of unrotted granite stood up like moldering houses. Pepé relaxed a little. He drank from his water bag and bit off a piece of jerky. A single eagle flew over, high in the light.

Without warning Pepé's horse screamed and fell on its side. He was almost down before the rifle crash echoed up from the valley. From a hole behind the struggling shoulder, a stream of bright crimson blood pumped and stopped and pumped and stopped. The hooves threshed on the ground. Pepé lay half stunned beside the horse. He looked slowly down the hill. A piece of sage clipped off beside his head and another crash echoed up from side to side of the canyon. Pepé flung himself frantically behind a bush.

He crawled up the hill on his knees and on one hand. His right hand held the rifle up off the ground and pushed it ahead of him. He moved with the instinctive care of an animal. Rapidly he wormed his way toward one of the big outcroppings of granite on the hill above him. Where the brush was high he doubled up and ran, but where the cover was slight he wriggled forward on his stomach, pushing the rifle ahead of him. In the last little distance there was no cover at all. Pepé poised and then he darted across the space and flashed around the corner of the rock.

He leaned panting against the stone. When his breath came easier he moved along behind the big rock until he came to a narrow slit that offered a thin section of vision down the hill. Pepé lay on his stomach and pushed the rifle barrel through the slit and waited.

The sun reddened the western ridges now. Already the buzzards were settling down toward the place where the horse lay. A small brown bird scratched in the dead sage leaves directly in front of the rifle muzzle. The coasting eagle flew back toward the rising sun.

Pepé saw a little movement in the brush far below. His grip tightened on the gun. A little brown doe stepped daintily out on the trail and crossed it and disappeared into the brush again. For a long time Pepé waited. Far below he could see the little flat and the oak trees and the slash of green. Suddenly his eyes flashed back at the trail again. A quarter of a mile down there had been a quick movement in the chaparral. The rifle swung over. The front sight nestled in the V of the rear sight. Pepé studied for a moment and then raised the rear sight a notch. The little movement in the brush came again. The sight settled on it. Pepé squeezed the trigger. The explosion crashed down the mountain and up the other side, and came rattling back. The whole side of the slope grew still. No more movement. And then a white streak cut into the granite of the slit and a bullet whined away and a crash sounded up from below. Pepé felt a sharp pain in his right hand. A sliver of granite was sticking out from between his first and second knuckles and the point protruded from his palm. Carefully he pulled out the sliver of stone. The wound bled evenly and gently. No vein nor artery was cut.

Pepé looked into a little dusty cave in the rock and gathered a handful of spider web, and he pressed the mass into the cut, plastering the soft web into the blood. The flow stopped almost at once.

The rifle was on the ground. Pepé picked it up, levered a new shell into the chamber. And then he slid into the brush on his stomach. Far to the right he crawled, and then up the hill, moving slowly and carefully, crawling to cover and resting and then crawling again.

In the mountains the sun is high in its arc before it penetrates the gorges. The hot face looked over the hill and brought instant heat with it. The white light beat on the rocks and reflected from them and rose up quivering from the earth again, and the rocks and bushes seemed to quiver behind the air.

Pepé crawled in the general direction of the ridge peak, zig-zagging for cover. The deep cut between his knuckles began to throb. He crawled close to a rattlesnake before he saw it, and when it raised its dry head and made a soft beginning whirr, he backed up and took another way. The quick gray lizards flashed in front of him, raising a tiny line of dust. He found another mass of spider web and pressed it against his throbbing hand.

Pepé was pushing the rifle with his left hand now. Little drops of sweat ran to the ends of his coarse black hair and rolled down his cheeks. His lips and tongue were growing thick and heavy. His lips writhed to draw saliva into his mouth. His little dark eyes were uneasy and suspicious. Once when a gray lizard paused in front of him on the parched ground and turned its head sideways he crushed it flat with a stone.

When the sun slid past noon he had not gone a mile. He crawled exhaustedly a last hundred yards to a patch of high sharp manzanita, crawled desperately, and when the patch was reached he wriggled in among the tough gnarly trunks and dropped his head on his left arm. There was little shade in the meager brush, but there was cover and safety. Pepé went to sleep as he lay and the sun beat on his back. A few little birds hopped close to him and peered and hopped away. Pepé squirmed in his sleep and he raised and dropped his wounded hand again and again.

The sun went down behind the peaks and the cool evening came, and then the dark. A coyote yelled from the hillside, Pepé started awake and looked about with misty eyes. His hand was swollen and heavy; a little thread of pain ran up the inside of his arm and settled in a pocket in his armpit. He peered about and then stood up, for the mountains were black and the moon had not yet risen. Pepé stood up in the dark. The coat of his father pressed on his arm. His tongue was swollen until it nearly filled his mouth. He wriggled out of the coat and dropped it in the brush, and then he struggled up the hill, falling over rocks and tearing his way through the brush. The rifle knocked against stones as he went. Little dry avalanches of gravel and shattered stone went whispering down the hill behind him.

After a while the old moon came up and showed the jagged ridge top ahead of him. By moonlight Pepé traveled more easily. He bent forward so that his throbbing arm hung away from his body. The journey uphill was made in dashes and rests, a frantic rush up a few yards and then a rest. The wind coasted down the slope rattling the dry stems of the bushes.

The moon was at meridian when Pepé came at last to the sharp back-bone of the ridge top. On the last hundred yards of the rise no soil had clung under the wearing winds. The way was on solid rock. He clambered to the top and looked down on the other side. There was a draw like the last below him, misty with moonlight, brushed with dry struggling sage and chaparral. On the other side the hill rose up sharply and at the top the jagged rotten teeth of the mountain showed against the sky. At the bottom of the cut the brush was thick and dark.

Pepé stumbled down the hill. His throat was almost closed with thirst. At first he tried to run, but immediately he fell and rolled. After that he went more carefully. The moon was just disappearing behind the mountains when he came to the bottom. He crawled into the heavy brush feeling with his fingers for water. There was no water in the bed of the stream, only damp earth. Pepé laid his gun down and scooped up a handful of mud and put it in his mouth, and then he spluttered and scraped the earth from his tongue with his finger, for the mud drew at his mouth like a poultice. He dug a hole in the stream bed with his fingers, dug a little basin to catch water; but before it was very deep his head fell forward on the damp ground and he slept.

The dawn came and the heat of the day fell on the earth, and still Pepé slept. Late in the afternoon his head jerked up. He looked slowly around. His eyes were slits of wariness. Twenty feet away in the heavy brush a big tawny mountain lion stood looking at him. Its long thick tail waved gracefully, its ears erect with interest, not laid back dangerously. The lion squatted down on its stomach and watched him.

Pepé looked at the hole he had dug in the earth. A half inch of muddy water had collected in the bottom. He tore the sleeve from his hurt arm, with his teeth ripped out a little square, soaked it in the water and put it in his mouth. Over and over he filled the cloth and sucked it.

Still the lion sat and watched him. The evening came down but there was no movement on the hills. No birds visited the dry bottom of the cut. Pepé looked occasionally at the lion. The eyes of the yellow beast drooped as though he were about to sleep. He yawned and his long thin red tongue curled out. Suddenly his head jerked around and his nostrils quivered. His big tail lashed. He stood up and slunk like a tawny shadow into the thick brush.

A moment later Pepé heard the sound, the faint far crash of horses' hooves on gravel. And he heard something else, a high whining yelp of a dog.

Pepé took his rifle in his left hand and he glided into the brush almost as quietly as the lion had. In the darkening evening he crouched up the hill toward the next ridge. Only when the dark came did he stand up. His energy was short. Once it was dark he fell over the rocks and slipped to his knees on the steep slope, but he moved on and on up the hill, climbing and scrabbling over the broken hillside.

When he was far up toward the top, he lay down and slept for a little while. The withered moon, shining on his face, awakened him. He stood up and moved up the hill. Fifty yards away he stopped and turned back, for he had forgotten his rifle. He walked heavily down and poked about in the brush, but he could not find his gun. At last he lay down to rest. The pocket of pain in his armpit had grown more sharp. His arm seemed to swell out and fall with every heartbeat. There was no position lying down where the heavy arm did not press against his armpit.

With the effort of a hurt beast, Pepé got up and moved again toward the top of the ridge. He held his swollen arm away from his body with his left hand. Up the steep hill he dragged himself, a few steps and a rest, and a few more steps. At last he was nearing the top. The moon showed the uneven sharp back of it against the sky.

Pepé's brain spun in a big spiral up and away from him. He slumped to the ground and lay still. The rock ridge top was only a hundred feet above him.

The moon moved over the sky. Pepé half turned on his back. His tongue tried to make words, but only a thick hissing came from between his lips.

When the dawn came, Pepé pulled himself up. His eyes were sane again. He drew his great puffed arm in front of him and looked at the angry wound. The black line ran up from his wrist to his armpit. Automatically he reached in his pocket for the big black knife, but it was not there. His eyes searched the ground. He picked up a sharp blade of stone and scraped at the wound, sawed at the proud flesh and then squeezed the green juice out in big drops. Instantly he threw back his head and whined like a dog. His whole right side shuddered at the pain, but the pain cleared his head.

In the gray light he struggled up the last slope to the ridge and crawled over and lay down behind a line of rocks. Below him lay a deep canyon exactly like the last, waterless and desolate. There was no flat, no oak trees, not even heavy brush in the bottom of it. And on the other side a sharp ridge stood up, thinly brushed with starving sage, littered with broken granite. Strewn over the hill there were giant outcroppings, and on the top the granite teeth stood out against the sky.

The new day was light now. The flame of sun came over the ridge and fell on Pepé where he lay on the ground. His coarse black hair was littered with twigs and bits of spider web. His eyes had retreated back into his head. Between his lips the tip of his black tongue showed.

He sat up and dragged his great arm into his lap and nursed it, rocking his body and moaning in his throat. He threw back his head and looked up into the pale sky. A big black bird circled nearly out of sight, and far to the left another was sailing near.

He lifted his head to listen, for a similar sound had come to him from the valley he had climbed out of; it was the crying yelp of hounds, excited and feverish, on a trail.

Pepé bowed his head quickly. He tried to speak rapid words but only a thick hiss came from his lips. He drew a shaky cross on his breast with his left hand. It was a long struggle to get to his feet. He crawled slowly and mechanically to the top of a big rock on the ridge peak. Once there, he arose slowly, swaying to his feet, and stood erect. Far below he could see the dark brush where he had slept. He braced his feet and stood there, black against the morning sky.

There came a ripping sound at his feet. A piece of stone flew up and a bullet droned off into the next gorge. The hollow crash echoed up from below. Pepé looked down for a moment and then pulled himself straight again.

His body jarred back. His left hand fluttered helplessly toward his breast. The second crash sounded from below. Pepé swung forward and toppled from the rock. His body struck and rolled over and over, starting a little avalanche. And when at last he stopped against a bush, the avalanche slid slowly down and covered up his head.

Roald Dahl *born 1916 in Llandaff, South Wales. Before the war, in 1939, he worked with the Shell Oil Company in London, and later in Dar-es-Salaam. At the outbreak of war he enlisted in the R.A.F. serving in the Libyan Desert, where he was wounded, and in Greece and Syria. In 1942, in Washington, where he had been sent as Assistant Air Attache, he began to write short stories. His collections include* OVER TO YOU, SOMEONE LIKE YOU, *and* KISS KISS.

THE CHAMPION OF THE WORLD

Roald Dahl

ALL DAY, IN BETWEEN SERVING CUSTOMERS, WE HAD BEEN CROUCHING over the table in the office of my filling station, preparing the raisins. They were plump and soft from being soaked in water, and when you nicked them with a razor blade the skin sprang open and the jelly stuff inside squeezed out as easily as you could wish. But we had a hundred and ninety-six of them to do altogether, and the evening was nearly upon us before we had finished.

'Don't they look marvellous!' Claud cried, rubbing his hands together hard. 'What time is it, Gordon?'

'Just after five.'

Through the window, we could see a station wagon pulling up at the petrol pumps, with a woman at the wheel and about eight children in the back eating ice creams.

'We ought to be moving soon,' Claud said. 'The whole thing'll be a washout if we don't arrive before sunset, you realize that.' He was getting twitchy now. His face had the same flushed and popeyed look it got before a dog race.

We both went outside, and Claud gave the woman the number of gallons she wanted. When she had gone, he remained standing in the middle of the driveway, squinting anxiously up at the sun, which was now only the width of a man's hand above the line of trees along the crest of the ridge on the far side of the valley.

'All right,' I said. 'Lock up.'

He went quickly from pump to pump, securing each nozzle in its holder with a small padlock.

'You'd better take off that yellow pullover,' he said.

'Why should I?'

'You'll be shining like a beacon out there in the moonlight.'

'I'll be all right.'

'You will not,' he said. 'Take it off, Gordon, please. I'll see you in three minutes.' He disappeared into his caravan behind the filling station, and I went indoors and changed my yellow pullover for a blue one.

When we met again outside, Claud was dressed in a pair of black trousers and a dark-green turtleneck sweater. On his head he wore a brown cloth cap with the peak pulled down low over his eyes, and he looked like an apache actor out of a night club.

'What's under there?' I asked, seeing the bulge at his waistline.

He pulled up his sweater and showed me two thin but very large white cotton sacks bound neat and tight around his belly. 'To carry the stuff,' he said.

'I see.'

'Let's go,' he said.

'I still think we ought to take the car.'

'It's too risky. They'll see it parked.'

'But it's over three miles up to that wood.'

'Yes,' he said. 'And I suppose you realize we can get six months in the clink if they catch us.'

'You never told me that.'

'Didn't I?'

'I'm not coming,' I said. 'It's not worth it.'

'The walk will do you good, Gordon. Come on.'

It was a calm, sunny evening, with little wisps of brilliant white cloud hanging motionless in the sky, and the valley was cool and very quiet as the two of us began walking along the grass on the side of the road that ran between the hills toward Oxford.

'You got the raisins?' Claud asked.

'They're in my pocket.'

'Good,' he said. 'Marvellous.'

Ten minutes later, we turned left off the main road into a narrow lane with high hedges on either side, and from then on it was all uphill.

'How many keepers are there?' I asked.

'Three.'

Claud threw away a half-finished cigarette. A minute later, he lit another. 'It'll be a milestone in the history of poaching,' he said. 'But don't you go telling a single soul how we've done it, you understand? Because if this ever leaked out, we'd have every fool in the district doing the same thing, and there wouldn't be a pheasant left.'

'I won't say a word.'

'You ought to be very proud of yourself,' he went on. 'There's been men with brains studying this problem for hundreds of years, and not one of them's ever come up with anything even a quarter as artful as you have. Why didn't you tell me about it before?'

'You never invited my opinion,' I said.

And that was the truth. In fact, up until the day before, Claud had never even offered to discuss with me the sacred subject of poaching. Often enough, on a summer's evening when work was finished, I had seen him, with cap on head, sliding quietly out of his caravan and disappearing up the road towards the woods; and sometimes, watching him through the window of the filling station, I would find myself wondering exactly what he was going to do, what tricks he was going to practice all alone up there under the trees in the night. He seldom came back until very late, and never, absolutely never, did he bring any of the spoils with him on his return. But the following afternoon—I couldn't imagine how he did it—there would always be a pheasant or a hare or a brace of partridges hanging up in the shed behind the filling station.

This summer, he had been particularly active, and during the past couple of months he had stepped up the tempo to a point where he was going out four and sometimes five nights a week. But that was not all. It seemed to me that recently his whole attitude towards poaching had undergone a subtle and mysterious change. He was more purposeful about it now, more tight-lipped and intense than before, and I had formed the impression that this was not so much a game any longer as a sort of private war that he was waging against the famous Mr Victor Hazel himself. Mr Hazel was a pie and sausage manufacturer, with an unbelievably arrogant manner. He was rich beyond words, and his property stretched for miles along either side of the valley. He was a self-made man, with no charm at all and precious few virtues. He loathed all persons of humble station, having once been one of them himself, and he strove desperately to mingle with what he believed were the right kind of folk. He hunted with the hounds and gave shooting parties and wore fancy waistcoats, and every weekday he drove an enormous black Rolls-Royce past the filling station on his way to and from the factory. As he flashed by, we would sometimes catch a glimpse of his great, glistening butcher's face above the wheel, pink as a ham, all soft and inflamed from eating too much meat.

Anyway, the day before, which was Wednesday, Claud had suddenly said to me, right out of the blue, 'I'll be going on up to Hazel's woods again tonight. Why don't you come along?'

'Who, me?'

'It's about the last chance this year for pheasants,' he had said. 'The shooting season opens Saturday, and the birds'll be scattered all over the place after that—if there's any left.'

'Why the sudden invitation?' I had asked.

'No special reason, Gordon. No reason at all.'

'I suppose you keep a gun or something hidden away up there?'

'A gun!' he cried disgusted. 'Nobody ever *shoots* pheasants, didn't you know that? You've only got to fire a *cap pistol* in Hazel's woods and the keepers'll be on you.'

'Then how do you do it?'

'Ah,' he said. There was a long pause. Then he said, 'Do you think you could keep your mouth shut if I was to tell you a thing or two?'

'Definitely.'

'I've never told this to anyone else in my whole life, Gordon.'

'I am greatly honoured,' I said. 'You can trust me completely.'

He turned his head, fixing me with pale eyes, 'I am now about to let you in on the three best ways in the world of poaching a pheasant,' he said. 'And, seeing that you're the guest on this little trip, I am going to give you the choice of which one you'd like us to use tonight. How's that?'

'There's a catch in this.'

'There's no catch, Gordon. I swear it.'

'All right, go on.'

'Now, here's the thing,' he said. 'Here's the first big secret.' He paused and took a long suck at his cigarette. 'Pheasants,' he whispered softly, 'is *crazy* about raisins.'

'Raisins?'

'Just ordinary raisins. It's like a *mania* with them. My dad discovered that more than forty years ago, just like he discovered all three of these methods.'

'I thought you said your dad was a drunk.'

'Maybe he was. But he was also a great poacher, Gordon. Possibly the greatest there's ever been in the history of England. My dad studied poaching like a scientist.'

'Is that so?'

'I mean it. I really mean it.'

'I believe you.'

'Do you know,' he said, 'my dad used to keep a whole flock of prime cockerels in the back yard, purely for experimental purposes.'

'Cockerels?'

'That's right. And whenever he thought up some new stunt for catching a pheasant, he'd try it out on a cockerel first, to see how it worked. That's how he discovered about raisins. It's also how he invented the horsehair method.'

Claud paused and glanced over his shoulder, as though to make sure there was nobody listening. 'Here's how it's done,' he said. 'First you take a few raisins and you soak them overnight in water to make them nice and plump and juicy. Then you get a bit of good stiff horsehair and you cut it up into half-inch lengths. Then you push one of these lengths of horsehair through the middle of each raisin, so that there's about an eighth of an inch of it sticking out on either side. You follow?'

'Yes.'

'Now. The old pheasant comes along and eats one of these raisins. Right? And you're watching him from behind a tree. So, what then?'

'I imagine it sticks in his throat.'

'That's obvious, Gordon. But here's the amazing thing. Here's what my dad discovered. The moment this happens, the bird *never moves his feet again!* He becomes absolutely rooted to the spot, and there he stands

108

pumping his silly neck up and down, and all you've got to do is walk
calmly out from the place where you're hiding and pick him up in your
hands.'

'I don't believe that.'

'I swear it,' he said. 'Once a pheasant's had the horsehair, you can fire a
rifle in his ear and he won't even jump. It's just one of these unexplainable
little things. But it takes a genius to discover it.'

He paused, and there was a gleam of pride in his eyes as he dwelt for a
moment upon the memory of his father, the great inventor.

'So that's Method Number One,' he said. 'Method Number Two is
even more simple still. All you do is you have a fishing line. Then you
bait the hook with a raisin, and you fish for the pheasant just like you fish
for a fish. You pay out the line about fifty yards, and you lie there on your
stomach in the bushes, waiting till you get a bite. Then you haul him in.'

'I don't think your father was the first to invent that one.'

'It's very popular with fishermen,' he said, choosing not to hear me.
'Keen fishermen who can't get down to the seaside as often as they want.
It gives them a bit of the old thrill.'

'What is Method Number Three?' I asked.

'Ah,' he said. 'Number Three's a real beauty. It was the last one my
dad ever invented before he passed away.'

'His final great work?'

'Exactly, Gordon. And I can remember the very day it happened—
a Sunday morning it was—and suddenly my dad comes into the kitchen
holding a huge white cockerel in his hands, and he says, "I think I've
got it." There's a little smile on his face and a shine of glory in his eyes,
and he comes in very soft and quiet, and he puts the bird down right in
the middle of the kitchen table, and he says, "By God, I think I've got a
good one this time." "A good what?" Mum says, looking up from
the sink. "Horace, take that filthy bird off my table." The cockerel has a
funny little paper hat over its head, like an ice-cream cone upside down,
and my dad is pointing to it proudly. "Stroke him," he says. "He won't
move an inch." The cockerel starts scratching away at the paper hat
with one of its feet, but the hat seems to be stuck on with glue, and it
won't come off. "No bird in the world is going to run away once you
cover up his eyes," my dad says, and he starts poking the cockerel with
his finger and pushing it around on the table, but it doesn't take the
slightest bit of notice. And then straightaway he takes me by the arm
and marches me quickly out the door, and off we go over the fields and
up into the big forest the other side of Haddenham, which used to belong
to the Duke of Buckingham, and in less than two hours we get five
lovely fat pheasants with no more trouble than it takes to go out and
buy them in a shop.'

Claud paused for breath. His eyes were huge and moist and dreamy as they gazed back into the wonderful world of his youth.

'I don't quite follow this,' I said. 'How did he get the paper hats over the pheasants' heads up in the woods?'

'You'd never guess it.'

'I'm sure I wouldn't.'

'Then here it is. First of all you dig a little hole in the ground. Then you twist a piece of paper into the shape of a cone and you fit this into the hole, hollow end upward, like a cup. Then you smear the paper cup all around the inside with birdlime, and drop in a few raisins. At the same time, you lay a trail of raisins along the ground leading up to it. Now, the old pheasant comes pecking along the trail, and when he gets to the hole, he pops his head inside to gobble the raisins, and the next thing he knows he's got a paper hat stuck over his eyes and he can't see a thing. Isn't it marvellous what some people think of, Gordon? Don't you agree?'

'Your dad was a genius,' I said.

'Then take your pick. Choose whichever one of the three methods you fancy, and we'll use it tonight.'

'You don't think they're all just a trifle on the crude side, do you?'

'Crude!' he cried, aghast. 'Oh, my God! And who's been having roasted pheasant in the house nearly every single day for the last six months and not a penny to pay?'

He walked away toward the door of the workshop. I could see that he was deeply pained by my remark.

'Wait a minute,' I said. 'Don't go.'

'You want to come or don't you?'

'Yes, but let me ask you something first. I've just had a bit of an idea.'

'Keep it,' he said. 'You are talking about a subject you don't know the first thing about.'

'Do you remember that bottle of sleeping pills the doc gave me last month when I had a bad back?'

'What about them?'

'Is there any reason why those wouldn't work on a pheasant?'

Claud closed his eyes and shook his head pityingly.

'Wait,' I said.

'It's not worth discussing,' he said. 'No pheasant in the world is going to swallow those lousy red capsules. Don't you know any better than that?'

'You are forgetting the raisins,' I said. 'Now listen to this. We take a raisin. Then we soak it till it swells. Then we make a tiny slit in one side of it with a razor blade. Then we hollow it out a little. Then we open up one of my red capsules and pour all the powder into the raisin. Then we get a needle and cotton, and very carefully we sew up the slit. Now...'

Out of the corner of my eye, I saw Claud's mouth slowly beginning to open.

'Now,' I said. 'We have a nice, clean-looking raisin with two and a half grains of seconal inside it, and let me tell *you* something now. That's enough dope to knock the average *man* unconscious, never mind about *birds!*'

I paused for ten seconds to allow the full impact of this to strike home.

'What's more, with this method we could operate on a really grand scale. We could prepare *twenty* raisins if we felt like it, and all we'd have to do is scatter them around the feeding grounds at sunset and then walk away. Half an hour later, we'd come back, and the pills would be beginning to work, and the pheasants would be up in the branches by then, roosting, and they'd be starting to feel groggy, and soon every pheasant that had eaten *one single raisin* would keel over unconscious and fall to the ground. My dear boy, they'd be dropping out of the trees like apples, and all we'd have to do is walk around picking them up!'

Claud was staring at me, rapt.

'And they'd never catch us, either. We'd simply stroll through the woods, dropping a few raisins here and there as we went, and even if the keepers were *watching* us, they wouldn't notice anything.'

'Gordon,' he said, laying a hand on my knee, 'if this thing works, it will revolutionize poaching.'

'I'm glad to hear it.'

'How many pills have you got left?' he asked.

'Forty-nine. There were fifty in the bottle, and I've only used one.'

'Forty-nine's not enough. We want at least two hundred.'

'Are you mad!' I cried.

He walked slowly away and stood by the door with his back to me, gazing at the sky. 'Two hundred's the bare minimum,' he said quietly. 'There's really not much point in doing it unless we have two hundred.'

What is it now, I wondered. What the hell's he trying to do?

'This is almost the last chance we'll have before the season opens,' he said.

'I couldn't possibly get any more.'

'You wouldn't want us to come back empty-handed, would you?'

'But why so *many*?'

Claud looked at me with large, innocent eyes. 'Why not?' he said gently. 'Do you have any objection?'

My God, I thought suddenly. The lunatic is out to wreck Mr Victor Hazel's opening-day shooting party.

Mr Hazel's party took place on the first of October every year, and it was a very famous event. Debilitated gentlemen in tweed suits, some with titles and some who were merely rich, motored in from miles around, with their gunbearers and dogs and wives, and all day long the noise of shooting rolled across the valley. There were always enough pheasants to go around, for each summer the woods were methodically restocked with dozens and dozens of young birds, at incredible expense. I had heard it said that the cost of rearing and keeping each pheasant up to the time when it was ready to be shot was well over five pounds. But to Mr Hazel it was worth every penny of it. He became, if only for a few hours, a big cheese in a little world, and even the Lord Lieutenant of the county slapped him on the back and tried to remember his first name when he said goodbye.

'You get us two hundred of those pills,' Claud said, 'and then it'll be worth doing.'

'I can't.'

'How would it be if we just reduced the dose?' he asked.

'Why couldn't we divide the contents of one capsule among four raisins?'

'I suppose you could, if you wanted to.'

'But would a quarter of a capsule be strong enough for each bird?'

One simply had to admire the man's nerve. It was dangerous enough to poach a single pheasant up in those woods at this time of year, and here he was planning to knock off the lot.

'A quarter would be plenty,' I said.

'You're sure of that?'

'Work it out for yourself. It's all done by body weight. You'd still be giving about twenty times more than is necessary.'

'Then we'll quarter the dose,' he said, rubbing his hands. He paused, and calculated for a moment. 'We'll have one hundred and ninety-six raisins!'

'Do you realize what that involves?' I said. 'They'll take hours to prepare.'

'What of it!' he cried. 'We'll go tomorrow instead. We'll soak the raisins overnight and then we'll have all morning and afternoon to get them ready.'

And that was precisely what we did.

We had been walking steadily for about forty minutes, and we were nearing the point where the lane curved around to the right and ran along the crest of the hill toward the big wood where the pheasants lived. There was about a mile to go.

'I don't suppose by any chance these keepers might be carrying guns?' I asked.

'All keepers carry guns,' Claud said.

I had been afraid of that.

'It's for the vermin mostly,' he added.

'Ah.'

'Of course, there's no guarantee they won't take a pot at a poacher now and again.'

'You're joking.'

'Not at all. But they only do it from behind—only when you're running away. They like to pepper you in the legs at about fifty yards.'

'They can't do that!' I cried. 'It's a criminal offence!'

'So is poaching,' Claud said.

We walked on awhile in silence. The sun was below the high hedge on our right now, and the lane was in shadow.

'You can consider yourself lucky this isn't thirty years ago,' he went on. 'They used to shoot you on sight in those days.'

'Do you believe that?'

'I know it,' he said. 'There wasn't a man in the whole village who didn't have a bit of shot in him. But my dad was the champion.'

'Good luck to him,' I said.

'I wish to hell he was here now,' Claud said, wistful. 'He'd have given anything in the world to be coming with us on this job tonight.'

'He could take my place,' I said. 'Gladly.'

We had reached the crest of the hill and now we could see the wood ahead of us, huge and dark, with the sun going down behind the trees and little sparks of gold shining through.

'You'd better let me have those raisins,' Claud said.

I gave him the bag, and he slid it gently into a trouser pocket.

'No talking once we're inside,' he said. 'Just follow me, and try not to go snapping any branches.'

Five minutes later, we were there. The lane ran right up to the wood itself and then skirted the edge of it for about three hundred yards, with only a little hedge between. Claud slipped through the hedge on all fours, and I followed.

It was cool and dark inside the wood. No sunlight came in at all.

'This is spooky,' I said.

'Sh-h-h!'

Claud was very tense. He was walking just ahead of me, picking his feet up high and putting them down gently on the moist ground. He kept his head moving all the time, the eyes sweeping slowly from side to side, searching for danger. I tried doing the same, but soon I began to see a keeper behind every tree, so I gave it up.

Then a large patch of sky appeared ahead of us in the roof of the forest, and I knew that this must be the clearing. Claud had told me that the clearing was the place where the young birds were introduced into the woods in early July, where they were fed and watered and guarded by the keepers, and where many of them stayed, from force of habit, until the shooting began. 'There's always plenty of pheasants in the clearing,' he had said.

We were now advancing in a series of quick, crouching spurts, running from tree to tree and stopping and waiting and listening and running on again, and then at last we knelt safely behind a big clump of alder, right on the edge of the clearing, and Claud grinned and nudged me in the ribs and pointed through the branches at the pheasants.

The place was absolutely stiff with birds. There must have been two hundred of them, at least, strutting around among the tree stumps.

'You see what I mean?' Claud whispered.

It was an astonishing sight—a poacher's dream come true. And how close they were! Some of them were not more than ten paces from where we were kneeling. The hens were plump and creamy brown, and so fat that their breast feathers almost brushed the ground as they walked. The cocks were slim and beautiful, with long tails and brilliant red patches around the eyes, like scarlet spectacles. I glanced at Claud. His big oxlike face was transfigured with ecstacy. The mouth was slightly open, and the eyes had a kind of glazy look about them as they stared at the pheasants.

There was a long pause. The birds made a queer rustling noise as they moved about among the dead leaves in the clearing. 'Ah-ha,' Claud said softly a minute later. 'You see the keeper?'

'Where?'

'Over the other side, standing by that big tree. Look carefully.'

'My God!'

'It's all right. He can't see *us*.'

We crouched close to the ground, watching the keeper. He was a smallish man with a cap on his head and gun under one arm. He never moved. He was like a little post standing there.

'Let's go,' I whispered.

The keeper's face was shadowed by the peak of his cap, but it seemed to me that he was looking directly at us.

'I'm not staying here,' I said.

'Hush!' Claud said.

Slowly, never taking his eyes from the keeper, he reached into his pocket and brought out a single raisin. He placed it in the palm of his right hand, and then quickly, with a little flick of the wrist, he threw the raisin high into the air. I watched it as it went sailing over the bushes, and I saw it land within a yard or so of two hen birds standing together beside an old tree stump. Both birds turned their heads sharply at the drop of the raisin. Then one of them hopped over and made a quick peck at the ground.

I glanced up at the keeper. He hadn't moved.

Claud threw a second raisin into the clearing; then a third, and a fourth, and a fifth. At this point, I saw the keeper turn his head away to survey the woods behind him. Quick as a flash, Claud pulled the paper bag out of his pocket and tipped a huge pile of raisins into the cup of his right hand.

'Stop,' I said.

But with a great sweep of the arm he flung the whole handful high over the bushes into the clearing. They fell with a soft little patter, like rain-drops on dry leaves, and every single pheasant in the place must have heard them fall. There was a flurry of wings and a rush to find the treasure.

The keeper's head flicked round as though there were a spring inside his neck. The birds were all pecking away madly at the raisins. The keeper took two quick paces forward, and for a moment I thought he was going to investigate. But then he stopped, and his face came up, and his eyes began travelling slowly around the perimeter of the clearing.

'Follow me,' Claud whispered. 'And *keep down*.' He started crawling away swiftly on all fours, under cover of the bushes.

I went after him, and we went along like this for about a hundred yards.

'Now run,' Claud said.

We got to our feet and ran, and a few minutes later we emerged through the hedge into the lovely open safety of the lane.

'It went marvellous,' Claud said, breathing heavily. 'Didn't it go absolutely marvellous?' The big face was scarlet and glowing with triumph. 'In another five minutes, it'll be pitch-dark inside the wood, and that keeper will be sloping off home to his supper.'

'I think I'll join him,' I said.

'You're a great poacher,' Claud said. He sat down on the grassy bank under the hedge and lit a cigarette.

The sun had set now and the sky was a pale smoke-blue, faintly glazed with yellow. In the wood behind us, the shadows and the spaces in between the trees were turning from grey to black.

'How long does a sleeping pill take to work?' Claud asked.

'Look out!' I said. 'There's someone coming.'

The man had appeared suddenly and silently out of the dusk, and he was only thirty yards away when I saw him.

'Another keeper,' Claud said.

We both looked at the keeper as he came down the lane toward us. He had a shotgun under his arm, and there was a black Labrador walking at his heels. He stopped when he was a few paces away, and the dog stopped with him and stayed behind him, watching us through the keeper's legs.

'Good evening,' Claud said, nice and friendly.

This one was a tall bony man of about forty, with a swift eye and a hard cheek and hard dangerous hands.

'I know you,' he said softly, coming closer. 'I know the both of you.'

Claud didn't answer this.

'You're from the fillin' station. Right?' His lips were thin and dry. 'You're Cubbage and Hawes and you're from the fillin' station on the main road. Right?'

'What are we playing?' Claud said. 'Twenty Questions?'

The keeper took a step forward. 'Beat it,' he said. 'Go on. Get out.'

Claud sat on the bank, smoking his cigarette and looking at the keeper's feet.

'Go on,' the man said. 'Get out.' When he spoke, the upper lip lifted above the gum, and I could see a row of small discoloured teeth, one of them black, the others quince and ochre.

'This happens to be a public highway,' Claud said. 'Kindly do not molest us.'

The keeper shifted the gun from his left arm to his right. 'You're loiterin',' he said, 'with intent to commit a felony. I could run you in for that.'

'No, you couldn't,' Claud said.

All this made me rather nervous.

'I've had my eye on you for some time,' the keeper said, looking at Claud.

'It's getting late,' I said. 'Shall we stroll on?'

Claud flipped away his cigarette and got slowly to his feet, 'All right,' he said. 'Let's go.'

We wandered off down the lane the way we had come, leaving him standing there, and soon the man was out of sight in the half darkness behind us.

'That's the head keeper,' Claud said. 'His name is Rabbetts.'

'Let's get the hell out,' I said.

'Come in here,' Claud said.

There was a gate on our left leading into a field, and we climbed over it and sat down behind the hedge.

'Mr Rabbetts is also due for his supper,' Claud said. 'You mustn't worry about him.'

We sat quietly behind the hedge, waiting for the keeper to walk past us on his way home. A few stars were showing, and a bright three-quarter moon was coming up over the hills behind us in the east.

'Here he is,' Claud whispered. 'Don't move.'

The keeper came loping softly up the lane with the dog padding quick and soft-footed at his heels, and we watched them through the hedge as they went by.

'He won't be coming back tonight,' Claud said.

'How do you know that?'

'A keeper never waits for you in the wood if he knows where you live. He goes to your house and hides outside and watches for you to come back.'

'That's worse.'

'No, it isn't. Not if you dump the loot somewhere else before you go home. He can't touch you then.'

'What about the other one—the one in the clearing?'

'He's gone, too.'

'You can't be sure of that.'

'I've been studying these fellows for months, Gordon. Honest I have. I know all their habits. There's no danger.'

A few minutes later, I reluctantly followed Claud back into the wood. It was pitch-dark in there now, and very silent, and as we moved cautiously forward, the noise of our footsteps seemed to go echoing around the walls of the forest as though we were walking in a cathedral.

'Here's where we threw the raisins,' Claud said.

I peered through the bushes. The clearing lay dim and milky in the moonlight.

'You're quite sure the keeper's gone?'

'I *know* he's gone.'

I could just see Claud's face under the peak of his cap—the pale lips, the soft, pale cheeks, and the large eyes with a little spark of excitement dancing in each.

'Are they roosting?' I asked.

'Yes. In the branches.'

'Whereabouts?'

'All around. They don't go far.'

'What do we do next?'

'We stay here and wait. I brought you a light,' he added, and he handed me one of those small pocket flashlights shaped like a fountain pen. 'You may need it.'

I was beginning to feel better. 'Shall we see if we can spot some of them sitting in the trees?' I said.

'No.'

'I should like to see how they look when they're roosting.'

'This isn't a nature study,' Claud said. 'Please be quiet.'

We stood there for a long time, waiting for something to happen.

'I've just had a nasty thought,' I said. 'If a bird can keep its balance on a branch when it's asleep, then surely there isn't any reason why the pills should make it fall down.'

Claud looked at me quick.

'After all,' I said, 'it's not dead. It's still only sleeping.'

'It's doped,' Claud said.

'But that's just a *deeper* sort of sleep. Why should we expect it to fall down just because it's in a deeper sleep?'

There was a gloomy silence.

'We should've tried it with chickens,' Claud said. 'My dad would've done that.'

'Your dad was a genius,' I said.

At that moment, there came a soft thump from the woods behind us.

'Hey!' I said.

'Sh-h-h!'

We stood listening.

Thump!

'There's another!'

It was a deep, muffled sound, as though a small bag of sand had been dropped from about shoulder height.

Thump!

'They're pheasants!' I cried.

'Wait!'

'I'm sure they're pheasants!'

Thump! Thump!

'You're right!'

We ran back into the wood.

'Where were they?' I asked.

'Over here! Two of them were over here!'

'I thought they were this way.'

'Keep looking!' Claud shouted. 'They can't be far.'

We searched for about a minute.

'Here's one!' he called.

When I got to him, he was holding a magnificent cockbird in both hands. We examined it closely with our flashlights.

'It's doped to the gills,' Claud said. 'It's still alive, I can feel its heart, but it's doped to the gills.'

Thump!

'There's another!' he cried.

Thump! Thump!

'Two more!'

Thump!

Thump! Thump! Thump!

Thump! Thump! Thump! Thump!
Thump! Thump!

All around us, the pheasants were starting to rain down out of the trees. We began rushing around madly in the dark, sweeping the ground with our flashlights.

Thump! Thump! Thump! This lot fell almost on top of me. I was right under the tree as they came down, and I found all three of them immediately—two cocks and a hen. They were limp and warm, the feathers wonderfully soft in the hand.

'Where shall I put them?' I called out. I was holding them by the legs.

'Lay them here, Gordon! Just pile them up here where it's light!'

Claud was standing on the edge of the clearing with the moonlight streaming down all over him and a great bunch of pheasants in each hand. His face was bright, his eyes big and bright and wonderful, and he was staring around him like a child who had just discovered that the whole world is made of chocolate.

Thump!
Thump! Thump!

'I don't like it,' I said. 'It's too many.'

'It's beautiful!' he cried, and he dumped the birds he was carrying and ran off to look for more.

Thump! Thump! Thump! Thump!
Thump!

It was easy to find them now. There were one or two lying under every tree. I quickly collected six more, three in each hand, and ran back and dumped them with the others. Then six more. Then six more after that. And still they kept falling.

Claud was in a whirl of ecstacy now, dashing about like a mad ghost under the trees. I could see the beam of his flashlight waving around in the dark, and each time he found a bird he gave a little yelp of triumph.

Thump! Thump! Thump!

'Mr Victor Hazel ought to hear this!' he called out.

'Don't shout,' I said. 'It frightens me.'

'What?'

'Don't *shout*. There might be keepers.'

'To hell with the keepers!' he cried. 'They're all eating!'

For three or four minutes, the pheasants kept on falling. Then suddenly they stopped.

'Keep searching!' Claud shouted. 'There's plenty more on the ground!'

'Don't you think we ought to get out while the going's good?'

'No,' he said.

We went on searching. Between us, we looked under every tree within a hundred yards of the clearing—north, south, east, and west—and I

119

think we found most of them in the end. At the collecting point, there was a pile of pheasants as big as a bonfire.

'It's a miracle,' Claud said. 'It's a miracle.' He was staring at them in a kind of trance.

'We'd better just take a half a dozen each and get out quick,' I said.

'I would like to count them, Gordon.'

'There's no time for that.'

'I must count them.'

'No,' I said. 'Come on.'

'One. Two. Three. Four . . .' He began counting them very carefully, picking up each bird in turn and laying it gently to one side. The moon was directly overhead now, and the whole clearing was brilliantly illuminated.

'I'm not standing around here like this,' I said. I walked back a few paces and hid myself in the shadows, waiting for him to finish.

'A hundred and seventeen, a hundred and eighteen, a hundred and nineteen, *a hundred and twenty!*' he cried. '*One hundred and twenty birds!* It's an all-time record!'

I didn't doubt it for a moment.

'The most my dad ever got in one night was fifteen, and he was drunk for a week afterward!'

'You're the champion of the world.' I said. 'Are you ready now?'

'One minute,' he answered, and he pulled up his sweater and began to unwind the two big white cotton sacks from around his belly. 'Here's yours,' he said, handing one of them to me. 'Fill it up quick.'

The light of the moon was so strong that I could read the small print along the base of the sack. 'J. W. Crump,' it said. 'Keston Flour Mills, London S.W. 17.'

'You don't think that keeper with the brown teeth is watching us this very moment, from behind a tree?'

'There's no chance of that,' Claud said. 'He's down at the filling station, like I told you, waiting for us to come home.'

We started loading the pheasants into the sacks. They were soft and floppy-necked, and the skin underneath the feathers was warm.

'There'll be a taxi waiting for us in the lane,' Claud said.

'What?'

'I always go back in a taxi, Gordon. Didn't you know that? A taxi is anonymous. Nobody knows who's inside a taxi except the driver. My dad taught me that.'

'Which driver?'

'Charlie Kinch. He's only too glad to oblige.'

We finished loading the pheasants, and I tried to hump my bulging sack onto my shoulder. My sack had about sixty birds inside it, and it must have weighed a hundredweight and a half, at least. 'I can't carry this,' I said. 'We'll have to leave some of them behind.'

'Drag it,' Claud said. 'Just pull it behind you.'

We started off through the pitch-black woods, pulling the pheasants behind us. 'We'll never make it all the way back to the village like this,' I said.

'Charlie's never let me down yet,' Claud said.

We came to the margin of the wood and peered through the hedge into the lane. The taxi was there, not five yards away. Claud said, 'Charlie boy,' very softly, and the old man behind the wheel poked his head out into the moonlight and gave us a sly, toothless grin. We slid through the hedge, dragging the sacks after us.

'Hullo!' Charlie said. 'What's this?'

'It's cabbages,' Claud told him. 'Open the door.'

Two minutes later, we were safely inside the taxi, cruising slowly down the hill toward the village.

It was all over now bar the shouting. Claud was triumphant, bursting with pride and excitement, and he kept leaning forward and tapping Charlie Kinch on the shoulder and saying, 'How about it, Charlie? How about this for a haul?' and Charlie kept glancing back popeyed at the huge, bulging sacks lying on the floor between us and saying, 'How did you do it?'

'There's six brace of them for you, Charlie,' Claud said.

Charlie said, 'I reckon pheasants is going to be a bit scarce up at Mr Victor Hazel's opening-day shoot this year,' and Claud said, 'I imagine they are, Charlie, I imagine they are.'

'What are you going to do with a hundred and twenty pheasants?' I asked.

'Put them in cold storage for the winter,' Claud said. 'Put them in with the dog meat in the deep freeze at the filling station.'

'Not tonight, I trust?'

'No, Gordon, not tonight. We leave them at Bessie's house tonight.'

'Bessie who?'

'Bessie Organ.'

'Bessie *Organ!*' I was completely stunned. Mrs Organ was the wife of the Reverend Jack Organ, the local vicar.

'Bessie always delivers my game, didn't you know that?'

'I don't know anything,' I said.

'Always choose a respectable woman to deliver your game,' Claud announced. 'That's correct, Charlie, isn't it?'

'Bessie's a right smart girl,' Charlie said.

We were driving through the village now and the street lamps were still on and the men were wandering home from the pubs. I saw Will

Prattley letting himself in quietly by the side door of his fishmonger's shop, and Mrs Prattley's head was sticking out the window just above him, but he didn't know it.

'The vicar is very partial to roasted pheasant,' Claud said.

'He hangs it eighteen days,' Charlie said. 'Then he gives it a couple of good shakes and all the feathers drop off.'

The taxi turned left and swung in through the gates of the vicarage. There were no lights on in the house, and nobody met us. Claud and I dumped the pheasants in the coal shed at the rear, and then we said good-bye to Charlie Kinch and walked back in the moonlight to the filling station, empty-handed. Whether or not Mr Rabbetts was watching us as we went in, I do not know. We saw no sign of him.

'Here she comes,' Claud said to me the next morning. He was looking through the window of the filling station.

'Who?'

'Bessie—Bessie Organ.' He spoke the name proudly and with a slight proprietary air, as though he were a general referring to his bravest officer.

I followed him outside.

'Down there,' he said, pointing.

Far away down the road, I could see a small female figure advancing toward us. 'What's she pushing?' I asked.

Claud gave me a sly look. 'There's only one safe way of delivering game,' he announced, 'and that's under a baby.'

'Yes,' I murmured. 'Yes, of course.'

'That'll be young Christopher Organ in the pram, aged one and a half. He's a lovely child, Gordon.'

I could just make out the small dot of a baby sitting high up in the pram, which had its hood folded down.

'There's sixty or seventy pheasants at least under that little nipper,' Claud said happily. 'Just imagine that.'

'You can't fit sixty or seventy pheasants into a pram,' I said.

'You can if it's got a good deep well underneath it, and if you take out the mattress and pack them in tight, right up to the top. All you need is a sheet. You'll be surprised how little room a pheasant takes up when it's limp.'

We stood beside the pumps, waiting for Bessie Organ to arrive. It was one of those warm, windless September mornings, with a darkening sky and a smell of thunder in the air.

'Right through the village, bold as brass,' Claud said. 'Good old Bessie.'

'She seems in rather a hurry to me.'

Claud lit a new cigarette from the stub of the old one. 'Bessie is never in a hurry,' he said.

'She certainly isn't walking normal,' I told him. 'You look.'

He squinted at her through the smoke of his cigarette. Then he took the cigarette out of his mouth and looked again.

'Well?' I said.

'She does seem to be going a tiny bit quick, doesn't she?' he said carefully.

'She's going damn quick.'

There was a pause. Claud was beginning to stare hard at the approaching woman. 'Perhaps she doesn't want to be caught in the rain, Gordon. I'll bet that's exactly what it is—she thinks it's going to rain, and she don't want the baby to get wet.'

'She's *running!*' I cried. 'Look!' Bessie had suddenly broken into a full sprint.

Claud stood very still, watching the woman; and in the silence that followed I fancied I could hear a baby screaming.

'There's something wrong with that baby,' I said. 'Listen.'

At this point, Bessie was about two hundred yards away from us, but closing fast.

'Can you hear him now?' I said.

'Yes.'

'He's yelling his head off.'

The small shrill voice in the distance was growing louder every second—frantic, piercing, almost hysterical.

'He's having a fit,' Claud announced.

'I think he must be.'

'That's why she's running, Gordon. She wants to get him in here quick and put him under a cold tap.'

'I'm sure you're right,' I said.

Claud shifted his feet uneasily on the gravel of the driveway. 'There's a thousand and one different things keep happening every day to little babies like that,' he said.

'Of course.'

'Whatever it is,' Claud said, 'I wish she'd stop running.'

A long lorry loaded with bricks came up alongside of Bessie, and the driver slowed down and poked his head out the window to stare. Bessie flew on, and she was so close now that I could see her big red face, with the mouth wide open, panting for breath. I noticed she was wearing white gloves on her hands, very prim and dainty, and there was a funny little white hat to match perched right on the top of her head, like a mushroom.

Suddenly, out of the pram, straight up into the air, flew an enormous pheasant.

Claud let out a cry of horror.

The fool in the truck going along beside Bessie roared with laughter. The pheasant flapped around drunkenly for a few seconds, then it lost height and landed in the grass by the side of the road. Bessie kept on running.

Then—*whoosh!*—a second pheasant flew up out of the pram.

Then a third and a fourth. Then a fifth.

'My God!' I said. 'It's the pills! They're wearing off!'

Bessie covered the last fifty yards at a tremendous pace, and she came swinging into the driveway of the filling station with birds flying up out of the pram in all directions.

'What the hell's going on?' she cried.

'Go round the back!' I shouted. 'Go round the back!' But she pulled up sharp beside the first pump in the line, and before we could reach her, she had seized the screaming infant in her arms and dragged him clear.

'No! No!' Claud cried, racing towards her. 'Don't lift the baby! Put him back! Hold down the sheet!' But she wasn't even listening, and with the weight of the child suddenly lifted away, a great cloud of pheasants rose up out of the pram—forty or fifty of them, at least—and the whole sky above us was filled with huge brown birds clapping their wings furiously to gain height.

Claud and I started running up and down the driveway, waving our arms to frighten them off the premises. 'Go away!' we shouted. 'Shoo! Go away!' But they were too dopey still to take any notice of us, and within half a minute down they came again and settled themselves like a swarm of locusts all over the front of my filling station. The place was covered with them. They sat wing to wing along the edges of the roof and on the concrete canopy that came out over the pumps, and a dozen, at least, were clinging to the sill of the office window. Some had flown down onto the rack that held the bottles of lubricating oil, and others were sliding about on the bonnets of my second-hand cars. One cock-bird with a fine tail was perched superbly on top of a petrol pump, and quite a number simply squatted in the driveway at our feet, fluffing their feathers and blinking their small eyes.

Across the road, a line of cars had already started forming behind the brick lorry, and people were opening their doors and getting out and beginning to cross over to have a closer look. I glanced at my watch. It was twenty to nine. Any moment now, I thought, a large black car is going to come streaking along the road from the direction of the village, and the car will be a Rolls, and the face behind the wheel will be the great butcher's face of Mr Victor Hazel, maker of sausages and pies.

'They near pecked him to pieces!' Bessie was shouting, clasping the screaming baby to her bosom.

'You go on home, Bessie,' Claud said, white in the face.

'Lock up,' I said. 'Put out the sign. We've gone for the day.'

James Thurber born in Columbus, Ohio, in 1894, and educated at Ohio University. He lost the sight in one eye when young, and became totally blind in later life. He explained that this dictated the form of his line drawings, as he had only partial cognisance of the shape and area of the objects he was drawing. He worked as a code clerk with the United States State Department, and as a journalist for the Columbus DISPATCH, and then the Chicago TRIBUNE. In 1926 he joined the EVENING POST, and became a regular contributor of line drawings and witty stories to THE NEW YORKER, in which most of his best work appeared. He collaborated with Elliott Nugent in writing 'THE MALE ANIMAL' which, like 'THE SECRET LIFE OF WALTER MITTY', was later made into a film.

'To me', he once wrote, 'humour is a kind of emotional chaos told about calmly and quietly in retrospect.' His stories employ the natural, vernacular tradition established by Mark Twain. His more symbolic, imaginative stories, like 'IN THE MAZE', include an element of irony characteristic of more recent American writers dealing with folk characters and situations. Yet in both his stories and his line drawings, he is an admirable technician, who achieves a highly personal idiom. The fantasies of his small, sad men are at once hilarious and evocative of pathos. His parodies are both incisively critical and sympathetic.

Probably the best collection of his work is to be found in THE CREAM OF THURBER, *1939*.

He died in 1961.

THE SECRET LIFE OF WALTER MITTY

James Thurber

'WE'RE GOING THROUGH!' THE COMMANDER'S VOICE WAS LIKE THIN ICE breaking. He wore his full-dress uniform, with the heavily braided white cap pulled down rakishly over one cold grey eye. 'We can't make it, sir. It's spoiling for a hurricane, if you ask me.' 'I'm not asking you, Lieutenant Berg,' said the Commander. 'Throw on the power lights! Rev her up to 8,500! We're going through!' The pounding of the cylinders increased: ta-pocketa-pocketa-pocketa-*pocketa-pocketa*. The Commander stared at the ice forming on the pilot window. He walked over and twisted a row of complicated dials. 'Switch on No. 8 auxiliary!' he shouted. 'Switch on No. 8 auxiliary!' repeated Lieutenant Berg. 'Full strength in No. 3 turret!' shouted the Commander. 'Full strength in No. 3 turret!' The crew, bending to their various tasks in the huge, hurtling eight-engined Navy hydroplane, looked at each other and grinned. 'The Old Man'll get us through,' they said to one another. 'The Old Man ain't afraid of Hell!' . . .

'Not so fast! You're driving too fast!' said Mrs Mitty. 'What are you driving so fast for?'

'Hmm?' said Walter Mitty. He looked at his wife, in the seat beside him, with shocked astonishment. She seemed grossly unfamiliar, like a strange woman who had yelled at him in a crowd. 'You were up to fifty-five,' she said. 'You know I don't like to go more than forty. You were up to fifty-five.' Walter Mitty drove on towards Waterbury in silence, the roaring of the SN202 through the worst storm in twenty years of Navy flying fading in the remote, intimate airways of his mind. 'You're tensed up again,' said Mrs Mitty. 'It's one of your days. I wish you'd let Dr Renshaw look you over.'

Walter Mitty stopped the car in front of the building where his wife went to have her hair done. 'Remember to get those overshoes while I'm having my hair done,' she said. 'I don't need overshoes,' said Mitty. She put her mirror back into her bag. 'We've been all through that,' she said, getting out of the car. 'You're not a young man any longer.' He raced the engine a little. 'Why don't you wear your gloves? Have you lost your gloves?' Walter Mitty reached in a pocket and brought out the gloves. He put them on, but after she had turned and gone into the building and he had driven on to a red light, he took them off again. 'Pick it up, brother!' snapped a cop as the lights changed, and Mitty hastily pulled on his gloves and lurched ahead. He drove round the streets aimlessly for a time, and then he drove past the hospital on his way to the parking lot.

. . . 'It's the millionaire banker, Wellington McMillan,' said the pretty nurse. 'Yes?' said Walter Mitty, removing his gloves slowly. 'Who has the case?' 'Dr Renshaw and Dr Benbow, but there are two specialists here, Dr Remington from New York and Mr Pritchard-Mitford from London. He flew over.' A door opened down a long, cool corridor and Dr Renshaw came out. He looked distraught and haggard. 'Hello, Mitty,' he said. 'We're having the devil's own time with McMillan, the millionaire banker and close personal friend of Roosevelt. Obstreosis of the ductal tract. Tertiary. Wish you'd take a look at him.' 'Glad to,' said Mitty.

In the operating room there were whispered introductions: 'Dr Remington, Dr Mitty, Mr Pritchard-Mitford, Dr Mitty.' 'I've read your book on streptothricosis,' said Pritchard-Mitford, shaking hands. 'A brilliant performance, sir.' 'Thank you,' said Walter Mitty. 'Didn't know you were in the States, Mitty,' grumbled Remington. 'Coals to Newcastle, bringing Mitford and me up here for a tertiary.' 'You are very kind,' said Mitty. A huge, complicated machine, connected to the operating table, with many tubes and wires, began at this moment to go pocketa-pocketa-pocketa. 'The new anaesthetizer is giving way!' shouted an intern. 'There is no one in the East who knows how to fix it!' 'Quiet man!' said Mitty, in a low cool voice. He sprang to the machine, which was now going pocketa-pocketa-queep-pocketa-queep. He began fingering delicately a row of glistening dials. 'Give me a fountain pen!' he snapped. Someone handed him a fountain pen. He pulled a faulty piston out of the machine and inserted the pen in its place. 'That will hold for ten minutes,' he said. 'Get on with the operation.' A nurse hurried over and whispered to Renshaw, and Mitty saw the man turn pale. 'Coreopsis has set in,' said Renshaw nervously. 'If you would take over, Mitty?' Mitty looked at him and at the craven figure of Benbow, who drank, and at the grave, uncertain faces of the two great specialists. 'If you wish,' he said. They slipped a white gown on him; he adjusted a mask and drew on thin gloves; nurses handed him shining . . .

'Back it up, Mac! Look out for that Buick!' Walter Mitty jammed on the brakes. 'Wrong lane, Mac,' said the parking-lot attendant, looking at Mitty closely. 'Gee. Yeh,' muttered Mitty. He began cautiously to back out of the lane marked 'Exit Only'. 'Leave her sit there,' said the attendant. 'I'll put her away.' Mitty got out of the car. 'Hey, better leave the key.' 'Oh,' said Mitty, handing the man the ignition key. The attendant vaulted into the car, backed it up with insolent skill, and put it where it belonged.

They're so damn cocky, thought Walter Mitty, walking along Main Street; they think they know everything. Once he had tried to take his chains off, outside New Milford, and he had got them wound round the axles. A man had had to come out in a wrecking car and unwind them, a young, grinning garageman. Since then Mrs Mitty always made him drive to a garage to have the chains taken off. The next time, he thought, I'll wear my right arm in a sling; they won't grin at me then. I'll have my right arm in a sling and they'll see I couldn't possibly take the chains off myself. He kicked at the slush on the sidewalk. 'Overshoes,' he said to himself, and he began looking for a shoe store.

When he came out into the street again, with the overshoes in a box under his arm, Walter Mitty began to wonder what the other thing was his wife had told him to get. She had told him twice, before they set out from their house for Waterbury. In a way he hated these weekly trips to town—he was always getting something wrong. Kleenex, he thought, Squibb's, razor blades? No. Toothpaste, toothbrush, bicarbonate, carborundum, initiative and referendum? He gave it up. But she would remember it. 'Where's the what's-its-name?' she would ask. 'Don't tell me you forgot the what's-its-name.' A newsboy went by shouting something about the Waterbury trial.

. . . 'Perhaps this will refresh your memory.' The District Attorney suddenly thrust a heavy automatic at the quiet figure on the witness stand. 'Have you ever seen this before?' Walter Mitty took the gun and examined it expertly. 'This is my Webley-Vickers 50.80,' he said calmly. An excited buzz ran around the courtroom. The judge rapped for order. 'You are a crack shot with any sort of firearms, I believe?' said the District Attorney, insinuatingly. 'Objection!' shouted Mitty's attorney. 'We have shown that the defendant could not have fired the shot. We have shown that he wore his right arm in a sling on the night of the fourteenth of July.' Walter Mitty raised his hand briefly and the bickering attorneys were stilled. 'With any known make of gun,' he said evenly, 'I could have killed Gregory Fitzhurst at three hundred feet *with my left hand.*' Pandemonium broke loose in the courtroom. A woman's scream rose above the bedlam and suddenly a lovely, dark-haired girl was in Walter Mitty's arms. The District Attorney struck at her savagely. Without rising from his chair, Mitty let the man have it on the point of the chin. 'You miserable cur!' . . .

'Puppy biscuit,' said Walter Mitty. He stopped walking and the buildings of Waterbury rose up out of the misty courtroom and surrounded him again. A woman who was passing laughed. 'He said "Puppy biscuit" ', she said to her companion. 'That man said "Puppy biscuit" to himself.' Walter Mitty hurried on. He went into an A. &. P., not the first one he came to but a smaller one farther up the street. 'I want some biscuit for small, young dogs,' he said to the clerk. 'Any special brand, sir?' The greatest pistol shot in the world thought a moment. 'It says "Puppies Bark for It" on the box,' said Walter Mitty.

His wife would be through at the hairdresser's in fifteen minutes, Mitty saw in looking at his watch, unless they had trouble drying it; sometimes they had trouble drying it. She didn't like to get to the hotel first; she would want him to be there waiting for her as usual. He found a big leather chair in the lobby, facing a window, and he put the overshoes and the puppy biscuit on the floor beside it. He picked up an old copy of *Liberty* and sank down into the chair. 'Can Germany Conquer the World Through the Air?' Walter Mitty looked at the pictures of bombing planes and of ruined streets.

. . . 'The cannonading has got the wind up in young Raleigh, sir,' said the sergeant. Captain Mitty looked up at him through tousled hair. 'Get him to bed,' he said wearily. 'With the others. I'll fly alone.' 'But you can't sir,' said the sergeant anxiously. 'It takes two men to handle that bomber and the Archies are pounding hell out of the air. Von Richtman's circus is between here and Saulier.' 'Somebody's got to get that ammunition dump,' said Mitty. 'I'm going over. Spot of brandy?' He poured a drink for the sergeant and one for himself. War thundered and whined around the dugout and battered at the door. There was a rend of wood and splinters flew through the room. 'A bit of a near thing,' said Captain Mitty carelessly. 'The box barrage is closing in,' said the sergeant. 'We only live once, Sergeant,' said Mitty, with his faint, fleeting smile. 'Or do we?' He poured another brandy and tossed it off. 'I never see a man could hold his brandy like you, sir,' said the sergeant. 'Begging your pardon, sir.' Captain Mitty stood up and strapped on his huge Webley-Vickers automatic. 'It's forty kilometres through hell, sir,' said the sergeant. Mitty finished one last brandy. 'After all,' he said softly, 'what isn't?' The pounding of the cannon increased; there was the rat-tat-tatting of machine guns, and from somewhere came the menacing pocketa-pocketa-pocketa of the new flamethrowers. Walter Mitty walked to the door of the dugout humming 'Auprès de Ma Blonde.' He turned and waved to the sergeant. 'Cheerio!' he said . . .

Something struck his shoulder. 'I've been looking all over this hotel for you,' said Mrs Mitty. 'Why do you have to hide in this old chair? How do you expect me to find you?' 'Things close in,' said Walter Mitty vaguely. 'What?' Mrs Mitty said. 'Did you get the what's-its-name? The puppy biscuit? What's in that box?' 'Overshoes,' said Mitty. 'Couldn't you have put them on in the store?' 'I was thinking,' said Walter Mitty. 'Does it ever occur to you that I am sometimes thinking?' She looked at him. 'I'm going to take your temperature when I get you home,' she said.

They went out through the revolving doors that made a faintly derisive whistling sound when you pushed them. It was two blocks to the parking lot. At the drugstore on the corner she said, 'Wait here for me. I forgot something. I won't be a minute.' She was more than a minute. Walter Mitty lighted a cigarette. It began to rain, rain with sleet in it. He stood up against the wall of the drugstore, smoking. . . . He put his shoulders back and his heels together. 'To hell with the handkerchief,' said Walter Mitty scornfully. He took one last drag on his cigarette and snapped it away. Then, with that faint, fleeting smile playing about his lips, he faced the firing squad; erect and motionless, proud and disdainful, Walter Mitty the Undefeated, inscrutable to the last.

Judah Waten born in Odessa, Russia, in 1911. Just before the First World War his family migrated to Western Australia, and he himself travelled widely in Australia and abroad before settling in Victoria. An intense interest in politics as well as literature make him one of the most politically controversial of today's Australian writers and his works have been translated into Russian and Chinese. In addition to writing on cultural and political questions, he has produced five novels and many short stories. Waten's interest in the problems of migrants appears in much of his work.

In 'THE KNIFE' the author gives a perceptive account of the way of life that has influenced Plinio's personality before he narrates the events of his character's fateful night. The climax of the story is more impressive for its close description of the confused boy's reactions and its lack of moralizing comment.

THE KNIFE

Judah Waten

MANY MEMORIES—SAD, GAY, TENDER—DANCED THROUGH PLINIO'S MIND whenever he looked at his father's knife. That knife was his most definite link with home. A well-knit, good-looking young fellow of twenty-three —the new kitchen-hand at the Café Milano—he had come from a poor village in Calabria, in a very desolate part of Southern Italy. Most of the men had emigrated to America and Australia; women easily outnumbered them in the villages. And many a mother had to bring up children without ever hearing again from a father who had vanished without a trace into one of the new lands.

Not Plinio's father who had died in his native village nearly fourteen years before. Old Bonelli had never cared to leave his wife and his large brood of children even for a week. For them he had worked hard as a day labourer on the roads and in the fields, and in his spare time he had carved things with the knife that had come down to him from his grandfather. It was his most valued possession, his mark of self sufficiency, a symbol of poverty, yet a very proud poverty.

Now in Melbourne, Plinio always carried his father's knife and he wore his father's black corduroy trousers. In the new land. ' >nely, pining for the village he had never before left, Plinio thought more than ever of his father; it was as if the new country had made him conscious of being an orphan. As vividly as if it had happened the day before, he could remember his father dying; he could remember the dying man's continuous cries like an endless litany of anguish.

'Christ save me. Bring me a doctor. Christ save me.'

But there was no doctor for miles around. Before a doctor could be brought from the district centre his calls had changed to a death rattle. Plinio could remember seeing his mother and her sister close the dead man's eyelids, and then begin their lament declaiming in high voices the death story. From time to time they put their heads out of the window to announce the death to the world and then they drew back into the room to continue their lamentations. They were joined by other women from the village and the wailing lasted for two days without stopping until the funeral.

The memory of this long-drawn-out, repetitious, agonizing lament always filled Plinio with a feeling of physical distress; it brought a lump to his throat and he could hardly keep back his tears. And with that came more recollections. He recalled how his mother, Maddalena, went out to work for a stonemason, a relative of hers, and how she had carried great weights on her head, bags of sand and even ceiling boards. Yet hard as she worked she earned very little and her children lived in daily need of food.

133

Their most constant meal was black bread made of hard wheat, in great round loaves weighing five or ten pounds. A loaf would last a whole week. On the few holidays, as on the feast day of the Virgin Mary, the bread was spiced with a little garlic, dipped in oil and eaten with pieces of the ferociously hot Spanish pepper. Sometimes there was also a thin broth. These rare feasts were among the happiest of Plinio's childhood memories. He had not had a long childhood. A year after his father's death, when he turned ten, he began to work as a day labourer on farms around the villages.

It was then as a symbol of his coming of age as it were, of his manhood, that Maddalena gave Plinio his father's knife which had hung on a rack on the wall since his death. It was a small knife with a bony handle covered by a patina of dark green rust from the sweat of many palms, and it had a worn-down, sharp, shiny blade no more than half an inch wide. With this knife Plinio's father had whittled and carved the wooden chairs they sat on, the wooden plates and forks they used. Although old Bonelli would never have thought of himself as an artist or a craftsman, he had carved exquisitely the sacred wooden statue in the corner of the room they lived in and it had been his ambition to complete a miniature of the Palermo Cathedral, a job that would have taken him ten years.

In the fields Plinio proudly wore the knife at his belt just as his father had. But he did not have any of his father's skill at wood carving nor did he want to carve. He used the knife for cutting the sausage and cheese that he ate sometimes now that he was working. Occasionally he used it to cut the black bread, holding the loaf against his chest and drawing the knife towards him, expertly taking care not to cut his chin. As he mostly broke the bread with his hands like a good Christian, the knife more than anything else was for him the symbol of his manliness, of his being on a level with his fellows, irrespective of age.

Plinio was a quiet youth but he had not turned his back on the pleasures of the village. He was one of the best dancers in the district although he had a heavy, awkward gait from walking barefoot except on Sundays. He was always among those young people who danced to the shepherd's bagpipes, circling round each other, barely touching fingers as if in a harmonious courtship, or taking hands and spinning round like tops.

The women of the village liked the grace and ardour with which he danced. Altogether he was a most attractive youth, with his black curly hair and his rather sad, black eyes that seemed a heritage of generations of tears and sufferings and reflected a kind of deep inner sadness. It was a sadness that for the women only enhanced his beauty. Behind their veils their gaze was frank, franker now with so many men in foreign lands or dead on the battlefields of North Africa and Europe, and they spoke of love-making with a great directness and simplicity. Whenever Plinio walked across the village square, their black eyes looked him up and down with a relentless physical familiarity and they whispered judgments on his hidden charms.

But Plinio's pleasures were only fleeting, slight incidents in a life of work. He never worked less hard because of them, but always harder, and all the time he yearned for a good meal that would stop the everlasting gnawing of his stomach. This constant half-hunger often made him irritable as it did the animals of the district, the skinny donkey braying in anguish, the goat looking for grass in the barren ground, staring with blank, yellow eyes at the bitter world. Then Plinio would go into a tavern with his fellow labourers, drink wine and play a certain game of cards that was the recognized first stage in a kind of oratory tournament. The interminable speeches made by the players revealed a vast amount of rancour and bitterness towards each other and it often ended in quarrels and scuffling. But never once did Plinio think of drawing his father's knife which he did not associate with violence, even when there was murder in his eyes. The knife was not something to be used in defence or offence but it might have been drawn to defend his honour or the honour of his family, especially if the honour of the women of his family had been impugned.

One day when he returned from the fields his mother held up a letter she had received from a distant relative in far away Australia. As she could not read herself she had taken the letter to the parish priest who had read it to her and she had memorized it word for word. The relative waited on tables at the Café Milano and could not only arrange an assisted passage for Plinio but could also get him a good job in the kitchen of the café.

Plinio had stood for a while without speaking, thinking of the good food that was promised him, thinking of the wonders of a sea-trip across half the world; then the horror of being separated from the family he loved with passionate tenderness broke over him.

'No, I won't go. Why should I go? I'll stay here.'

'You will help us very much by going, Plinio,' said Maddalena with grave eyes.

He would be able to send them money from the good wages he earned, she argued, and she would even save some money for him for the day when he would return to the village to marry the bride she would choose for him.

There was no denying her wisdom. As with most of the men in the village, there seemed to be no alternative but emigration if he wanted to eat and feed his family.

So the day came when Plinio's mother, brothers, sisters, relatives and friends from the village escorted him to the railway station at the district centre on the first stage of his journey to Naples where he would catch the boat to Australia. Plinio and his mother walked slightly ahead of the others. She bore herself with dignity and she walked erect with the stately carriage of one accustomed to balancing heavy weights. She was dressed in a black cotton blouse, black bell-shaped skirt and high boots, and her solemn face was framed in a veil folded several times and falling over her shoulders, a mantle which had come down to her from her family.

The emotions of that leave-taking often swept over Plinio as he lay in bed in his lodgings. They were in a single-fronted, two-storey apartment house in North Melbourne where at least twenty other young Italian newcomers were crowded into four rooms. Most were from the south of Italy and were friendly with each other, and with Plinio: they talked to him as if they had known him all their lives. But he could not make much conversation with them; they came from other villages and towns and to him they were like foreigners. His village had been his world and his conversation mirrored that narrow world. But he listened intently to their chatter, groping for knowledge of the new land. They talked of their jobs and their future which seemed rosy to them, yet he knew they suffered from the same loneliness as he. There were not enough Italian women to go round and the Australian women were hard to approach. Nor was it easy to make friends with Australian men who sometimes showed resentment towards them. Newcomers had to live to themselves. Even the church to which they took Plinio had Italian priests and an almost wholly Italian congregation.

After three months in the kitchen of the Café Milano, Plinio still felt as if he had been cut adrift from everything that gave life meaning. There was his relative who was good to him but seemed to belong to another world, having already lived in Australia over five years. Plinio yearned for his family, his friends and those women of the village who had made such a fuss of him, and he entered the new life not with hope or enthusiasm but with resignation. But he did not dislike his job. It was the easiest work he had ever done although he worked long hours, six days a week. He scrubbed floors, washed dishes and occasionally his large, heavy hands were put to smaller tasks, peeling and cutting vegetables. And he had never had so much food before. Sometimes, without thinking, he would take out his father's knife and use it to cut bread and meat. But this habit became rare as he grew accustomed to the metal cutlery.

Every night after work he walked from the Café Milano to his home in North Melbourne. It would not have occurred to him to spend money on a bus fare; that would have been so many lire off the money to be sent home.

Sometimes beyond the markets he dropped into one of the new Espresso bars to see if he could find a kinsman, a man from his own district, and when he met one he would sit talking with him for hours over a cup of coffee. But mostly there was nobody and he went quickly on his way.

One night outside a milk bar a pretty girl with bright eyes and a pert expression caught his eye. She was with a group of seven or eight youths and girls on the footpath, tapping their feet to the music of the juke box, while they talked and argued.

Plinio saw her several times standing outside the milk bar with her companions, the same youths and girls. She turned her head and looked at him: he stared back frankly and greedily just as he might have done back home.

'Cop the cheeky dago,' one of her companions said.

It was Tommy Lawler, a tall, strong, good-looking youth of nineteen who wore an open-necked Hawaiian style shirt and a two-toned coat, almost reaching down to his knees. The girl, Mavis Keer, laughed and stared back at Plinio until he disappeared round the corner into his street.

'I can't stick dagos,' Tommy went on rancorously.

His companions were well aware of his dislike. He was just like his father with whom he worked at the Victoria Market. Old Lawler never tired of saying that dagos could live on the smell of an oil rag; that way back in the depression when returned soldiers were forced off their farms, they had taken them over, and in the cities they had taken the jobs of Australians.

Young Tommy repeated his father's words as if they were holy writ. But until Plinio had appeared on the scene he had not railed against any particular Italian, but Italians in general. Now he began to fasten all his antipathy on this olive-skinned youth in the cap and dark corduroy trousers.

One night when Mavis cast a provocative sideways glance at Plinio, Tommy swore loudly at the Italian who did not understand one word. One of the others turned to the girl with a grin.

'Garn, you're keen on that dago, Mavis.'

'He's not bad looking,' she said provocatively.

Something in her eyes roused Tommy. Until Plinio had come on the scene he had not considered Mavis his special property, but just one of the girls with whom all of the boys could flirt equally. Now he wanted Mavis for himself. His jealousy amused his companions.

'Never thought you'd let a dago do you for a girl,' one of them said teasingly. Mavis giggled and an ugly light shone from Tommy's eyes.

'Another crack like that and I'll drop you.' He knew how to use his fists, having fought in prelims at the West Melbourne stadium.

'I was only joking, Tommy,' his companion said, edging back.

As if now compelled to maintain his mastery, the next time Plinio walked past the milk bar and looked at Mavis, Tommy went straight up to him, aggressively.

'Whadya think you're up to, mug?'

'No understand,' Plinio said, shaking his head, his eyes darting to the left and right of him.

'That's what they all say,' Tommy sneered. 'You understand all right when you want to.'

Plinio began to feel alarmed. He stepped back and made to move away. But Tommy did not want him to go yet. With a quick movement of his hand he sent Plinio's cap flying into the gutter. As he stooped down to find his cap the youths and girls laughed and shouted approval to Tommy who watched Plinio with a contemptuous leer. Their laughter could be heard right down Victoria Street when Plinio found his cap and holding it in his hand ran past Tommy.

For days the young people continued to joke about the incident.

'It was funny as a circus,' one said.

'He went like a rabbit,' said another.

'They've got no guts, those dagos,' declared Tommy authoritatively.

Plinio decided he would not go past the milk bar any more. He could not bear to tell anyone about his humiliating experience, yet from the talk he had heard among the cooks and the other kitchen hands, he could guess what would happen to him the next time he walked past those youths. He would be hit by the one who had knocked off his cap and if he fell all the others would gather round and kick him. In the stomach, in the face! Sometimes men died from a kicking, he had heard said. Although he was almost stonily indifferent to his fate he did not want to die in the new land; death seemed so much more awful on alien soil. At times he would fearfully wonder if someone had placed a death curse on him. Yet he kept brooding on what had happened to him and always before his eyes appeared the face of Tommy Lawler. His manhood had been outraged and, gentle, passive and resigned as he was, he felt stirring within him a bitter resentment.

Next Saturday Plinio left the Café Milano later than usual. Although he would avoid the milk bar he would go up as far as the Espresso bar: tonight might be a lucky one for him—he might happen upon a man to whom he could talk. It was well after eleven when he walked up the street. The picture theatres had already emptied and there were only few people about. Only here and there in the shadows of the markets there were couples whispering and on street corners small groups of men stood and talked.

Plinio walked on ploddingly, not looking this way or that. Unexpectedly he heard laughter in the distance. It had an ominously reminiscent sound. He peered down the street patchily lit by overhead lights. Tommy and Mavis and their companions had just come out of a side street where they had been to a dance and they were walking towards him.

'Hey! Here's that dago coming,' shouted Tommy suddenly.

Mavis laid a restraining hand on his arm.

'Don't start anything, Tommy. Don't.'

That settled it for him.

'You don't want him hurt, eh?'

'This is going to be good,' another youth said.

They moved across the footpath and blocked Plinio's way. The Italian crouched involuntarily and glanced back over his shoulder as if looking for an escape.

'Don't let the cow get away,' someone shouted.

'No, don't let him run this time.'

Tommy placed himself in front of Plinio and thrust his face at him. 'Still around, you dago . . . !'

Plinio put out his hands as if to keep Tommy away and his eyes darted from the brick wall of the factory on his left to the excited expectant faces of the youths in front of him.

'Let him have it, Tommy,' one of them said.

'Yes, let him have it.'

'I'll fix him,' Tommy said out of the side of his mouth.

The girls crouched across the wall as Tommy suddenly raised his fists and struck Plinio across the ear. He staggered back, his face going white as if drained of blood. He was hurt but his mind was clear. He would not suffer any more indignities; in his village only a parent could strike him without affronting his honour.

As Tommy stepped in to deliver another blow, a kind of unreasoning ferocity was awakened in Plinio. He shouted something in Italian and quickly pulled out of his pocket his father's small sharp knife. With a short, swift upwards movement he thrust it at Tommy with all his force. Tommy saw the onrushing point and tried to shield himself from it, but without avail. The knife slipped off his defensive left arm into his body. He fell back against the wall, blood flowing out of him.

A short and desperate scream came from one of the girls.

'He's been stabbed!' a youth cried.

'Th' ambulance,' Tommy moaned in a voice that sounded far away. 'Get th' ambulance.'

He had slumped to the footpath, his back against the wall, his eyes staring down at the ever-widening dark pool.

The other girls and youths huddled in a frightened group, staring at Plinio who had not moved from the centre of the footpath, the small knife in his hand; but one by one they slipped off into the night. Only Mavis remained. She squatted down beside Tommy, talking to him, reassuring him, but every now and again casting bewildered glances at Plinio.

He did not look at her. He was filled with dark confusion and his heart was oppressed. He took a few steps and stopped. He did not know what to do—whether to stay or move away. He kept staring in an unseeing way at the small blade of steel in his hand.

Suddenly the thoroughfare became alive with shouts and cries. The red light of an ambulance was bearing down upon them; a police-car had just turned into Victoria Street. People had begun to crowd around, those in front pressing the others back.

'It's a dago! . . . He's got a knife.'

'Look out! He'll use it again.'

All their secret images of evil seemed to flow together and take a single shape.

'A knife! . . . He's got a knife.'

T. A. G. Hungerford born 1915 in Perth, Western Australia, and educated there. From 1940 to 1945 he served with the A.I.F. and was in the Occupation Force in Japan during 1946 and 1947. His army experience gave him the background for THE RIDGE AND THE RIVER, one of the best Australian war novels, and SOWERS OF THE WIND. His other novels are RIVERSLAKE and SHAKE THE GOLDEN BOUGH. His two war novels were prize winners in SYDNEY MORNING HERALD literary competitions. His short stories, sensitive to problems of place, show an effective use of local background. He has recently produced with Richard Woldendorp an illustrated book on Western Australia, A MILLION SQUARE.

THE ONLY ONE WHO FORGOT

T. A. G. Hungerford

ON A SMOOTH ROCK THAT JUTTED OUT OF A DEEP CLEAR POOL IN THE REEF, a black boy sat and idly watched the flashing gulls stab into a school of mackerel in the shallows off shore. They scattered the water into flung diamonds as they struck, and filled the air with their thin, savage cries. Far out, the big boomers thundered on the edge of the reef, and at his feet the water slid hissing over the coarse sand, clucking and sucking in the holes, never still, never silent; behind him, at the other end of the gleaming white shell road, the little town slumbered already in the golden threat of midday heat, not quite alive, but not quite dead. It was all he had ever known, this rock, this beach, this sea, and this little town, and he was content, when his work at the hotel was done, to sit and watch the luggers come in, and the great clouds roll over the edge of the world.

Hearing a sound behind him, a gentle, furtive sound like a goanna stirring in grass, he turned round quickly. A little girl stood on the sand looking up at him—the bright glare of the coral sand made her wrinkle her eyes and her nose, and her mouth was screwed up into a tight little red dot of conjecture. Her skin, he saw, was pale gold, and soft pale curls bobbed on her shoulders beneath a big straw hat.

'Hullo, boy,' she said brightly. 'You see any ships?'

The black boy jumped from his rock and stood beside her.

'No,' he replied gravely, 'no ships. Only luggers, sometimes.'

He spoke the language of the hotel and the post-office, unaccented, the language of Miss Bella and Bob Mayo and Dan, the mailman. It was the only sort he ever heard, apart from occasional travellers staying overnight at the hotel; to anyone else but the little girl standing at his side, it would have sounded strangely out of place on his thick, plum-covered lips.

'There's plenty of ships where I come from.' She stooped to pick up a shell, and held it against her ear, listening intently, listening for a moment to the sigh of the wind and the ghosts of tales that the great waves had breathed into it. 'Down Perth, that is. Where'd you come from, boy?'

The black boy frowned slightly, for he didn't rightly know where he came from. He couldn't know, and nobody had thought to tell him, that he had been brought back to the settlement one day twelve years ago by the mailman and deposited, a smelly little bundle of rags and bright eyes, in the kitchen of the Royal, the only pub in hundreds of miles of that barren nor'west coastline. Dan, who had found him, was a bachelor, so took him to Miss Bella.

'Poor little cow,' was her comment when Dan deposited the picca-ninny on the cool linoleum of the floor. 'What is it, Dan, a he or a she?'

'A little buck—found 'im bellerin' 'is head 'orf 'longside a bit of a

143

swamp a few miles out. I dunno—'is mammy might'a been took with a 'gator, or somethin', but there wasn't no niggers round. I brought 'im in—couldn't leave 'im there.'

'No, a course not—how old is he, Dan, d'you reckon?'

'I dunno,' the mailman replied, removing his wide felt hat and scratching his head. "Bout three, I guess. Give 'im some tucker, Bell.'

Miss Bella moved over to the cooler. 'What you going to do with him?' she demanded.

'Aw—I dunno. 'E can live at the post-office, until 'is mob comes in for 'im.'

'Well, I suppose that'll be all right—what are you going to call him?'

Dan's eyes roved over the ceiling in search of inspiration and lighted on a bottle on top of the dresser.

'Brandy!' he said with a dry chuckle. 'That's a bonzer name. Brandy Smith!'

'It'll do,' the woman said, with a wry grimace. 'He won't be here long enough for it to stick, anyway!'

But no mob came in looking for the piccaninny, and he stayed on to live with Dan, doing odd jobs round the post-office and occasionally, when he got old enough, cutting the wood at the Royal and sweeping out the bar. Through the years, his mind forgot, and his heart forgot, the thousand nomad lives that dreamed in his blood.

He frowned again, deeply, but the little girl didn't press her question. She picked a limpet off the rock with her fingernail and made the universal approach of childhood. 'My name's Shelagh,' she said engagingly. 'What's yours, boy?'

'Brandy,' said the black boy.

She laughed, a high, silvery sound, and a gull wheeling near sheered off into the higher air. 'Brandy?' she cried. 'That's not a name—it's something you drink!'

'It's my name,' he insisted, without heat. 'Dan gave it to me. You know, Dan at the post-office. You've come to live at the pub, haven't you? You're Mr Bob's little girl, from Perth?'

'Yes, I've been at school there, and I only got here last Sat'd'y, but I've been down the beach every day—where've you been?'

The boy pointed towards the horizon. 'On a lugger,' he said shortly. 'Been out three days.'

'Oh, are you a sailor?' The little girl looked at him with renewed interest. 'Can you swim?'

''Course. You watch!'

He helped her up on the rock, where without self-consciousness, he peeled off his jersey. Beneath it, the skin was lustrous black, smooth and glowing and hairless, and as he raised his arms above his head, the smooth forming muscles rippled over his ribs and down his back. He plunged into the water, and the girl watched him, breathless. The water was clear and she could see his black body, strangely fluid and distorted, snaking round the rocks on the bottom like a long black fish; sometimes it disappeared wholly, only to float into view again from some shadowy little cavern, and sometimes he would turn slowly over on his back and send a great wobbling bubble of air up to break the surface with a fat plop. Then all of a sudden, his black head burst out into the sunshine, showering glittering drops in every direction. He shook it violently, smiling a broad, happy grin.

'Oh, Brandy, you are good!' The child clapped her hands excitedly, the long curls dancing on her shoulders. Brandy laughed aloud, turned like a seal in the water, and swam lazily back to drag himself out easily and lie beside her in the hot sunshine.

'You like perclums?' he inquired, and put his hands into a pocket of his ragged khaki shorts.

'Perclums?' she said. 'I don't know—why?'

He pulled several small weed-furred shells from his pocket and sat up. 'You look,' he said, placing one of them under her small nose. 'You see him—a little blue feller?'

She could see it now, a tiny button of blue enamel that closed the shell-fish's front door. The boy placed his long fingernail under it and flipped it into her lap. She squealed with pleasure.

'Oh, isn't it pretty! I could make a necklace out of them—get me some more!'

The black boy grinned, slid noiselessly into the pool and disappeared. He came up at long intervals to breathe, and then disappeared again. Shelagh could see him most of the time and watched fascinated, clapping every time his black arm reached up to deposit a heap of the shells on the rock. When she had a glowing pile of the little blue buttons he crawled on to the rock and sat beside her, watching her as she rolled them in her handkerchief and placed them carefully under a ledge. When she looked up, he said casually: 'I know a bonzer cave—you like to see it?'

Together they picked their way across the exposed reef which was all enchantment. In shallow pools in the rocks, scarlet and green flags of weed floated lazily, anemones spread their greedy plum-coloured lips on the still water, and sea-urchins drilled meticulously with their long scarlet spines; tiny multicoloured crabs scuttled in panic round them, and beneath the ledges there were shells of all colours and shapes, spotted and spiked, some with green pearly sheen on their insides and some that had two beady eyes and two daintily curved claws poling out at the front door. The day was all brightness and cool salty wind, the sky a limitless blue and the sea a peacock's tail that touched the sky's rim out beyond the reef. Gulls wheeled and screamed, and great black divers sat like lacquered birds on the rocks, holding out their wings to dry. The beach shimmered in the heat, and noontime quiet put its fingers against the lips of the white town in the hollow.

'Where you been, Shely—it's after lunch!' When the child stepped into the cool cavern of the hotel kitchen from the glare of the yard, Miss Bella almost shouted the question at her. She was making bread, with Mayo standing beside her; she watched the girl intently, blowing hard at a strand of mousy hair that hung over her forehead.

'Down to the beach, Miss Bella.' Shelagh skipped to the table and held out the flags of crimson weed she had brought home with her. 'Hullo, daddy. Look what—'

'Who you been with?' the woman demanded.

'With Brandy. He knows all the best places, and catches crabs and things for me. He showed me a cave, and he says he'll always be there when I go down.'

'A cave . . . ?' The woman glared at the child's father and muttered, mouthing the words rather than saying them, 'See, you fool!' Then she walked round the table to where the child stood. The man followed her with his eyes, slid his gaze from her to the little girl watching almost apprehensively as the woman approached her. I should have sold out up here and gone down to be near her, he thought. I don't even know her, or what to say to her or what to do for her. But as he thought, he knew that he could never live away from the hot little town, the trembling boom of the surf and the gleaming miles of beach that stretched away into the shimmering heat haze until sea and sky and sand all met in a shifting mirage. He couldn't forego the talks with the drovers and cattlemen from the vast wild plains behind the red ranges east of the town, the mad miners who came in from the desert with their earnest tales about lost reefs in some forgotten gorge where the gold stuck out of the rock in lumps and you were lucky if you got away from the niggers—the pearlers who anchored in the bay sometimes to escape the cock-eyed-bobs that sprang up so suddenly along those desolate, treacherous coasts. They came into the bar, nights, and in the flickering light of hurricane lanterns, traced their rough maps in the beer on the counter, produced their little nuggets and tobacco tins of gold-dust, their round white iridescent pearls, and talked far into the night while outside the surf drummed against the reef and the soft darkness was stabbed by a furious gusher of great yellow stars that sprayed across the black sky. He couldn't leave it, and live—breathe, perhaps, but never live.

The woman stopped beside the child, rubbed the dough off her hands and picked up one of the big shells.

'Put it to your ear, and hear the sea!' Shelagh cried, excited and pleased to share her secret. 'You listen—you can hear the wind and the waves, and everything!' Miss Bella looked down into the shining eyes and smiled gently, put the shell to her ear and stood in the gloomy kitchen and listened to the sea.

She sighed.

'Shelagh,' she said presently. 'I don't want you to go down the beach with Brandy again. You can play at the pub, or wait until he's busy. Don't go down with him.'

Mayo shrugged uncomfortably. 'God, Bella,' he muttered, 'the boy's all right!'

She shut him up with a glare. 'D'you hear me, Shelagh?' she demanded.

The child looked at them in amazement. 'Why, Miss Bella! Brandy c'n swim and everything. He gets me perclums—oh!'

She stopped sharply and her distress showed plainly on her face.

'What is it? What's the matter?' The woman cried with strange urgency. 'Oh—what?'

'My perclums. I left them on the rock!'

'Oh, is that all!' There was undisguised relief in the woman's voice, and she avoided Mayo's half-triumphant glance.

'You can get them another time, when Brandy's not there.'

'But, why, Miss Bella?' the child demanded, almost tearfully. 'Why when Brandy's not there?'

'Well, he might hurt you,' Miss Bella said lamely, and Mayo muttered inaudibly, shaking his head and shrugging impatiently. 'He might knock you over and steal your purse, or something. You can't always trust a black.'

Black? The child looked at her, uncomprehendingly, and then at her father. To her, Brandy was Brandy, who dived off the rock and shook his head like a woolly dog in the water, who got perclums and caught crabs, and who had showed her the cave in the rocks. She wrinkled her brow and said in a puzzled tone, 'But, Miss Bella, I don't take my purse down the beach!'

The woman lost patience. 'Purse or no purse,' she cried sharply, 'you'll do as you're told, my lady. You won't go to the beach again with Brandy, d'you hear, and that's final! Now, get them shells off the table, an' don't let me have to speak to you about it again. Now get!'

Shelagh ran from the kitchen almost in tears, and the man and the woman stood in silence and watched her go. In her room she snivelled for a while, and then comforted herself by laying the weed and the shells across her bed, idly making a pattern. Soon, the enchantment of the morning flowed over her again, and she stood with a shell against her

ear and let the imprisoned song of the sea wash away the memory of
Miss Bella's threats.

It was dark and cool in the kitchen, when she crept through it after
her afternoon nap. The blinds were drawn, and Miss Bella was upstairs
having a lie-down. She took her hat from the peg and ran into the sunny
yard. The afternoon was a virgin sheet on which she might write anything
she fancied, and the few golden hours left to the day were limitless—
before tea, she would have time enough to go round the world. There
was a lonely pig in a sty behind the sandstone garage; wrinkling her nose
at the odour surrounding him, she wandered down and spent some
minutes idly throwing stones at him until he charged the fence, whereupon she retired with a pleasurable thrill of danger. At the kitchen door
she knelt and gathered the crimson berries of the peppercorn-tree, and
then with a head-long decision of childhood, did what she knew she
would do all the time., There was no sound from the hotel, and the yard
and the white road outside it were deserted. With a quick glance at
the window of Miss Bella's room, she slipped out at the gate and ran down
the road towards the beach.

The black boy, sitting on the rock beside the pool, jumped lightly
to the sand and stood waiting for her.

'Brandy,' she said without preamble when she stood beside him,
'what's a black?'

'I dunno, Miss Shely,' he replied uncertainly, and then, brightening,
'Look, Miss Shely—I got something for you.' He stopped and took a
grubby bundle of paper from a ledge at the base of the rock and handed
it to her. 'You have a look!'

Shelagh unwrapped the parcel and stood transfixed. It contained a
small pearl-shell, the rough edges smoothed away, the lustrous sheen of
its inside surface gleaming with all the sea's cool colours in the bright
sunshine.

'Oh, Brandy, isn't it lovely!' she breathed. 'I'll keep it till I di, I
promise I will. Did you make it?'

The black boy's eyes danced with pleasure, and every gleaming tooth
was displayed as he grinned. 'Yeah,' he said. 'I done it—I smoothed it
off with a file. You like it, eh?'

'It's beautiful.' She wrapped it again reverently. 'Thank you, Miss
Bella'll like it, too.'

'I know.' The boy's eyes shone. 'She's always looked after me, like my
mother. I live at the pub, too, sometimes.'

The little girl looked at him, suddenly remembering something.
'Brandy,' she said, 'Miss Bella listened to the shell. She was cross, and she
said I mustn't come and play with you. It's silly, isn't it?'

The black boy wrinkled his heavy forehead. 'Why?' he demanded.

'She said you might take my purse, or something. That's silly, too, because I don't bring my purse, do I?'

Brandy turned and looked out at the sun-splintered sea. His soft eyes were clouded and his heavy brow wrinkled again as he wrestled with what he had just heard. Miss Bella ... When he spoke again, his voice was rough and harsh.

'Miss Bella—why'd she say that? I don't steal!'

Shelagh stepped back, her hand at her lips. 'Brandy,' she said uncertainly, 'you aren't cross, too, now, are you?'

He turned and looked at her closely. Gradually his eyes cleared as her presence blotted out what his brain had been vainly trying to encompass. 'No, not cross, Miss Shely,' he said eventually. 'We'll get your perclums, eh?' He smiled as she placed her hand in his and tugged him towards the pool.

The afternoon wore on and cooled while they pottered round the reef, collecting the shells and crabs and every pretty thing that took the little girl's fancy. Brandy was tireless in pleasing her, and his eyes shone as he watched her, fair head bent, peering at the wonders in the depths of some clear pool or excitedly manoeuvring a tiny crab or fish into a corner for capture. She looked up suddenly, dismayed.

'Oh, Brandy, I've got to go! It must be getting late, and Miss Bella'll be cross again!'

'Orright, we'll race to the road, eh?' The boy stood up while she gathered the silk scarf, the shells and the seaweed and the pearl-shell, and then with a squeal of excitement, scampered up the beach. He dropped behind purposely to let her gain a lead.

Suddenly, before she had gone far, she sprawled headlong, and with a shrill cry of pain, clutched at her knee. All about her, little blue specks on the creamy sand, lay the perclums, the pearl-shell, shed of its wrappings, gleaming in the hot sunshine, and for a moment, the red spurt of her blood showed almost indistinguishable from the scarlet weed she had dropped. She whimpered at first, and then when she saw the blood flow, she opened her mouth to its fullest extent and howled like a dog baying the moon, great long quivering howls that carried well and stopped only for breath in between.

Miss Bella heard it on her way to the beach, stopped and stood stock still, almost smelling the wind, glaring in the direction of the sound. Her mind conjured up a picture not of the girl, but of the black boy, his brown eyes and hair, his thick lips, his satiny black skin and his strong boy's body, so soon to be a man's. She had nursed him and coddled him, even loved him, but now—black boy and white girl! She gave a short, dry sob, almost of terror, and started to run.

149

Brandy hurried round the corner of a shelf of rock with a streamer of bright weed and a crab held by its two long claws. As he saw the blood, he dropped them and knelt on the sand alongside the child.

'Why, don' cry, Miss Shely,' he murmured tenderly, as many a time Miss Bella had murmured to him. 'It's on'y a little cut, look!'

He leant over her gingerly and touched her knee with his black finger; the nail was long and filbert-shaped and startlingly pink, and in between the fingers the skin was creamy brown. 'There,' he said softly. Right beneath his nose the light fair hair curled on the little girl's sunburnt neck. The child turned and put her arms round his neck and howled against his faded jersey.

Brandy's arm strayed helplessly in the air, and then came to rest softly, naturally, on her shoulders. 'Don't you cry,' he murmured. 'It's all right. Don' cry!'

Miss Bella came down the white track, and stopped when she saw them squatting in the sand. Her hand went to her breast.

'Shelagh!' she screamed. The gulls wheeling in the fathomless blue sky answered her hoarsely. The black boy watched her as she ploughed through the thick shimmering sand, her black skirt held above her flaccid calves, her bosom heaving. She stopped a yard away from them; her face was crimson and a pulse beat wildly in her neck.

'You!' she flung hoarsely at him, and hate and fear burnt in the word. Behind him, the white sand sloped evenly to the soft green shallows, and then there was spread the deep blue and the flashing white where the great combers crashed on the black reef. Beyond that, to the edge of the world and beyond, the vast, timeless sea. The salty wind and the sunshine wrapped them round, the gulls, like silver boomerangs, swooped and soared, splashed and soared again, and at the end of the white road the half-dozen buildings of the little town gleamed almost unbearably in the late afternoon heat. Yet she saw only thick lips and black hair and heavy jutting forehead, the puzzled frown in the brown eyes, the black hands on the girl's shoulders.

'You—!' she spat at him again, and catching the child's hand, yanked her roughly to her feet. 'Get home, Shelagh!'

Brandy clambered to his feet. 'Why, Miss Bella—'

She swung her hand across his mouth, hard. The blood ran from his lips, and he stood still, his fingers creeping slowly along his jaw. The woman's eyes blazed.

'Nigger!' she cried, shrill with fear. 'Black, damned nigger!'

Unaccustomed tears swam in the boy's troubled eyes. At the sight of them, her hand fled, as his had, to her mouth; she seemed to shrink inside her black dress, and stood staring at him with dilated eyes.

'Why, Miss Bella—' he began again, but without a word she turned and trudged across the sand, dragging the little girl by the hand.

The boy's black fingers touched his lips, at last. He stared dully at their smeared tips, and then at the blackened patch on the sand where the girl's blood had dried and caked hard. The ghosts of a million years postured all about him, grimacing, daubed with mud and blood and feathers, gleaming with sacred kidney-fat, crying to the unresponsive blood that pounded in his questioning heart. Only he could not hear, did not see. Only he had forgotten. Little crabs scuttled across his bare feet, carrying off the scarlet weed he had dropped, but he did not move. He stood staring up the white road where Miss Bella and the little girl had disappeared in the direction of the white town.

Alan Sillitoe born in Nottingham, in 1928, and 'educated at various elementary schools until the age of fourteen'. He is considered, like John Osborne, the author of the play LOOK BACK IN ANGER, to be representative of the 'angry young men' school of social realist writers of the 1950's. Much of his best writing is to be found in the collection of short stories THE LONELINESS OF THE LONG DISTANCE RUNNER, 1959, and derives from his own experience of Nottingham working class life, described in the early parts of his long, auto-biographical novel KEY TO THE DOOR. The narrator in 'ON SATURDAY AFTER-NOON', unlike narrators in more traditional forms of short story, is highly implicated: directly involved in the action, and conscious of strong social attitudes, he offers us a perspective upon the action which we can compare and contrast with our own.

ON SATURDAY AFTERNOON

Alan Sillitoe

I ONCE SAW A BLOKE TRY TO KILL HIMSELF. I'LL NEVER FORGET THE DAY because I was sitting in the house one Saturday afternoon, feeling black and fed-up because everybody in the family had gone to the pictures, except me who'd for some reason been left out of it. 'Course, I didn't know then that I would soon see something you can never see in the same way on the pictures, a real bloke stringing himself up. I was only a kid at the time, so you can imagine how much I enjoyed it.

I've never known a family to look as black as our family when they're fed-up. I've seen the old man with his face so dark and full of murder because he ain't got no fags or was having to use saccharine to sweeten his tea, or even for nothing at all, that I've backed out of the house in case he got up from his fireside chair and came for me. He just sits, almost on top of the fire, his oil-stained Sunday-joint maulers opened out in front of him and facing inwards to each other, his thick shoulders scrunched forward, and his dark brown eyes staring into the fire. Now and again he'd say a dirty word, for no reason at all, the worst word you can think of, and when he starts saying this you know it's time to clear out. If mam's in it gets worse than ever, because she says sharp to him: 'What are yo' looking so bleddy black for?' as if it might be because of something she's done, and before you know what's happening he's tipped up a tableful of pots and mam's gone out of the house crying. Dad hunches back over the fire and goes on swearing. All because of a packet of fags.

I once saw him broodier than I'd ever seen him, so that I thought he'd gone crackers in a quiet sort of way—until a fly flew to within a yard of him. Then his hand shot out, got it, and slung it crippled into the roaring fire. After that he cheered up a bit and mashed some tea.

Well, that's where the rest of us get our black looks from. It stands to reason we'd have them with a dad who carries on like that, don't it? Black looks run in the family. Some families have them and some don't. Our family has them right enough, and that's certain, so when we're fed-up we're really fed-up. Nobody knows why we get as fed-up as we do or why it gives us these black looks when we are. Some people get fed-up and don't look bad at all: they seem happy in a funny sort of way, as if they've just been set free from clink after being in there for something they didn't do, or come out of the pictures after sitting plugged for eight hours at a bad film, or just missed a bus they ran half a mile for and seen it was the wrong one just after they'd stopped running—but in our family it's murder for the others if one of us is fed-up. I've asked myself lots of times what it is, but I can never get any sort of answer even if I sit and

153

think for hours, which I must admit I don't do, though it looks good when I say I do. But I sit and think for long enough, until mam says to me, at seeing me scrunched up over the fire like dad: 'What are yo' looking so black for?' So I've just got to stop thinking about it in case I get really black and fed-up and go the same way as dad, tipping up a tableful of pots and all.

Mostly I suppose there's nothing to look so black for: though it's nobody's fault and you can't blame anyone for looking black because I'm sure it's summat in the blood. But on this Saturday afternoon I was looking so black that when dad came in from the bookie's he said to me: 'What's up wi' yo'?'

'I feel badly,' I fibbed. He'd have had a fit if I'd said I was only black because I hadn't gone to the pictures.

'Well have a wash,' he told me.

'I don't want a wash,' I said, and that was a fact.

'Well, get outside and get some fresh air then,' he shouted.

I did as I was told, double-quick, because if ever dad goes as far as to tell me to get some fresh air I know it's time to get away from him. But outside the air wasn't so fresh, what with that bloody great bike factory bashing away at the yard-end. I didn't know where to go, so I walked up the yard a bit and sat down near somebody's back gate.

Then I saw this bloke who hadn't lived long in our yard. He was tall and thin and had a face like a parson except that he wore a flat cap and had a moustache that drooped, and looked as though he hadn't had a square meal for a year. I didn't think much o' this at the time: but I remember that as he turned in by the yard-end one of the nosy gossiping women who stood there every minute of the day except when she trudged to the pawnshop with her husband's bike or best suit, shouted to him: 'What's that rope for, mate?'

He called back: 'It's to 'ang messen wi', missis,' and she cackled at his bloody good joke so loud and long you'd think she never heard such a good 'un, though the next day she cackled on the other side of her fat face.

He walked by me puffing a fag and carrying his coil of brand-new rope, and he had to step over me to get past. His boot nearly took my shoulder off, and when I told him to watch where he was going I don't think he heard me because he didn't even look round. Hardly anybody was about. All the kids were still at the pictures, and most of their mams and dads were downtown doing the shopping.

The bloke walked down the yard to his back door, and having nothing better to do because I hadn't gone to the pictures I followed him. You see, he left his back door open a bit, so I gave it a push and went in. I stood there, just watching him, sucking my thumb, the other hand in my pocket. I suppose he knew I was there, because his eyes were moving more natural now, but he didn't seem to mind. 'What are yer going to do wi' that rope, mate?' I asked him.

'I'm going ter 'ang messen, lad,' he told me, as though he'd done it a time or two already, and people had usually asked him questions like this beforehand.

'What for, mate?' He must have thought I was a nosy young bogger.

' 'Cause I want to, that's what for,' he said, clearing all the pots off the table and pulling it to the middle of the room. Then he stood on it to fasten the rope to the light-fitting. The table creaked and didn't look very safe, but it did him for what he wanted.

'It wain't hold up mate,' I said to him, thinking how much better it was being here than sitting in the pictures and seeing the Jungle Jim serial.

But he got nettled now and turned on me. 'Mind yer own business.'

I thought he was going to tell me to scram, but he didn't. He made ever such a fancy knot with that rope, as though he'd been a sailor or summat, and as he tied it he was whistling a fancy tune to himself. Then he got down from the table and pushed it back to the wall, and put a chair in its place. He wasn't looking black at all, nowhere near as black as anybody in our family when they're feeling fed-up. If ever he'd looked only half as black as our dad looked twice a week he'd have hanged himself years ago, I couldn't help thinking. But he was making a good job of that rope all right, as though he'd thought about it a lot anyway, and as though it was going to be the last thing he'd ever do. But I knew something he didn't know, because he wasn't standing where I was. I knew the rope wouldn't hold up, and I told him so, again.

'Shut yer gob,' he said, but quiet like, 'or I'll kick yer out.'

I didn't want to miss it, so I said nothing. He took his cap off and put it on the dresser, then he took his coat off, and his scarf, and spread them out on the sofa. I wasn't a bit frightened, like I might be now at sixteen, because it was interesting. And being only ten I'd never had a chance to see a bloke hang himself before. We got pally, the two of us, before he slipped the rope around his neck.

'Shut the door,' he asked me, and I did as I was told. 'Ye're a good lad for your age,' he said to me while I sucked my thumb, and he felt in his pockets and pulled out all that was inside, throwing the handful of bits and bobs on the table: fag-packet and peppermints, a pawn-ticket, and old comb, and a few coppers. He picked out a penny and gave it to me, saying: 'Now listen ter me, young 'un. I'm going to 'ang messen, and when I'm swinging I want you to gi' this chair a bloody good kick and push it away. All right?'

I nodded.

He put the rope around his neck, and then took it off like it was a tie that didn't fit. 'What are yer going to do it for, mate?' I asked again.

'Because I'm fed-up,' he said, looking very unhappy. 'And because I want to. My missus left me, and I'm out o' work.'

I didn't want to argue, because the way he said it, I knew he couldn't do anything else except hang himself. Also there was a funny look in his face: even when he talked to me I swear he couldn't see me. It was different to the black looks my old man puts on, and I suppose that's why my old man would never hang himself, worse luck, because he never gets a look into his clock like this bloke had. My old man's look stares *at* you, so that you have to back down and fly out of the house: this bloke's look looked *through* you, so that you could face it and know it wouldn't do you any harm. So I saw now that dad would never hang himself because he could never get the right sort of look into his face, in spite of the fact that he'd been out of work often enough. Maybe mam would have to leave him first, and then he might do it; but no—I shook my head—there wasn't much chance of that even though he did lead her a dog's life.

'Yer wain't forget to kick that chair away?' he reminded me, and I swung my head to say I wouldn't. So my eyes were popping and I watched every move he made. He stood on the chair and put the rope around his neck so that it fitted this time, still whistling his fancy tune. I wanted to get a better goz at the knot, because my pal was in the scouts, and would ask to know how it was done, and if I told him later he'd let me know what happened at the pictures in the Jungle Jim serial, so's I could have my cake and eat it as well, as mam says, tit for tat. But I thought I'd better not ask the bloke to tell me, and I stayed back in my corner. The last thing he did was to take the wet dirty butt-end from his lips and sling it into the empty firegrate, following it with his eyes to the black fireback where it landed—as if he was then going to mend a fault in the lighting like any electrician.

Suddenly his long legs wriggled and his feet tried to kick the chair, so I helped him as I'd promised I would and took a runner at it as if I was playing centre-forward for Notts Forest, and the chair went scooting back against the sofa, dragging his muffler to the floor as it tipped over. He swung for a bit, his arms chafing like he was a scarecrow flapping birds away, and he made a noise in his throat as if he'd just took a dose of salts and was trying to make them stay down.

Then there was another sound, and I looked up and saw a big crack come in the ceiling, like you see on the pictures when an earthquake's happening, and the bulb began circling round and round as though it was a space ship. I was just beginning to get dizzy when, thank Christ, he fell down with such a horrible thump on the floor that I thought he'd broke every bone he'd got. He kicked around for a bit, like a dog that's got colic bad. Then he lay still.

I didn't stay to look at him. 'I told him that rope wouldn't hold up,' I kept saying to myself as I went out of the house, tut-tutting because he hadn't done the job right, hands stuffed deep into my pockets and nearly crying at the balls-up he'd made of everything. I slammed his gate so hard with disappointment that it nearly dropped off its hinges.

Just as I was going back up the yard to get my tea at home, hoping the others had come back from the pictures so's I wouldn't have anything to keep on being black about, a copper passed me and headed for the bloke's door. He was striding quickly with his head bent forward, and I knew that somebody had narked. They must have seen him buy the rope and then tipped-off the cop. Or happen the old hen at the yard-end finally caught on. Or perhaps he'd even told somebody himself, because I supposed that the bloke who'd strung himself up hadn't much known what he was doing, especially with the look I'd seen in his eyes. But that's how it is, I said to myself, as I followed the copper back to the bloke's house, a poor bloke can't even hang himself these days.

When I got back the copper was slitting the rope from his neck with a pen-knife, then he gave him a drink of water, and the bloke opened his peepers. I didn't like the copper, because he'd got a couple of my mates sent to approved school for pinching lead piping from lavatories.

'What did you want to hang yourself for?' he asked the bloke, trying to make him sit up. He could hardly talk, and one of his hands was bleeding from where the light-bulb had smashed. I knew that rope wouldn't hold up, but he hadn't listened to me. I'll never hang myself anyway, but if I want to I'll make sure I do it from a tree or something like that, not a light fitting. 'Well, what did you do it for?'

'Because I wanted to,' the bloke croaked.

'You'll get five years for this,' the copper told him. I'd crept back into the house and was sucking my thumb in the same corner.

'That's what yo' think,' the bloke said, a normal frightened look in his eyes now. 'I only wanted to hang myself.'

'Well,' the copper said, taking out his book, 'it's against the law, you know.'

'Nay,' the bloke said, 'it can't be. It's my life, ain't it?'

'You might think so,' the copper said, 'but it ain't.'

He began to suck the blood from his hand. It was such a little scratch though that you couldn't see it. 'That's the first thing I knew,' he said.

'Well I'm telling you,' the copper told him.

'Course, I didn't let on to the copper that I'd helped the bloke to hang himself. I wasn't born yesterday, nor the day before yesterday either.

'It's a fine thing if a bloke can't tek his own life,' the bloke said, seeing he was in for it.

'Well he can't,' the copper said, as if reading out of his book and enjoying it. 'It ain't your life. And it's a crime to take your own life. It's killing yourself. It's suicide.'

The bloke looked hard, as if every one of the copper's words meant six-months cold. I felt sorry for him, and that's a fact, but if only he'd listened to what I'd said and not depended on that light-fitting. He should have done it from a tree, or something like that.

He went up the yard with the copper like a peaceful lamb, and we all thought that that was the end of that.

But a couple of days later the news was flashed through to us—even before it got to the *Post* because a woman in our yard worked at the hospital of an evening dishing grub out and tidying up. I heard her spilling it to somebody at the yard-end. 'I'd never 'ave thought it. I thought he'd got that daft idea out of his head when they took him away. But no. Wonders'll never cease. Chucked 'issen from the hospital window when the copper who sat near his bed went off for a pee. Would you believe it? Dead? Not much 'e ain't.'

He'd heaved himself at the glass, and fallen like a stone on to the road. In one way I was sorry he'd done it, but in another I was glad, because he'd proved to the coppers and everybody whether it was his life or not all right. It was marvellous though, the way the brainless bastards had put him in a ward six floors up, which finished him off, proper, even better than a tree.

All of which will make me think twice about how black I sometimes feel. The black coal-bag locked inside you, and the black look it puts on your face, doesn't mean you're going to string yourself up or sling yourself under a double-decker or chuck yourself out of a window or cut your throat with a sardine-tin or put your head in the gas-oven or drop your rotten sack-bag of a body on to a railway line, because when you're feeling that black you can't even move from your chair. Anyhow, I know I'll never get so black as to hang myself, because hanging don't look very nice to me, and never will, the more I remember old what's-his-name swinging from the light-fitting.

More than anything else, I'm glad now I didn't go to the pictures that Saturday afternoon when I was feeling black and ready to do myself in. Because you know, I shan't ever kill myself. Trust me. I'll stay alive half-balmy till I'm a hundred and five, and then go out screaming blue murder because I want to stay where I am.

Ray Bradbury born *Waukegan, Illinois, in 1920. Educated at Los Angeles High School. Between 1941 and 1944 many of his stories appeared in leading American magazines, and after the war in numerous anthologies of Science Fiction and in the annual collections of* BEST AMERICAN SHORT STORIES. *Among the most successful of his works are the short stories in* THE GOLDEN APPLES OF THE SUN, THE SILVER LOCUSTS (*published in the United States as* THE MARTIAN CHRONICLES) *and the novels,* DANDELION WINE *and* FAHRENHEIT 451.

Bradbury's short stories and novels show a deep concern with the effects of a technological revolution on human society. This concern is dramatized in situations where individuals try, often vainly, to assert their humanity in the face of uncontrollable, impersonal but man-made forces.

The neutral tone and precise detail of the narration in 'THERE WILL COME SOFT RAINS' *intensify the horror of the situation. Not only does this story look forward to a horribly plausible future; technically, the device of announcing time passing in a setting from which characters are obliterated, looks forward to some of the more experimental methods of narration in* SPECTRUM TWO: MODERN SHORT STORIES.

THERE WILL COME SOFT RAINS

Ray Bradbury

THE HOUSE WAS A GOOD HOUSE AND HAD BEEN PLANNED AND BUILT BY THE people who were to live in it, in the year 1980. The house was like many another house in that year; it fed and slept and entertained its inhabitants, and made a good life for them. The man and wife and their two children lived at ease there, and lived happily, even while the world trembled. All of the fine things of living, the warm things, music and poetry, books that talked, beds that warmed and made themselves, fires that built themselves in the fireplaces of evenings, were in this house, and living there was a contentment.

And then one day the world shook and there was an explosion followed by ten thousand explosions and red fire in the sky and a rain of ashes and radio-activity, and the happy time was over.

In the living room the voice-clock sang, *Tick-tock, seven* A.M. *o'clock, time to get up!* as if it were afraid nobody would. The house lay empty. The clock talked on into the empty morning.

The kitchen stove sighed and ejected from its warm interior eight eggs, sunny side up, twelve bacon slices, two coffees, and two cups of hot cocoa. *Seven nine, breakfast time, seven nine.*

'Today is April 28th, 1985,' said a phonograph voice in the kitchen ceiling. 'Today, remember, is Mr Featherstone's birthday. Insurance, gas, light and water bills are due.'

Somewhere in the walls, relays clicked, memory tapes glided under electric eyes. Recorded voices moved beneath steel needles:

Eight one, run, run, off to school, off to work, run, run, ticktock, eight one o'clock!

But no doors slammed, no carpets took the quick tread of rubber heels. Outside, it was raining. The voice of the weather box on the front door sang quietly: 'Rain, rain, go away, rubbers, raincoats for today.' And the rain tapped on the roof.

At eight thirty the eggs were shrivelled. An aluminium wedge scraped them into the sink, where hot water whirled them down a metal throat which digested and flushed them away to the distant sea.

Nine fifteen, sang the clock, *time to clean.*

Out of warrens in the wall, tiny mechanical mice darted. The rooms were acrawl with the small cleaning animals, all rubber and metal. They sucked up the hidden dust, and popped back in their burrows.

Ten o'clock. The sun came out from behind the rain. The house stood alone on a street where all the other houses were rubble and ashes. At night, the ruined town gave off a radioactive glow which could be seen for miles.

Ten fifteen. The garden sprinkler filled the soft morning air with golden fountains. The water tinkled over the charred west side of the house where it had been scorched evenly free of its white paint. The entire face of the house was black, save for five places. Here, the silhouette, in paint, of a man mowing a lawn. Here, a woman bent to pick flowers. Still farther over, their images burned on wood in one titanic instant, a small boy, hands flung in the air—higher up, the image of a thrown ball—and opposite him a girl, her hands raised to catch a ball which never came down.

The five spots of paint—the man, the woman, the boy, the girl, the ball—remained. The rest was a thin layer of charcoal.

The gentle rain of the sprinkler filled the garden with falling light.

Until this day, how well the house had kept its peace. How carefully it had asked, 'Who goes there?' and getting no reply from rains and lonely foxes and whining cats, it had shut up its windows and drawn the shades. If a sparrow brushed a window, the shade snapped up. The bird, startled, flew off! No, not even an evil bird must touch the house.

And inside, the house was like an altar with nine thousand robot attendants, big and small, servicing, attending, singing in choirs, even though the gods had gone away and the ritual was meaningless.

A dog whined, shivering, on the front porch.

The front door recognized the dog voice and opened. The dog padded in wearily, thinned to the bone, covered with sores. It tracked mud on the carpet. Behind it whirred the angry robot mice, angry at having to pick up mud and maple leaves, which, carried to the burrows, were dropped down cellar tubes into an incinerator which sat like an evil Baal in a dark corner.

The dog ran upstairs, hysterically yelping at each door. It pawed the kitchen door wildly.

Behind the door, the stove was making pancakes which filled the whole house with their odour.

The dog frothed, ran insanely, spun in a circle, biting its tail, and died. It lay in the living room for an hour.

One o'clock.

Delicately sensing decay, the regiments of mice hummed out of the walls, soft as brown leaves, their electric eyes blowing.

One fifteen.

The dog was gone.

The cellar incinerator glowed suddenly and a whirl of sparks leaped up the flue.

Two thirty-five.

Bridge tables sprouted from the patio walls. Playing cards fluttered onto pads in a shower of pips. Martinis appeared on an oaken bench. But the tables were silent, the cards untouched.

At four-thirty the tables folded back into the walls.

Five o'clock. The bathtubs filled with clear hot water. A safety razor dropped into a wall-mould, ready.

Six, seven, eight, nine o'clock.

Dinner made, ignored, and flushed away; dishes washed; and in the study, the tobacco stand produced a cigar, half an inch of gray ash on it, smoking, waiting. The hearth fire bloomed up all by itself, out of nothing.

Nine o'clock. The beds began to warm their hidden circuits, for the night was cool.

A gentle click in the study wall. A voice spoke from above the crackling fireplace:

'Mrs McClellan, what poem would you like to hear this evening?' The house was silent.

The voice said, 'Since you express no preference, I'll pick a poem at random.' Quiet music rose behind the voice. 'Sara Teasdale. A favourite of yours, as I recall.'

> *'There will come soft rains and the smell of the ground,*
> *And swallows circling with their shimmering sound;*
>
> *And frogs in the pools singing at night,*
> *And wild plum-trees in tremulous white.*
>
> *Robins will wear their feathery fire*
> *Whistling their whims on a low fence-wire;*
>
> *And not one will know of the war, not one*
> *Will care at last when it is done.*
>
> *Not one would mind, neither bird nor tree!*
> *If mankind perished utterly:*
>
> *And Spring herself, when she woke at dawn,*
> *Would scarcely know that we were gone.'*

The voice finished the poem. The empty chairs faced each other between the silent walls, and the music played.

At ten o'clock, the house began to die.

The wind blew. The bough of a falling tree smashed the kitchen window. Cleaning solvent, bottled, crashed on the stove.

'Fire!' screamed voices. 'Fire!' Water pumps shot down water from the ceilings. But the solvent spread under the doors, making fire as it went, while other voices took up the alarm in chorus.

The windows broke with heat and the wind blew in to help the fire. Scurrying water rats, their copper wheels spinning, squeaked from the walls, squirted their water, ran for more.

Too late! Somewhere, a pump stopped. The ceiling sprays stopped raining. The reserve water supply, which had filled baths and washed dishes for many silent days, was gone.

The fire crackled upstairs, ate paintings, lay hungrily in the beds! It devoured every room.

The house was shuddering, oak bone on bone, the bared skeleton cringing from the heat, all the wires revealed as if a surgeon had torn the skin off to let the red veins quiver in scalded air. Voices screamed, '*Help, help, fire, run!*' Windows snapped open and shut, like mouths, undecided. *Fire, run!* the voices wailed a tragic nursery rhyme, and the silly Greek chorus faded as the sound-wires popped their sheathings. Ten dozen high, shrieking voices died, as emergency batteries melted.

In other parts of the house, in the last instant under the fire avalanche, other choruses could be heard announcing the time, the weather, appointments, diets; playing music, reading poetry in the fiery study, while doors opened and slammed and umbrellas appeared at the doors and put themselves away—a thousand things happening, like the interior of a clock shop at midnight, all clocks striking, a merry-go-round of squeaking, whispering, rushing, until all the film spools were burned and fell, and all the wires withered and the circuits cracked.

In the kitchen, an instant before the final collapse, the stove, hysterically hissing, could be seen making breakfasts at a psychopathic rate, ten dozen pancakes, six dozen loaves of toast.

The crash! The attic smashing kitchen down into cellar and subcellar. Deep freeze, armchairs, filmtapes, beds, were thrown in a cluttered mound deep under.

Smoke and silence.

Dawn shone faintly in the east. In the ruins, one wall stood alone. Within the wall, a voice said, over and over again and again, even as the sun rose to shine upon the heaped rubble and steam:

'Today is April 29th, 1985. Today is April 29th, 1985. Today is . . .'